THE SPERM KING

I0638855

William Mesusan

William Mesusan, Publisher

ISBN: 9781736460757

Cover Design by: Vila Design

Library of Congress Control Number: 2024904332

Printed in the United States of America

We are all guilty – all peoples,
all religions, all nations, all classes. Humanity itself is guilty.

--Erich Neumann

The first wealth is health.

-- Ralph Waldo Emerson

Book I

Spermaggedon

CHAPTER ONE

Clay Roberts became the most wanted man on Earth. Not yet realizing his fate, he pushed open the glass doors of a redwood and stucco building on the campus of Sonoma State University, in northern California, to leave the college's Student Health Center. Clay walked past outdoor planting beds whose original landscaped groundcover of roses and golden poppies had long ago been replaced by agave and cacti. He headed for the main walkway.

Clay had reported, as required, for mandatory testing to determine the overall potency of his sperm. He had given Government the requisite vial of his semen. They want that sample awfully bad, he thought to himself. They force us to ejaculate so they can get it while it's fresh. What's this world come to?

Clay turned onto West Redwood Drive and walked towards the parking lot. He heard footsteps approaching from behind as he continued walking along the pavement.

A voice called out to him.

"Wait!" came a shout. "We need to talk."

It was a man's voice.

Clay stopped and turned to see who was so determined to speak with him. An overweight male with a pug-dog face rapidly approached. Heavy breathing indicated physical distress, but neither man paid attention to this fact because a torrent of words began to flow out of the flat-faced mouth.

"I have a friend inside who tells me who tests for a high sperm count."

"A friend gives you that kind of information?" asked Clay, interrupting the stream before it gained velocity. "Isn't that illegal?"

1

"Alright," the guy confessed. "I pay someone to alert me when anyone has a high sperm count. I'm a fertility agent. I drive up here once a month, from San Francisco, for the mandatory testing.

"What's that have to do with me?"

"I want to represent you."

"You want to what?"

"I want to be your agent."

"Agent?" questioned Clay. "Why do I need an agent?"

"You don't know, do you?"

The question was accompanied by nervous laughter and an uneasy pause.

"They haven't shared your results with you," the stranger shouted in exasperation as he flung outstretched hands into the air. "Your sperm count is ca-ray-zee." The two syllable word had morphed into three syllables, creating an unusual delivery in the way it was spoken. "You're off the charts in all three criteria. You're a triple threat."

The stranger looked Clay over. Early to mid-twenties, he guessed. Six-foot one, maybe a hundred and ninety pounds. Muscular build. Brown eyes, dark hair, a day or twos worth of stubble, and a bit of a tan to the skin. Might explain his manly attributes.

"What do you mean off the charts?" asked Clay. "I'm not sure what you're talking about."

"Count, motility, and shape," the man answered. "You got it all, dude. Government will soon be after you, and Sperm Master himself, and the most lucrative Sperm Banks in the world. You owe it to yourself to maximize your potential. You'll get older and your count will decline. When it does, believe me, they'll drop you like you were radioactive waste."

A knot formed in Clay's stomach as the two men continued walking. They passed another building made from wood and stucco and glass. Carson Hall was named in honor of Rachel Carson, a conservationist working in the late 1950s and early 60s.

2

It had been almost a hundred years since her environmental science book, *Silent Spring*, had documented the harm caused by the indiscriminate use of synthetic pesticides. In the book, she accused the chemical industry of spreading disinformation and public officials of accepting the industry's marketing claims (and perhaps their money) a little too easily.

Clay lived during the aftermath.

By the year 2050, the evidence of a toxic and chemically imbalanced world, one that had failed to listen to Carson and scores of scientists warning mankind of pesticide and fossil fuel folly a century earlier, was visible to the eye.

What remained invisible was the hormonal imbalance at the heart of a precipitous decline in human reproductive development. One so dire as to hurtle humanity headlong towards extinction.

Clay fought through his discomfort.

"I don't know about this," he said, with hesitation in his voice.

"I need to talk with you," said the man, almost pleading. "I'll buy you lunch."

"Organics Café?"

"Sure," came the response, accompanied by a frown. "You got a car?"

They sat across from one another on a hot Monday morning, in early May.

The once scorching temperatures of July and August were now commonplace in the spring months, so restaurant staff had a couple of ceiling fans whirling overhead for the comfort of its patrons. They weren't allowed to use air conditioning, which was restricted to three hours a day during the late afternoon. Organics Café, being a breakfast and lunch establishment, hadn't even bothered to have AC installed on the premises.

They'd introduced each other on the way to Clay's truck.

Henry Gallagher, known to his friends as Hank, sat sizing up his prey. Like any sharp-clawed predator, he worked by instinct. He'd concluded that Clay Roberts was somewhat unsophisticated if not quite the country bumpkin.

Clay's innate intelligence didn't always shine through, but he had strong impressions of his own. The stranger wore a maroon polo shirt under a grey suit. Clay had observed his shiny black shoes in the car. His father had warned him to be wary of soft-shoed shufflers. The pudgy body underneath the fine clothes, and his heavy breathing earlier, indicated a man out of shape.

Clay ordered a Cobb salad and an iced tea. Hank Gallagher had a veggie burger, but only because there was no meat offered on the menu. He also asked for an iced coffee though he seemed hyper enough. They conversed between sips and bites.

"Any idea why your markers are so high?" Hank asked.

"I'm not sure," admitted Clay apologetically. "Maybe cause I grew up on an organic farm outside of town? Our parents were health conscious."

The word *were* registered with the agent. He decided against pursuing the subject because he didn't want Clay to feel like he was intruding into his personal life. Not just yet. Although it doesn't get much more personal than one's sperm count, he mused.

"I can help you."

"I need help?"

"You don't know the half of it," replied Hank. "You have a whole new world to navigate. First thing Government will do is order you to report to St. Francis Hospital, in San Francisco, for a mandatory follow-up session."

"I've never heard of that," said Clay with skepticism creeping into his voice.

"That's because only the top two percentile make the cut."

"You're serious."

"Damn right, I'm serious!"

4

Clay put down his fork. He took a long, slow sip of his iced-tea before setting the glass back down on the tabletop. A table made from wood with matching chairs. There wasn't an ounce of plastic inside the café unless it was brought in by customers. All wood and metal and glass and ceramics. A time warp. A link to the past.

"What is it you're suggesting I do?"

"I want you to let me represent you," Hank reminded him, trying his best to sound patient. His foot tapping nervously on the tile floor suggested otherwise.

"What exactly does that mean?"

"I'll keep you safe and help set up your interviews and negotiate the contracts for your services and endorsements," explained the wannabe agent. "My share will be twenty percent."

Clay smiled. He sat back in his chair and waited without saying a word.

The nervous foot continued to tap on the floor.

"Ten . . ."

"I'd love to represent you for ten percent, but I incur a lot of major expenses on my end," the agent maintained. "Do you know how much I spend on electricity alone?" He didn't wait for an answer to his question. "The electrical grid is crap, man. And the price of car rentals has gone through the roof. There's also the cost of paying . . . uh . . . associates at the testing sites."

Clay didn't know the agent well enough to know if he was being totally honest, but he wasn't greedy. Just testing the waters and looking for a reasonable share.

"Fifteen percent sounds fair."

Hank Gallagher frowned. He's not as dumb as I thought, but fifteen percent will still make me a rich man. A very rich man.

"I'll have the contract written up."

The agent extended a hand across the table. Clay grasped it and gave it a strong squeeze. Hank winced, but managed a smile.

They stood outside under the café's awning to protect themselves from the blistering sun.

Hank reached into his coat pocket and pulled out a pair of what looked to be wrap-around sunglasses. They were a recently introduced, streamlined version of the old Virtual Reality, also known as Augmented Reality, goggles that were popular decades earlier.

Their primary function was providing users a portal into the Metaverse, but they could be used to read emails and the news and to make phone calls. These new have-to-have high-tech Smart Glasses appealed to those who could afford them, especially to aficionados of Metaverse worlds. Others, less fortunate or perhaps more discerning, utilized older cell phone technology running on the latest 25G networks.

Gallagher wasn't a Metaverse kind of guy. He considered it an escape from reality. Many of his friends and social acquaintances differed in their opinion. They thought of it as a portal into reality. They challenged him to define the exact nature of reality which, of course, he couldn't do. He used them for one reason only. He simply didn't want to take time away from his principal pursuit. To find the most potent men and fertile women in northern California. Little else mattered to him. So he confined the use of his glasses to business.

He positioned the Smart Glasses over his ears and turned to Clay.

"Eve, bring me a ride."

"Eve?" Clay wondered aloud. "What happened to Siri?"

"They retired her long ago," he was informed. "Most people personalize the names, but I'm too lazy so I use the default name."

"I see . . . "

"Give me a minute," Hank said. "I want to check my emails."

Clay found the Smart Glasses intriguing, but he'd never felt a need to buy a pair. He knew that people were using them to gain access to alternate realities, something else he'd had no desire to explore. He viewed the Metaverse as fast food for the mind in a world where technology dominated and lured people away from the natural world.

"Here's the plan," Hank suddenly announced, having read through his emails. "You call me when Government contacts you for your appointment."

The agent pulled out his wallet and took out a business card. He handed it to Clay just as a shiny silver Tesla Model XXX arrived at the curb in front of them. Clay looked inside, but the vehicle sat empty.

"There's nobody in there!"

"It's fully automated and self-driving."

"You trust that car?"

"With my life."

"Apparently."

Elon Musk's vision of a Robo Taxi Network had come to fruition a decade earlier, but it had remained a largely urban phenomenon due to logistical and monetary restrictions. The inventive entrepreneur was one of the few influential voices sounding an alarm when, almost *three decades* earlier, he tweeted, "Population collapse is a major risk to the future of civilization."

His prophetic words had come to pass with a vengeance. One that had altered the course of a virile young man's life journey, and had him listening to a stranger offering to represent his much needed services in an effort to save their species.

"Once I hear from you, we'll arrange a time to meet back in the university parking lot," said Hank, taking charge of the situation.

"Do you think they'll be contacting me soon?"

"You can bet on it!" insisted the wannabe agent. " I'll drive you down to the hospital and we can talk over our strategy. Our plan of attack. How we're going to handle the offers."

"You own a car?"

"No, that doesn't make sense for me," laughed Hank. "I'll rent one just to put you at ease. I know the city, so I can take us where we need to go."

"Thanks."

"Do me a favor, Clay," requested the agent. "Watch your back. And don't tell anybody what's going on until after you meet with Government's officials."

Hank Gallagher left Clay in the shade of the awning and walked out to the curb. The passenger side door opened for him and he slid into the front seat next to an invisible driver.

All Clay could do was shake his head. You'll never get me to use one of those self-driving cars, he said to himself as the electric vehicle drove out into mid-day traffic.

Time for him to drive home.

Time to consider a life turned upside down.

CHAPTER 2

Clay and Hank met in the university parking lot two days later.

They'd agreed to meet near one of the electric vehicle charging stations. Clay recognized Hank in the driver's seat of a spotless, futuristic-looking electric car called the Gemini. A triangular roofline set it apart from all the other current models. The stylish rental's sleek lines were accentuated by a two-tone paint job. Royal blue and gunmetal gray.

Clay parked his used Ford F-150 Lightning electric pick-up in an unoccupied space, two cars away. He grabbed his water flask, opened the door and climbed out, and then hit the remote to lock the truck. He walked over to the Gemini.

That day brought blue skies and sunshine along with the expected sweltering heat. Hank had warned Clay that San Francisco might be shrouded in fog and suggested he bring a jacket. The agent wore the same grey suit only this time he sported a black polo shirt.

Clay had on a short-sleeved, plaid shirt and jeans. His shirt, made from organic cotton, remained unbuttoned at the collar and he'd dispensed with wearing a belt since his thick, muscular thighs and hips held the pants up without one. He'd disregarded the advice about bringing a coat.

The agent gave a verbal command and the front windows rolled down. Another request from the agent and the passenger side door opened to allow entry.

Clay swallowed hard.

"Hop in," Hank said in a welcoming tone.

Clay climbed in and the door closed automatically, with barely a sound.

"It has a driverless mode if I choose to use it," he informed Clay.

"But you won't."

"Relax, pal," chuckled Hank as he slapped Clay on the knee.

Gallagher pulled his rental vehicle out of the student parking lot and drove to the Rohnert Park Expressway. Next thing they knew, they were turning south onto Highway 101 and cruising along in the slow lane at seventy miles per hour while electric semi-trucks passed them going ninety in the fast lane.

San Francisco was located an hour away. Plenty of time for the agent to talk with his potential client. They hadn't yet signed the all-important contract.

"Our first stop will be St. Francis Hospital for your appointment with Government's people."

"First stop?"

"After that I've lined up a meeting with Hiroshi Tanaka," replied Hank. "They call him Sperm Master. He lives like a king. Owns his own island where he brings together the most fertile individuals left on the planet. He hires them at exorbitant salaries and treats them like royalty. He wants you to . . . huh . . . work for him, but he's going to fill you in on the details of his offer himself."

"This is so bizarre!" Clay exclaimed.

"Things are a little ca-ray-zy," agreed Hank. "That's what happens when a species faces extinction. Abnormal behavior becomes the norm. Small penises in alligators, panthers, and mink. Male turtles start humping male turtles. Female frogs become masculinized. Fish, birds, and frogs now have both male and female gonads. Been going on for decades."

"Weird."

Clay gazed out the window as they passed the charred remains of a once green highway windbreak. Black misshapen tree trunks, devoid of their canopies. Their ashes had blown away long ago. A stark reminder of how massive California wildfires had denuded the landscape of a bygone Golden State.

The earth had burned.

Day and night.

It wasn't just California. The scenario, played out on every continent on planet Earth, had almost reached the point of no return. And it was only the year 2050. Not some far-off futuristic world. There had been dire warnings, but the speed of the changes shocked even the most pessimistic in the scientific community.

Clay remembered the summers of his childhood years. They weren't fond memories. Weeks spent indoors as smoke turned the air a sickly charcoal color. The acrid taste of ash on the tongue. Rolling blackouts for days on end. Summer after summer until finally there wasn't much left to burn because wildfires had destroyed two-thirds of the state's forests. Entire towns perished. Mudslides from winter rains washed away many of the communities that had miraculously escaped the infernos.

They replanted the trees and some of them lasted another ten to twenty years, but there came new fires even though they'd finally learned to clear out the underbrush. Nobody could prevent lightning strikes.

A dark mood.

Clay didn't want to think about the ongoing drought that had devastated the western United States. Once thought to be the most extreme in over a thousand years, it had defied time as it sucked the earth dry, leaving chaos in its wake: rivers and lakes and reservoirs had dried up, the electrical grid had collapsed, unprecedented crop failures had decimated the nation's food supply, and millions of Americans had suddenly become climate refugees.

Along with millions of sea-rise casualties on both coasts.

Don't even go there, he said to himself as his thoughts returned to his personal situation. Three days ago he never would've imaged himself sitting in a car and being driven to San Francisco for an appointment with Government's hand-chosen physician. All because of his sperm count. Triple threat. Isn't that how Hank Gallagher had described him? He shook his head in disbelief.

"This is insane," he said out loud.

"Where have you been, buddy," laughed Hank. "We're living in a ca-ray-zee world. Like I said, it's been like this for some time. A long time. Which reminds me of an old joke my grandfather used to tell."

"Let's hear it."

"What's the main advantage of being a test tube baby?"

"I give . . . "

"You get a womb with a view."

Hank looked over to gauge Clay's response.

"Sick joke," Clay chuckled. "Really, not funny . . . "

"It was back in the day," insisted Hank. "Back when my grandfather was growing up."

The miles rolled on.

They spotted the turn-off sign for Sausalito, a small city originally known for its houseboat enclaves and fishermen's shacks converted into vacation homes by wealthy San Franciscans, at the close of the 19th Century. Others soon built houseboats and moored them in the cove.

The end of World War II, and the closing of the local shipyard, jump started an unregulated community. Created by artist squatters and other free spirits, using a treasure trove of unfinished boats, lumber, metal, machinery and parts that had been left behind in the shipyard, the floating homes were linked to the piers by ramshackle wooden walkways.

An art scene flourished here and gained traction with the coming of the beatniks and hippies. Half a century later, home prices on the waterfront and nearby hills were among the most expensive in America.

This didn't last.

The once tony enclave on the water, with its gorgeous views of the Golden Gate Bridge and the San Francisco skyline, became the victim of rising seas. Another miscalculation. One among many as coastal communities were literally swamped all over the planet once the Doomsday Glacier broke free in western Antarctica, in the year 2028. The one to two foot rise in sea levels projected by 2050 turned out to be a ten foot increase by 2040.

The change proved devastating for the town they were passing by, one whose name translates from Spanish as "little willow grove." Popular restaurants and shops on the major boulevard, along with homes and apartments and exclusive hotels close to the waterfront, had all but disappeared. The coveted and expensive real estate, in an already overpriced market, became virtually worthless.

Sausalito wasn't alone. Other prime seaside locations faced the same fate: the French Riviera, Spain's Costa del Luz, and Portugal's Algarve. Nobody had imagined the catastrophe that was to come. It seemed too inconceivable. It boggled the mind. Undermined by saltwater and erosion, beachfront high-rise condos and hotels collapsed into the seas. Entire beach communities were wiped out. Residents of cities, towns, and villages all over the world retreated inland.

Hank and Clay continued on their way south as the San Francisco skyline emerged in the distance. The agent drove on, descending down the Waldo Grade and then through the Robin Williams Tunnel, named in honor of the late actor and comedian who grew up and lived in the area.

They began their drive across the Golden Gate Bridge, an iconic suspension bridge built at the place where the waters of San Francisco Bay open out into the mighty Pacific Ocean.

When Clay gazed up at the bridge's seven hundred-foot high towers, painted a color described as International Orange, he felt his stomach churning. He swallowed hard, but his dry mouth wasn't cooperating. He reached for his metal water flask and took a sip. Then another.

13

Clay Roberts knew once they crossed over that bridge and entered San Francisco his life would never be the same.

CHAPTER 3

Homeless encampments lined the sidewalks with stoned drug addicts lying around on the pavement or sitting outside of tattered tents and make-shift huts fashioned from cardboard and duct tape. Many still had needles sticking out of their arms or up from between their toes.

Clay had never been to San Francisco.

"I thought they'd organized encampments for the homeless," he began "We heard that volunteers fed them and made sure they were living in sanitary conditions."

"The camps are overrun," Hank asserted. "Some of those people don't want to live there anyway. They don't like the rules. Some are mentally ill."

"This place is depressing," Clay said as he turned away.

"It's gotten better," Hank insisted. "We no longer have thousands of addicts dying in the streets every year. We're down to hundreds. When the drug dealers started adding fentanyl to everything the death rate soared. The city stopped providing free services and that slowed the tide streaming into San Francisco."

"How can you stand this?"

"This is the hellhole I grew up in," the agent told him. "You get used to it if you live here."

They cruised down a couple of blocks filled with boarded-up stores before they drove into the entrance of St. Francis Hospital. Hank climbed out of the vehicle. This surprised Clay because he thought his agent would find a nearby parking garage and wait there with the car. A smiling pimple-faced valet, dressed in royal blue with a hospital logo stitched on his jacket, came out to greet them as Clay disembarked from the passenger side.

"Keys are in the car," said Hank.

The valet handed Hank a ticket to present when it came time to retrieve the rental.

The agent ushered his client through the front doors of the hospital, one named for the patron saint of nature and animals. Once safely inside, he took Clay aside for some final instructions.

"You brought your ID?"

"Just like you said."

Clay gazed around the waiting room at the wretched faces of those waiting to be seen for a variety of maladies. The men, women, and children appeared listless and weighed down with the burdens of their lives. A couple of whimpering preschoolers hovered around their mother while she tried to console them.

"How can anyone get used to this?" asked Clay.

Hank ignored the question.

"They'll try to get you to commit to government service," he told Clay while lowering his voice. "Tell them that you'll think it over. Don't commit to anything today."

"Okay," replied Clay. "Anything else?"

"Be yourself," advised Hank. "You'll be fine."

"Guess I'd better go."

"I'll wait for you here in the lobby," Hank reassured him. "I've got some business I can work on while you're upstairs."

Clay smiled. It felt forced. A frown would have revealed the extent of his anxiety. He shrugged his shoulders and made for the elevator where he pushed the "Up" button and waited. The door opened, he entered, and then he turned to catch one last glimpse of Hank. The agent had already donned his sleek new Smart Glasses.

The elevator stopped at the fourth floor.

Clay stepped out to discover himself at the end of a long hallway. He found a wall to his left. Dead end, he observed. He scanned to his right. Down a short corridor, etched on the

16

glass of a nondescript door, the words United States Medical Service were written in big, bold letters.

A uniformed guard stood off to one side of the door. He appeared to be armed, but the weapon wasn't visible. Clay just sensed a threat. One that told him to be on his best behavior.

"ID," the man demanded in a brusque tone as Clay approached.

Clay took out his wallet and opened it to reveal his driver's license. The guard peered closely at the Photo ID and then studied Clay's features. He looked back and forth between the ID and the license. Finally, he gave a curt nod as he opened the door and allowed Clay to enter the waiting room.

Once inside, Clay took a deep breath and sighed. He found chairs arranged along three walls. Walls painted a soft green. Little square tables separated the chairs by threes and fours and the obligatory magazines lay atop them. A door, on the far side of the room, led to who knew where. Clay could only guess, but he suspected that he would soon find out.

A receptionist, dressed in a starched white nurse's uniform, sat at a duty station sealed off by a plexiglass partition with a half dome opening cut out from the center at the bottom of the panel.

Clay approached and waited for her to speak to him through the opening.

"May I help you?" she asked.

"I'm Clay Roberts," he responded. "I was told to report here for a ten o'clock appointment."

The woman searched her computer records. She printed out a document and slid it across the counter along with a pen.

"Complete this form and then bring it back," she instructed. "Be sure to sign and date it."

Clay filled out the questionnaire and returned the completed information back to the receptionist before resuming his seat.

He was wondering what exactly he'd agreed to when the door on the far side of the room opened and a tall, silver-haired gentleman appeared. The man wore an unbuttoned lab coat over a white shirt with a black tie and black slacks and shoes.

"Clay Roberts!"

Clay stood and walked towards the door.

"Come this way, please," the soothing voice requested of him. "I'm Doctor Sheridan."

Clay remained silent as he followed the man down a hallway with two office doors on each side. The doctor stopped at the last door on the right. It stood slightly ajar.

Dr. Sheridan opened it wider and beckoned for Clay to enter first.

"Please, after you."

His good manners were meant to charm visitors and put them at ease.

The doctor walked over behind a desk made from rich, dark walnut. He sat down in a matching wooden chair and motioned for Clay to sit. Once he was seated, Dr. Sheridan took control of the interview.

"Stop me if this gets too scientific for you," said the doctor. "I'll try to keep it simple."

"All right," agreed Clay.

"I want to talk about sperm in some detail so that you understand what makes you such an exceptional young man." The doctor folded his hands and placed them down on the desk in front of himself. "A healthy sperm cell contains DNA in its torpedo like head, energy providing mitochondria packed into its middle section, and a long tail to propel the little swimmers forward. I'll be showing you a sample of your own sperm in just a minute."

Clay's gaze went to one of the back walls where there was a table set up with a microscope and a small, stainless steel suitcase sitting next to it.

"It's not just the total sperm count that matters," continued Doctor Sheridan. "It's also about their shape and how they move. Physicians and scientists consider concentration, movement, and their size and shape as the *big three* factors in overall male fertility."

Clay thought back to one of Hank's earliest comments, "You're a triple threat." Now he understood what his agent had implied. He didn't have a chance to consider this further because Doctor Sheridan rose from his chair.

He motioned for Clay to follow as he walked over to the microscope. They stood side by side as Clay watched the physician unlatch what he thought was a suitcase. Inside there were a dozen labeled vials containing a cloudy, whitish liquid with a jelly-like consistency, similar to an egg white. They rested in little pockets tucked down into a red velvet lining.

Doctor Sheridan picked up a vial, unscrewed the dropper, and squeezed a drop of semen on the glass slide. He returned the dropper to the vial, screwed it on tight, and placed it carefully back down into the empty pocket.

He put the slide under the microscope, then turned a knob to adjust what he was seeing to match up with his own vision.

"Do you wear glasses, Clay?"

"No, Sir."

"Good, neither do I." Doctor Sheridan took a couple of steps back. "Come here and take a look."

Clay moved in closer, leaned over, and peered into the lens of the microscope.

"Tell me what you see . . . "

"They look like little tadpoles," laughed Clay. "They're swimming together like a school of fish."

"But they aren't swimming in a circle."

"No."

"That's good. They may actually be able to reach and penetrate an unfertilized egg. These days we see a lot of sperm that aren't moving at all. Just lying around the pool sipping margaritas."

Doctor Sheridan waited for a response to his little joke. When none was forthcoming, he resorted to his bland professional persona. "We call their swimming ability, motility. We also see sperm with abnormal shapes. Few have all the component parts."

Clay was given a minute to consider all of this as Doctor Sheridan closed the stainless steel case. He took a key from his coat pocket, inserted it into a lock on the suitcase, and turned it. Once he was satisfied the case was secure, he returned the key to his pocket.

"You're a very unusual young man," said the physician. "Almost all the young men that I talk with these days have only two strong markers at best. You're a rare specimen. Very rare."

This surprised Clay. He'd never viewed himself as special in any particular way.

"Come on," exclaimed Doctor Sheridan with enthusiasm in his voice. "I'd like you to meet a colleague of mine."

They stood across the hall, one door down.

Doctor Sheridan knocked on the door before entering. This courteous gesture gave the person or people inside time to compose themselves.

"Come in," said another soothing voice.

Only this time it was a woman's voice.

Doctor Sheridan opened the door, again allowing Clay to enter before him. A thirtyish brunette, dressed in a wrinkle-free, olive drab blouse with a matching skirt, rose to greet them. The attractive woman wore a small, military style hat on her well-coiffed hair, using a couple of strategically located hair pins to keep it in place.

"Hello, Doctor Sheridan," she cooed with a gracious smile.

"I'd like you to meet Clay Roberts."

"Hello, Clay," said the woman as she rose from her desk and extended her hand.

Clay approached her and took hold of the hand, careful not to squeeze too tight.

Her hand felt soft and warm.

"I'll leave you two to chat things over," said Doctor Sheridan as he quietly turned around and walked back through the open door before closing it shut.

"I'm Major Morgan," the woman told Clay while gesturing to the chair in front of him. "Make yourself comfortable."

Clay eased himself down. Everyone here is so nice, he thought. A more discerning individual might have wondered if the well-choreographed visit had been staged. It never crossed his mind. At least not at that point.

"Did Doctor Sheridan explain your qualifications?"

"Yes, Ma'am."

"So you understand why we think that you're such a very special person."

"Umm-hmm," he answered, nodding his head.

"We'd like for you to join us here at the National Fertility Service."

Hank had briefed him not to commit to anything during the interview, so Clay sat in his chair pretending he was thinking over the offer.

"We only select from the cream of the crop," she assured him.

Unperturbed by the silence, Major Morgan got up from the desk and walked to the back of the room where a slide projector awaited her.

A morning of slides of one type or another, Clay thought to himself as the little swimming tadpoles came to mind.

Major Morgan turned off the lights and the first image, in 3D color, quickly flashed on the bare white wall at the opposite side of the room.

An aerial view of The Pentagon building.

The images raced by in rapid succession: smiling recruits, both young men and women, some with thumbs up or two-fingers held up to form a V; a nursery full of giggling toddlers; a bulleted list of benefits enjoyed by the National Fertility Service team members; a park-like setting with couples picnicking on the grass; a row of condominiums with the Lincoln Monument superimposed upon the background; a gigantic American flag waving proudly in the breeze; and, a full-screen, airbrushed picture of the current President of the United States, her silver hair elegantly trimmed, sporting an NFS logo on her blouse.

The slides suddenly stopped.

The lights came back on.

Major Morgan went back to her desk and sat.

Clay, who'd barely had time to blink during the barrage of images, waited for her to speak.

"So you were home-schooled," she said. It was more a statement than a question.

"All my life," he admitted.

He couldn't help but wonder how she knew this.

"So was I," Major Morgan said with a smile. "And I'm grateful to my parents, as I'm sure you are."

There came no response as Clay sat waiting for her to continue.

"I have a personal reason for working at the National Fertility Service."

Clay waited to hear what it might be.

"I'm infertile," she sniffed as she leaned across the desk to make eye contact.

He saw that hers were hazel.

Major Morgan then shared some intimate details as her voice lowered to a whisper.

"I cried for days after the results came in. You can imagine how I felt. My parents were devastated. They encouraged me to join the National Fertility Service to help me overcome my personal misfortune. I found new meaning for myself at NFS. My mission in life is to enable capable men and women, and there aren't many, to bring healthy babies into this world."

Clay was at a loss for words. Was her story true or an imaginary account delivered by an accomplished actress? He wasn't sure who or what to believe. He had entered a hall of mirrors.

She certainly didn't appear to be infertile. Quite the opposite. She looked like she was in the prime of her life. Maybe that was the point. Most of the seemingly healthy looking individuals on the planet were incapable of reproduction.

"I'm sorry," Clay sympathized.

"Now you, too, have the opportunity to serve your country."

Another awkward silence.

"What I'm about to tell you stays in this room," she announced as a tone of steely determination crept into her voice. "I can trust you, right?"

Clay nodded affirmatively.

"We're at war, Clay. We all know that the World Council proclaims international solidarity, but that body is dominated by the United States, China, and Russia. Each of us is doing all we can, individually, to ensure the survival of our own country at the expense of the others. The National Fertility Service is leading the way for us here in America."

She gave Clay a moment to consider the importance of the information that she was sharing with him.

"Procreation is a patriotic duty. A new form of warfare as countries compete to see who can increase their dwindling populations and save themselves from generational disaster. The Chinese initiated mandatory testing and followed that up with monetary enticements for the most promising candidates. They had some minor successes, but not nearly enough to narrow the gap. They've never been able to alter the curve of their declining, aging population. Their one-child policy has come back to haunt them."

Major Morgan gave Clay more time to absorb everything she had conveyed to him.

He felt light-headed. What the hell's going on, he wondered.

She smiled.

He knew her pitch was about to continue.

"The victors will survive and we want to be among them, Clay. It's your patriotic duty to help us succeed, but we realize there are other suitors who will entice you with their generous offers to gain your services."

Clay sighed deeply.

Information overload.

"The most promising candidates have always been lured away by Sperm Master and there's nothing we can do about it except appeal to you to put your country first. You get the picture, right?" she asked, reverting to her soothing voice. "We need you."

You need my sperm, Clay thought to himself.

Major Morgan offered a knowing smile as she slid a contract and a pen across the desk towards him.

"Will you join us, Clay? Will you be a patriot fighting for the future of your country?"

Not the human race? questioned Clay. Just my own country. He could feel wet sweat under his arms beneath the short-sleeved cotton shirt. He sighed while experiencing a feeling of resignation. Hank had warned him this moment would come.

"I really need some time to think this over."

24

Major Morgan's shared secrets and appeal to patriotism usually got her the desired outcome, but her charm, the most important weapon in her emotional arsenal, didn't desert her.

"Of course, Clay," she agreed. She took a business card from its holder and handed it across the desk to him. "I'm a good judge of character and I know you'll do the right thing for your country."

Clay took the card and stared down like he was studying it, but he wasn't. He just gazed at the script and the logo. He could check out the details later.

Major Morgan extended her soft, warm hand back over to Clay.

"I'll be waiting for your call, Clay."

Clay shook her hand and offered an embarrassed smile as Major Morgan stood, signaling that their meeting had run its course.

"Come on, I'll walk you out," she told him.

He got up and as they walked to the door she placed her hand on his shoulder and gave it a gentle squeeze. A subliminal message or a gesture of encouragement. He couldn't be sure of anything.

"I'm counting on you, Clay."

He couldn't wait to get out of there.

"Your country is counting on you."

CHAPTER 4

They drove away from the hospital

Hank turned at Post Street and headed straight for Japantown.

"I thought Tanaka might stay at the St. Francis Hotel since it's so near the hospital," the agent observed. "Instead, he's staying at the Kabuki. Later, I found out why. He owns the place."

Clay didn't respond. He was lost in his own thoughts. All he could think about was his recent experience at the National Fertility Service offices. His stomach tightened.

"You know they were playing you, right?"

"I got that impression," replied Clay. "How can I be sure?"

Hank ignored the question.

"Once you enter National Service they own you. They control your movements. Maybe even your mind. They say that the orientation is more of an indoctrination. I heard they're all a bunch of professional actors and actresses."

"They seemed so sincere."

Hank rolled his eyes.

"Rumor has it that Tanaka is really Satoshi Nakamoto. Even that was a pseudonym. Nakamoto was credited for developing Bitcoin. You know, the world's first crypto-currency."

"Our dad taught us about financials," Clay interrupted before the agent delivered another long discourse. "Nakamoto mined the first blockchain of Bitcoin and he published the whitepaper for the digital currency."

"He'd be about seventy-years old," Hank rambled on, undeterred by his client's familiarity with the subject.

"Experts have estimated that he owns three-quarters of a million Bitcoin. Today one Bitcoin is worth almost a million dollars. I don't have to do the math to know that Nakamoto is probably the richest man in the world."

The Agent pulled into an open space at the curb of the hotel entrance. Another valet, this time a middle-aged Asian man, came out to greet them.

"Here we are," said Hank.

He left the keys in the ignition, with the car idling, and then waited until the street was clear before opening his door and getting out of the vehicle. Hank walked around the front of the car and opened the passenger door for Clay.

The valet bowed politely and then he handed the Agent a retrieval ticket. It had been time stamped. Hank returned the bow with much less grace while the valet waited for traffic to clear before making a move to get into the car.

"Let's go," said Hank with enthusiasm in his voice.

They entered the uncluttered, Zen-like lobby of the Hotel Kabuki.

The pagoda-style boutique hotel offered a calm and serene experience as potted plants and succulents mingled with wicker chairs and colorful throw pillows. Contemporary and traditional Japanese art adorned the walls. The cultural chic meets minimalism vibe was intended to relax the mind, body, and soul.

Hank appeared anything but relaxed as he pulled Clay aside.

"The staff used to be all Anglos if you can believe that," the agent informed his potential client before abruptly changing the subject. "I'll take care of the desk clerk. Just follow me."

"Yes, Sir!" joked Clay.

The agent shot Clay a sideways glance, and then his mouth stretched out into a grin.

"Like I said before," reminded Hank. "Just be yourself. Don't commit because we might get a better offer."

The reservationist, a young Asian woman with dancing eyes, looked up from her ledger as the two men approached:

"May I help you?"

"We . . . I mean my friend here . . . has an appointment with Mr. Tanaka."

"One moment, please."

The woman reached for a pair of Smart Glasses sitting nearby on the counter. She opened them and slid them over her ears as the dancing eyes disappeared behind dark lenses: "Mr. Tanaka's suite," she said before waiting for a response. It wasn't long in coming. "Would you tell Mr. Tanaka that his guest has arrived."

Hank and Clay couldn't hear the voice at the other end of the call, so they waited as the woman removed her glasses and placed them gently back down on the counter.

"Someone will be down in a minute," she said with a smile.

"Thank you," said Hank in a polite tone. "We'll just take a look around while we're waiting."

He walked Clay over to the lobby bar, careful to keep the elevator in clear sight. The bar spanned both indoors and outdoors, including fire pit seating by a well-stocked koi pond. The agent looked over the bar's offerings: Japanese whiskey, imported beer, sake, and a selection of California wines.

"I'm going to hang out here," the agent announced.

The elevator door opened and a couple, two attractive and well-dressed women, emerged from inside. They walked through the lobby, hand-in-hand, and left the hotel through automatic front doors leading out to the street.

Clay and Hank watched the elevator door close.

They waited some more, perhaps three minutes.

The elevator door suddenly opened and not one, but two men came out of the interior. Both looked like they might be retired Sumo wrestlers, their suits straining to hold their massive, bulky bodies. They appeared to be unarmed.

"Good luck with the interview, Clay," said Hank as he nudged Clay towards the two approaching behemoths.

The shorter of the two men spoke first.

"Please come with us, Mr. Roberts."

The unlikely trio made their way back to the elevator.

They rode it all the way to the top floor of the Hotel Kabuki.

The door opened and the three of them stepped out into a luxurious living room.

The two men escorting Clay disappeared through a door leading into a connecting suite.

Outside, on an adjoining balcony stood a tall, thin man. His head was shaved smoothly and he wore a khaki-colored linen shirt with matching trousers. His belt and shoes were identical brown suede. He had no socks covering his feet.

Once he saw the door to the attached suite close, he turned to begin the encounter.

The two men began walking towards one another.

Clay noticed that Tanaka's round face held features remarkably in proportion to one another. Nature had forgotten its universal asymmetry in his case. His light beige skin had a warm glow and Clay was surprised by the lack of wrinkles. He didn't think about these things. They were more like subliminal impressions, a fleeting gestalt.

A smiling Tanaka stopped and bowed gracefully.

Clay reciprocated.

A round table had been arranged for the two men. A white tablecloth with red velvet napkins set with flatware, two empty wine glasses, and two crystal goblets filled with water. Like a table setting at an elegant restaurant.

"Would you care for something to eat or drink, Mr. Roberts?" asked Tanaka as he gestured towards the table.

"I'm fine, thank you," replied Clay. He actually did feel pangs of hunger, but he didn't want to prolong the interview.

The two men sat at the table across from each other.

"Are you sure," coaxed his host with raised brows, a slight tilt of the head, and a beckoning smile. "We have excellent sushi here at Hotel Kabuki."

"I'm good."

"Very well, then I'll begin." said Tanaka, accepting the refusals graciously. "I'd like to tell you about our special place in the South Pacific where I've brought together the most fertile men and women on the earth. A little piece of paradise. Not surprisingly, some of our lucky residents find their mates on the island. Others prefer to offer their services to Sperm Centers and other Cryobanks. Everything done on our island is voluntary, and everyone has complete freedom to engage in any and all of the activities we provide. Unlike the various National Fertility Services--China, the United States, and Russia--we have no mandates or requirements if you choose to join us."

Tanaka paused from his long discourse to gaze across the table at Clay.

"I understand, Sir."

"Don't be fooled by Government," warned Tanaka. "You'll be safe from their reach on the island. Unlike them, we'll look after your health. Our optimal regimen and schedule will focus on your physical and spiritual well-being. You'll have an opportunity to work with wealthy clients if you like. The world's elite, at least in monetary terms."

Clay felt confused. Rich single women or couples where the husband was sterile? He couldn't be sure if Sperm Master was a guru or a businessman or a combination of both. He stole a look at the tight-lipped smile.

"You can just be a donor. You don't have to sleep with anyone."

Tanaka paused to take a sip of his water.

"We do seek a one-year commitment," he continued. "If you choose not to remain with us after that period of time, you are free to leave. People are coming and going all the time."

Tanaka folded his arms across his body.

"Do you have any questions?"

"Why are you doing this?" asked Clay. "I mean you, personally."

A warm smile.

"When I was a much younger man, still in my fifties, I was considered the most virile man on Earth. My services were much in demand as the looming threat of extinction became acknowledged after years of denial. The evidence existed much earlier, but few paid attention until the reality of the situation could no longer be ignored. I now choose to engage my energies in bringing together the men and women who might help prevent the total extinction of our species."

"I see . . . "

"We share something in common," Tanaka assured his guest. "We were both raised in rural environments. I believe this has something to do with our virility. A more natural upbringing, although we weren't completely spared the toxicities of the modern world."

A wistful look.

Another tight-lipped smile.

Clay struggled to understand how everyone he talked to knew so much about him. Major Morgan knew about his homeschooling, and Tanaka knows about the farm. It felt invasive. Like a door leading into his private life had been flung wide open.

Tanaka must have sensed his unease because he quickly changed the subject.

"I understand you've retained the services of an agent."

This was no secret. Hank had arranged the meeting.

"I'll negotiate the final contract with him, but first I'd like to explain the highlights of my offer in person. I usually have others perform these duties, but I wanted to meet with you personally to outline the basic terms, and to assure you that you'll be rewarded very well for your services."

"I'm honored, Sir."

"I'm certain you'll find my terms quite attractive, but first let me reiterate. We do not work for the continuation of any particular national polity. Our aims are not so narrow," asserted Tanaka. "We draw from a worldwide pool of applicants and in rare instances, such as yours, we recruit new members. We attract an international clientele who wish to avail themselves of our services. Our island is an eco-friendly zone whose aim is to foster the physical, spiritual, and emotional well-being of every individual that fate brings our way."

Tanaka paused to allow Clay time to consider all that he'd shared with him.

"Do you have any other questions, Clay?"

Clay thought about all that he'd been told.

"I don't think so."

"I am prepared to offer you forty million dollars a year."

"Forty million," repeated Clay.

"Fully guaranteed."

A silence ensued.

"I know that doesn't sound like much, Clay. But all your living expenses on the island will be taken care of as well."

Another long pause.

Clay Roberts gulped at the staggering offer he'd just been made.

"Then there's the matter of your signing bonus," Tanaka added. "I can give you one thousand bitcoin."

Clay smiled vacantly as the room spun around him. He sat stunned for a moment until the suite came back into focus.

Tanaka waited patiently until Clay realized that he was expected to give some sort of a response.

"That's very generous of you, but I'd like some time to think things over."

"Of course," responded Tanaka with a wan smile.

Clay had done just as Hank had advised.

"Take your time. I know the competition," smirked Tanaka.

That smirk was the first sign of . . . what was the word Clay sought . . . arrogance? An attitude hinting at a superiority complex. Maybe he was misreading the situation. Had Tanaka indicated his offer couldn't be beat? Why was he so certain?

Tanaka stood from the table indicating the meeting was drawing to its end. He took his wallet out of his back pocket and removed an embossed card. Clay got up as his host came around the table to hand him the second business card of the morning. Two more than he'd ever received in his entire life.

"After you've decided, you may call or text me anytime. Day or night," said Tanaka. "I'd appreciate it if you didn't share the information on that card."

"I understand."

"It's been a pleasure, Clay," said Tanaka in a soft, sincere voice as he extended his hand in-lieu of the ceremonial bow.

Clay hesitated, and then he realized this was a goodbye gesture. He shook the hand as both men looked each other in the eye.

"Until we meet again, Clay."

CHAPTER 5

Clay found Hank sitting at the bar.

"You good to drive, Hank?" he asked as he eased down on a stool next to the agent.

"I'm fine," the agent answered. "Just been hanging out here nursing a Sapporo. How'd things go?"

Clay spied the hall-filled glass of draft beer on the bar counter in front of Hank.

"Tanaka made me an offer," said Clay. "I couldn't believe it. The amount of money he offered is unbelievable."

"Care to share any of the details?"

"Forty million dollars a year, fully guaranteed," laughed Clay. "One thousand bitcoin for a signing bonus."

"Ca-ray-zee!"

Clay spied a bowl of mixed nuts sitting on the counter. He reached over and grabbed a handful to assuage his hunger while he waited for Hank to wrap his mind around the figures.

"Damn, we got ourselves a great offer!" exclaimed the agent. "You tempted?"

Clay surprised him by shaking his head no.

"Why not?" asked Hank. "One year frolicking around on his island and you'll be set for life."

I will be, too, thought the agent.

"The signing bonus is in Bitcoin."

"That's not unusual these days," Hank informed him.

"I know about the history of Bitcoin," Clay claimed. "Our dad taught us all about crypto. Bitcoin went through four major downturns in its first two decades. The more unstable the world got, the more appealing the use of crypto became. But the proof of mining work requires a lot of computing energy. Enough to power a small country. It's created billions of pounds of carbon emissions. It could be over a trillion by now."

"Sheesh! I had no idea," admitted Hank. "A matter of principle for you?"

"Exactly," replied Clay. "I think my parents would turn over in their graves if they'd actually been buried. My sister and I scattered their ashes in our orchards. That was what they wanted."

Hank decided to leave personal history alone and return to matters of business.

"Keep an open mind," Hank advised. "Even the National Fertility Service pays in crypto."

"Is it bitcoin?"

"Not sure," came the honest reply. "Might be that worthless Government token."

Clay let the matter drop as he reached for another handful of nuts.

"You want to stay at my place tonight?" inquired the agent. "It will give us time to talk things over."

"No thank you," said Clay, declining the offer. "I told my sister I'd be home after I was done."

"Then let's go," insisted Hank. He took a fifty dollar bill from his wallet and dropped it on the counter. "We've got a stop to make before we leave the city."

"What do you mean?"

"We need to pick up some burner phones," explained Hank. "They'll be able to track your phone, which means your location, through GPS. I heard a rumor that Government can find you and lock your car doors remotely and take control of the vehicle. Take you to some designated place of their choosing. You disappear. Vanish from the face of the earth so they can use you for their own purposes."

Clay appreciated that his agent was looking out for him. He hadn't considered the possibility that the National Fertility Service, or Tanaka, or another interested party might be tracking his whereabouts. He already felt that they had invaded his privacy and wormed their way into his once secluded life.

Now his sister Jodie's private life could be at stake.

That thought began to scare him.

Clay hadn't told her yet.

They cruised up the Waldo Grade.

It seemed like the scenery was nonexistent. It hadn't disappeared. In fact, it was much the same as on the ride down to San Francisco. Only now, Clay and Hank were fixated on the events of the morning and simply weren't interested in the desolate landscape.

"I've been thinking about Tanaka's offer," said Hank. "It sounded generous at first, but that's less than players in the NFL made before they banned the sport a decade ago. Do you remember?"

"Vaguely."

"There were massive demonstrations all over the country because the evidence proved that CTE was widespread and lethal. So many suicides and mental problems in the community of ex-athletes. The bans started with youth football and worked their way up to the colleges. They shut down the gladiatorial pipeline completely. That put an end to the NFL. Not that most of the world gave a shit. For a majority of countries, football means soccer. "

"Is there a point to all this, Hank?"

"Tanaka," answered the agent. "If you sign up with him, he's going to tokenize you. I'm sure of it. He'll make billions. He didn't mention anything about it?"

"No."

"We don't need him. We can do that ourselves. I got some people who can help us set it up. Get us on the GTE."

"GTE?"

"Global Token Exchange."

"Oh . . . "

"Getting back to football players," said Hank, not wanting to let the subject go. "Most of them had a short shelf life. A couple of years, if that. You're going to have to take good care of yourself if you want a long career."

"What kind of a career do you envision for me?"

"I'm leaning towards Sperm Banks," confessed Hank. "We'll have complete control over the process. Where and when to give specimens. All you've got to do is go into some room and jerk off into a plastic container."

"Not glass?"

"I don't think so, but we can make a special request. Whatever it takes. You're going to be treated like royalty. They usually have porn magazines available, but we can ask for porno flicks if you want. We could probably have them bring in a masseuse. There's going to be a high demand for your sperm all over the planet. I can see it now. You're going to be on the cover of Fertility Magazine. Person of the Year: "The Sperm King.""

"I could just use my own imagination," Clay protested. "I'm not into porn."

"Just as well," mused Hank. "It would work against you in the long run. Shorten your career."

"What do you mean?"

"They found that guys who consumed a lot of porn suffered from major erectile dysfunction," the agent told him. "Their dopamine reserves were depleted due to overstimulation."

Clay turned to consider the man sitting next to him. Perhaps he'd sold him short.

"How do you know all this, Hank?"

"It's my business, buddy," replied the agent. "I've learned more than I ever wanted about the nature of sperm. Did you know that the ancient Pharaohs married their sisters? The idea is now being widely promoted as a possible option to forestall extinction."

The thought of marriage to and physical intimacy with his sister grossed Clay out. He didn't even like her half the time because she possessed a superior intelligence and a biting tongue.

"Marry my sister? Good Lord!" sighed Clay. "What kind of a world is this?"

"A very dysfunctional one if you haven't noticed," came the reply.

"How could such a thing happen?"

"You really do live in your own little world, don't you?"

"Don't we all," shrugged Clay.

"Some more than others." said Hank. "They can't force you to do anything, but the pressure will be intense. They'll hound you day and night. That's the reason I got the burner phones."

Angels Island and Sausalito soon faded into the distance and then disappeared from the rear-view mirror. Back though the charred landscape they drove. Back past the black stumped windbreak.

"The Sperm King. Yeah, that's what they're going to call you," said Hank, with a certain degree of admiration. "Fertile women will be lining up for you. We can hold a lottery."

"You're not serious?"

"Hell yes," asserted the agent. "Most men would give anything to be in your place."

"I'm not most men."

You're telling me, Hank thought to himself.

"You still don't get it, do you," It was more a statement than a question. "We're talking about the survival of the fucking human race."

"I'm not sure I want humanity to survive," admitted Clay.

Hank's jaw dropped. His hands began shaking on the steering wheel as the car veered off the highway towards the side of the road.

Clay's heart started beating wildly. Has he lost control? Clay wondered as he grabbed the wheel and turned it back to the left until they had re-entered the slow lane.

Hank regained control of the car.

"Maybe you ought to use that driverless mode," quipped Clay.

"Fuck you!" shouted Hank as his emotions got the best of him.

Not another word passed between them until they reached the university parking lot.

CHAPTER 6

Hank tried to repair the damage.

As soon as they arrived back at the university parking lot, he turned to Clay to apologize.

"I guess I overreacted."

"No man. It was my fault," Clay reassured him. His response made it sound like he was full of remorse. He was. He actually felt bad for Hank after subjecting the wannabe agent to his vitriol.

"Sometimes my mind gets into a dark place and I get a little down about what we've done to the planet. I never know when my feelings are going to get the best of me. It all just comes out of nowhere."

"Yeah, I feel down at times, too," Hank confessed. "I haven't really had all that much success as an agent, and I feel guilty that I haven't been able to do more to prevent our extinction. That's the reason I got into this business."

"Why don't you spend the night at our farm?" Clay suggested in a spontaneous moment. "You can meet my sister, Jodie. We can all talk about what's going on with my situation."

Hank reflected for a moment. He hadn't expected the invite. He wasn't really prepared. No change of clothes. No toiletries. He was determined not to let these shortcomings defer him from his goal. Spending time with Clay and his sister might bode well for him. Perhaps for all concerned. He had brought the contract with him. It was inside his leather briefcase. He thought if he accepted the invitation he might convince Clay to sign on the dotted line.

"All right!" exclaimed the agent enthusiastically.

"Want to follow me out to my place in this car?"

"Do you think they'd tow it away if I leave it here?"

"You kidding? They're so desperate for students they've lifted all of the parking restrictions."

Clay wasn't exaggerating. The educational system in the United States, and worldwide for that matter, had fallen into disfavor because of its irrelevance in the face of human created climate change. Institutions of higher education didn't take the lead in pushing back against the vested interests responsible for global warming and they didn't adapt their curriculums in a timely manner. It made them appear complicit. It was another example of not understanding the difficulty of the challenges facing the planet and the speed of change. Maintain the status quo. Keep going with business as usual.

Sonoma State University now survived by contracting the Student Health Center out to Government for their mandated sperm testing program. Other universities also provided locations in an effort to keep the struggling educational system alive. Universities and colleges were too expensive. The student loan fiasco, along with a lack of students because of the declining population, hadn't helped matters. Then there was the bitter fact that most young people had to work their entire lives due to the collapse of safety nets like Social Security and Medicare.

"Remember that unique Wine Business Institute?"

"Vaguely."

"They had to close it down," Clay told him. "The demise of California's wine industry made it useless."

Though he wasn't sure how long he'd be at the farm, Hank Gallagher had his priorities and stuck to them. The things Clay had shared with him were interesting, but there was a decision to be made. He pondered it, but not for long.

"Let's leave the car here," said the agent. "I rented it for a week because the rate was cheaper."

Clay nodded his consent.

"I need to let my roommates know that I won't be back tonight," said Hank. "They might rent my room out from under me."

"You're joking."

"Yeah, I am, but it's almost impossible to find housing in San Francisco. I live with three other guys so we can make the rent payment. I don't want them thinking that I skipped out on them."

Clay waited patiently while the agent made his call.

It didn't take long.

"We're good to go," he announced.

"Grab your stuff," said Clay.

Hank didn't have much to take with him. His leather briefcase and a couple of candy bars he'd brought with him to snack on. He locked the vehicle and followed Clay over to an old pick-up truck parked a few spaces away.

"How old is this dinosaur?" Hank asked.

"About twenty years old," Clay replied. "A second generation Ford F-150 Lightning. I like it cause of the high clearance. They don't maintain the roads very well outside of town."

What had he gotten himself into, wondered Hank as the two men climbed up into the cab, settled into their seats, and buckled their seatbelts.

"Is this the model with the trunk in the front where the engine used to be?"

"Yeah, they call it a frunk," replied Clay. "It's still got the bed for hauling equipment and materials."

Soon they were leaving the university and driving south. At a small town called Cotati, named after a peaceful tribe of Coast Miwok Native Americans who'd once lived in the valley, they turned onto the Gravenstein Highway and proceeded in a northwesterly direction. The road, which wound its way south from the Russian River through small towns like Forestville and Sebastopol, was named in honor of the Gravenstein apple.

Thousands of acres once covered the area. The "Grav" was at the center of the local economy. Apples were sold fresh and processed at dozens of plants into applesauce, vinegar, and cider. Cuttings were first planted at Fort Ross, arriving with early 19th century Russian sailing vessels.

On the advice of plant wizard Luther Burbank, Nathanial Griffith created the first orchard in Sebastopol, in 1890. By the 1930s there were almost twenty-five square miles of "Gravs" and demand was enormous. The juicy, crisp apple eventually gave way to grapes as orchards were converted to vineyards to grow a crop worth ten times more per ton. Little evidence of the original industry remained by the time Clay turned off the highway at Lone Pine Road.

"How can Tanaka have an island with our rising seas?" Clay wondered aloud. It was a question he'd wanted to ask Hank earlier, but it had slipped his mind.

"His island is surrounded by a giant rock sea wall. They say it rivals the Great Wall of China. The place even has beaches," continued the agent. "And multiple plateaus leading up to a mountaintop. Unique to the planet. He wants to attract fertile people and a rich clientele who are desperate for heirs."

"How about you, Hank?" asked Clay. "What's your status?"

"Infertile. No doubt about it. I'm not alone. You're the exception. That's why I'm here talking to you. I mean the rest of us are like eunuchs. Only we weren't castrated. At least not manually. Nature performed that operation on us. A fitting kind of revenge for what we've done to the earth, I'd say."

"The sins of our fathers."

"Exactly."

"Not my father," Clay added as an afterthought.

Clay felt a sense of compassion for Hank. For all the millions, and once possibly billions, of men who had lost or never even possessed their reproductive birthright after being born into a chemically toxic world.

Clay still felt like he needed to make amends. He knew that at times he was given to a deep, dark despair. Hank seemed to be excitable, but apparently he had a kind heart. He cared for the future of the human race. He wasn't in this business just for the money.

They passed a field of blooming lavender waving gently in the afternoon breeze.

Clay rolled down the windows.

"Inhale that aroma, Hank."

"Man, that smells like expensive perfume."

"Only better."

Hank began to take a closer look at his surroundings as the road became lined with trees.

"What kind of trees are these," he wanted to know. "The ones we're driving through."

"Mostly Douglas fir. They're native to the area. There is also a sprinkling of spruce, pine, cypress, and cedar. A mixed bag."

They left the conifers behind as the countryside opened back out to expanses of rolling hills. A car soon appeared behind the pick-up. Clay caught a glimpse of it in his rear view mirror. It seemed to be following extremely close. Were they being tailed? He mentioned his suspicions to Hank.

"Pull over as soon as you have a chance," he was advised.

Clay turned into a long driveway and the car behind them passed. They waited for a time, but the car continued on without returning.

"Maybe I'm getting paranoid," admitted Clay.

"No worries," Hank reassured him. "You have good reason to be."

Clay frowned, threw the car into reverse, and backed down the long driveway. He got back on the road and followed it until it became Bloomfield Road. This led them down to Knowles Corner, a little hamlet consisting of a smattering of farms, ranches and large swatches of open land.

A right turn at the intersection, a few miles more, and then Clay reached the dirt road that would take him home.

"So green out here," observed Hank.

"We're only ten miles from the coast so we benefit from the fog that rolls in and out of these hills," explained Clay. "Our parents told us there used to be more trees in this area, but they succumbed to the worst drought in twelve centuries. You know, the one we were still experiencing."

"I heard that there used to be a lot more foggy days in San Francisco," said the agent, repeating what his mother and grandmother had told him.

Clay had no comment.

"I can't get over it," Hank said. "This is like a slice of paradise."

"Not really," responded Clay. "We never escaped the smoke from all the wildfires. Lucky for us my dad stockpiled HEPA filters. Otherwise, we might have had to leave the farm for long stretches at a time. We never knew when that might be since the fire season lasted year round."

He's opening up. Talking more. He feels more relaxed out here, thought Hank.

Clay slowed the pick-up as he turned into a narrow tree-lined lane. There was no address sign and no mailbox. Just the dirt road. Most people would have driven past the entrance without even seeing it, mused the agent. He knew that he would have, and he admitted this to himself as an afterthought.

The trees gave way to open land as Clay pulled up to a modest two-story 1930s farmhouse. It wasn't painted the traditional white, but a pleasant sage green. A color tone that blended nicely with the surroundings. This wasn't a custom home and nothing indicated that it was in any way special. At least not from appearances.

Clay drove up and parked outside the front entrance
"We're here."

Inside the house, Clay's sister Jodie heard his pick-up arrive and went out to greet him.

She was taken by surprise when she found someone sitting next to her brother in the front seat. A man that she didn't recognize. This seemed odd. She wasn't used to Clay bringing home strangers.

The two men emerged from the truck.

Hank smiled and looked her over. It was more observational, not the predatory ogling some men engage in. Still, he liked what he saw. Five-foot seven, blue eyes and blond shoulder-length hair. Slender and healthy looking in jeans, tennis shoes, and a Mexican style blouse with intricate embroidery. Hope she's friendly, he said to himself.

Jodie shot Clay a questioning look.

"We need to talk, sis."

"Does this have anything to do with the specimen that you left with Government the other day?"

She's so damned intuitive, thought Clay before he realized that he hadn't yet introduced his guest.

"This is Hank Gallagher," he said motioning to Hank.

The agent walked around to the front of the truck and extended his hand. Jodie gave it a limp squeeze. Not the friendly gesture Hank had hoped for, or even expected.

"Let's go inside," Jodie suggested. "It's too hot out here."

The two men followed her to the door and then into the house.

Clay closed the door behind Hank while the agent briefly surveyed the interior of the Robert's home.

It had an open floor plan with a cozy living room just off to the left of the front door. A butter yellow sofa, and a matching occasional chair, sat on a floor made from wide-planked, recycled wood. The floor was partially covered by a jute area rug. No television.

Hank spied a small table with a chess set and two chairs. Although he was curious, the agent decided not to look around any further. He didn't want to appear inattentive when

46

Clay and his sister engaged in conversation. One in which he might emerge as the principal subject.

"Shall we sit and talk?" asked Clay.

"Let's," agreed Jodie, anxiously awaiting an explanation. She walked into the living room and plopped herself down on the side chair, leaving the sofa to Clay and Hank. It would be easier to grill them if she could look them both directly in the eye.

"Hank wants to be my agent," Clay began.

"Agent?"

"I should start from the beginning," said Hank. "Tell you how this all came about."

Jodie looked the agent in the eye. He didn't squirm. He held his own. She interpreted this as a positive sign. Perhaps she would get an honest rendition.

"I'd like that, Hank."

Clay's stomach churned. He wanted the agent to sound sincere, but he sensed that his sister was already displeased with them both. Why hadn't he told her? Hank had asked him to wait. He hoped this salient fact would emerge from the agent's own mouth. Jodie might be more accepting of the situation once she' understood how this unbelievable scenario had unfolded.

An hour later.

They were nearing the end of their conversation. One in which Clay and Hank both recounted the events of the day. All except for the contentious incident on the return trip. They both decided to keep that under wraps.

"So you see, Jodie, I'm to blame for Clay not telling you about me," admitted Hank. "I asked him not to. I was trying to protect his privacy for as long as I could. Same reason I got us some burner phones. Things could become a little ca-ray-zee."

An uncomfortable silence ensued.

Jodie finally spoke up.

47

"Thank you for helping my brother," Jodie said with genuine appreciation.

Hank breathed a sigh of relief and decided it was time for a little light-hearted banter.

"You guys play chess?" he asked, gesturing over to the chessboard.

"Our dad taught us," replied Clay. "He used to always beat our mom. It drove her crazy."

"I think she beat him two or three times," added Jodie.

"How about you two?"

"Jodie wins most of the time," groused Clay.

Sometimes it was annoying having a younger sister. Especially one with a superior intellect. She was the smart one. Neither of them had any doubt about that. His sister was pursuing a degree. Studying online and taking classes at the university in town while he felt content working at the farm, attending to his handmade life.

That also annoyed him. She'd go into town, take a couple of classes, and spend the rest of the day with her friends. Sometimes he thought she was lazy and wondered if she might one day leave him to run the farm alone. Would she really do that? Maybe what he needed was to find someone special. A relationship that might lead to marriage. To meet someone new he'd probably have to take classes at the university himself, and mingle with other students.

"Do you play chess?" Jodie asked the agent.

"I played checkers when I was younger," he replied. "I never learned chess because I couldn't sit still long enough to finish a game."

There was an awkward pause in the conversation.

Nobody said a word because nobody knew what to say.

"You guys must be hungry," declared Jodie, finally breaking the uneasy silence. "Clay, why don't you show Hank around while I make us something to eat."

The threesome rose from their seats. The agent followed Clay and his sister as they turned a corner and made their way straight into a kitchen lined with white cabinets on white walls and a ceiling made from tongue and groove paneling, also painted a matching white. A long counter separated the cooking space from the seating area. Just beyond lay a set of French doors leading out to a back patio and garden.

"Let's go outside, Hank."

"Sounds good," said the agent as he headed towards the doors.

"You should have told me," whispered Jodie.

"Sorry."

Clay joined Hank and opened both doors to heighten the effect of what he was about to share with him.

CHAPTER 7

Clay led Hank back to a fenced area about a hundred feet from the farmhouse.

The multipurpose garden space. A seventy-by-seventy foot-square surrounded by fig trees, grapevines, and blackberry bushes.

"When our parents bought this place it was berry vines and dirt," Clay informed the agent. "It was owned by an older couple and they had given up on all the outdoor work. The place had become too much for them to maintain. Our mom and dad said that it was pretty run down. So the old folks sold it to our family and moved into town."

Hank surveyed eight raised vegetable beds made from stacked four-by-fours with two-by-six boards set on top. The boards doubled as bench seating.

"Our Dad put greywater lines under the tile floors from the bathrooms and laundry room to help water these beds."

"Clever."

"He also ran potable water from the house to a cast iron sink that he installed near our outdoor eating area. We use it for washing up and for rinsing our vegetables after we pick them. He ran a drainpipe from the sink to the fig trees. We have to buy garden safe soap for the house, but we can purchase that at that lavender farm we passed on the way here. We trade them for lots of things. They produce essential oils, soaps, olive oil, and they even raise honey. We can only eat so much of our garden. So we barter and sell some at the Farmer's Market, up in Sebastopol."

Hank looked over the thriving vegetables to see which ones he recognized. He ambled over to one of the plots.

"This is zucchini," he observed. "My grandmother used to grow it."

Clay joined Hank and gave him the run-down on the rest of the beds.

"We have summer squash on the backside of this bed," he pointed out. "Behind the zucchini. We have different varieties of tomatoes and peppers along with some eggplant, cucumbers, and melons." One of the plots had green beans winding their way up tall bamboo poles. "During the winter months we grow broccoli, onions, carrots, chard, garlic, kale, arugula, beets, and a number of loose-leaf lettuces."

"How can you remember all that?"

"A labor of love."

They continued their tour of the raised beds.

"Hey, a berry patch!" exclaimed Hank. "That's cool."

"Strawberries and raspberries."

"I don't see any corn," the agent said.

"It takes too much water."

"Oh, I see . . . that makes sense."

They reached another section, closer to the house, where herbs, both culinary and medicinal, grew: basil, rosemary, thyme, marjoram, oregano, sage, and tarragon. Next to this, in another raised bed, Hank observed a variety of cut flowers displaying all the colors of the rainbow.

"Jodie likes to grow heirloom flowers," said Clay. "She gets that from our Mom."

"You produce enough to feed yourself?"

"The garden used to feed all four of us," Clay said with an air of sadness in his voice. "Like I said, we also exchange things with our neighbors and sell at the Farmer's Market. Come on . . . "

They passed the last raised bed. Leafy greens grew in this one. Atop this bed was a framework of steel and galvanized metal screens. All the other beds were completely uncovered. Clay noticed the look of curiosity on Hank's face and explained the reason for the protective measure.

"My Dad made the screens to keep rogue chickens out of the greens. They can be quite voracious."

They soon found themselves entering a quiet niche surrounded by berry vines laden with scores of blackberries, a semi-shaded lounging area.

"The berries used to ripen during the middle of summer," Clay said matter-of-factly. "Now it's by the end of spring."

An L-shaped furniture set sat on large thirty-inch square pavers laid on crushed gravel. The cozy-looking sectional, made with a wooden frame and wire backs, came complete with comfortable pads and pillows. A single chair turned the L into a U-shaped setting.

A table stood in the center of this collection along with two glazed pots overflowing with pink, white, coral, and violet geraniums.

"Jodie grew these?" guessed Hank.

"You got it."

Hank hoped they might sit and take a break, but Clay had other ideas.

They continued on to the outdoor dining area.

"This is where we'll eat," said Clay. "Mostly garden to grill around here. We consume a lot of fruits and vegetables. Almost all is home grown."

"Al fresco," smiled Hank. "Cool, man."

A brick barbeque, with a grilling surface and a grease tray below it, stood next to a long table with wood benches on both sides. A couple of wooden chairs were stacked nearby for the empty spaces at the ends of the table.

"Check this out," said Clay in reference to the outdoor table. "My dad made this table and the benches out of old redwood beams. Redwood is disease resistant."

"Your dad was a handy guy."

"He told me working in an office used to drive him nuts."

"Yeah, it's not for everyone."

"He was tired of living in the city. He said San Francisco wasn't the same place he'd grown up in. He told us the changes weren't positive."

"You seemed surprised by what you saw in the city, but it sounds like your parents had already told you about it."

"It was worse than I ever imagined. Not all of it. Just the street addicts and the boarded-up storefronts."

"I guess that makes sense."

"My parents quit their day jobs after finding this two-acre property. They sold their house in San Francisco. My dad left the tech world behind. They didn't want to raise kids in the city. They chose this area because they liked the idea of the fog rolling in off the coast. Only a lot more sunny days up here. They renovated our farmhouse from top to bottom. Tore out old carpets and updated the bathrooms. They painted the kitchen cabinets because they didn't want to tear out usable wood just to replace it with new. They always tried to reuse or repurpose things if they could."

"Admirable."

"Let's go see the orchard."

They pushed open a wooden gate that led to the back of the property.

Beyond the orchard lay a mixed conifer forest.

"I'm happiest when I'm out here working with the land," said Clay as he began to share his feelings with the agent. "I don't consider it work. It's a labor of love."

Clay led Hank down through the middle of two rows of fruit trees and served as guide, pointing out each of the many varieties. They walked along and stopped to take a closer look at every individual tree. Not a traditional orchard growing one or two varieties, but a small grove of about three dozen species, a plethora of fruit: apples, plums, pears, peach, and cherries. And oranges and lemons and limes.

The scent of blossoms filled the air.

"This is Mikey, a semi-dwarf Meyer lemon, announced Clay. "My favorite of all because you can eat their skins. They also produce year round."

"You name your trees?"

"They're my friends," asserted Clay. "I've always named our trees. Ever since I was a little boy."

"I had a teddy bear when I was a kid," mused Hank. "Not quite the same thing, but I did give him a name. Teddy. Not very original, but I was a little kid and I liked the name."

"We specialize in growing a wide variety of fruits. We trade our neighbors, the Keatings, for their poultry and Mrs. Keating bakes breads and pastries. We exchange with one of our neighbors for services we need. Mr. Hernandez can fix anything mechanical or electrical. Calls himself a *miluso*. Means he has a thousand uses. He helped my dad keep a lot of things going around here. I haven't had to ask him for help yet, but I know he's there for me."

"I remember you telling me that you and Jodie scattered your parents ashes out here."

"Yeah, they're feeding these trees."

Hank didn't want to seem like he was prying, so he didn't ask about the about the details of how Clay and Jodie's mom and dad had met their untimely deaths.

David and Clare Roberts were celebrating their thirtieth wedding anniversary.

They'd driven up to Sebastopol to enjoy a quiet dinner for two at a small bistro. They knew the owners and often supplied the restaurant with fresh fruits and vegetables. They might have accepted cash in return, but an occasional free meal appealed to them more.

They'd left Clay and Jodie home alone. It was just the two of them taking a break from their labors and reminiscing about a fulfilling thirty year relationship. They had done well and had reason to be pleased with themselves. They'd known

54

from the beginning that city life didn't suit either one of them.

The two wanted to raise a family, a cooperative venture fueled by love. They saw each other as equals. A couple relying upon their strengths and weaknesses to overcome any adversity life might throw their way.

They had been searching rural locations, north of the city, for more than a year. It was important to them not to be too far away from family and friends. One day, their real estate agent called and described the farm. They quickly made arrangements for a viewing. An older couple, unable to keep up with the maintenance needs required of acreage, was eager to sell. The place needed a lot of work, but that suited David and Clare just fine since their goal was to create as natural a living environment as they possibly could.

Clare resigned from a teaching position and David turned his back on a successful career in the Tech world. They sold their overpriced San Francisco home and cashed out. Friends and co-workers thought they were either the bravest or craziest people they knew.

The loving couple, from the City by the Bay, capped off their romantic dinner with chocolate cake and espressos.

A dark winter sky greeted them when they left the restaurant after the leisurely two-hour meal, one accompanied by wine from one of the few local vineyards still operating in a region once known worldwide for the excellent quality of its varietals.

They were about a mile north of Lone Pine Road when the unthinkable happened. Headlights in the distance. As a speeding car approached, the driver swerved into their lane at the last minute. Straight at them. David didn't have time to react to the unforeseen danger as the two vehicles met head on. Aluminum bodies crunched and compacted upon collision.

Inside the cabin of the twenty-year old vehicle, David and Clare's airbags deployed outwards at 300 miles per hour, the explosive equivalent of 20 shotgun shells. Deployed from both the front and sides. It was a freak occurrence. One attributed to the age of the truck. And to negligence on the part of the manufacturer. Few models were left on the road, and the recall should have covered them all. David and Clare never received notice of the problem. Their isolated lifestyle may have contributed to the omission.

A young man sat dazed and drunk inside the second vehicle, a three-year-old EV with functional air bags and its seat detection sensors calibrated properly.

The police used the address on David's driver's license as a reference and drove to the farmhouse to notify any potential occupants of the tragedy.

It was later determined that the teenager causing the accident had received bad news regarding his sperm markers from Government that same afternoon. The results weren't what he'd anticipated. They came as quite a shock to this apparently healthy, at least to the outer eye, nineteen year old.

So he drank too much and drove a little crazy and caused a fatal, two-car head-on collision. He somehow walked away with no life-threatening injuries while two beautiful, innocent people breathed their last.

Clay led the way back to the house by a different route.

Much as he appreciated the tour, Hank still had his mind on business.

"Would you take Ethereum?" he asked. "They don't mine like Bitcoin."

"Our dad warned us to use the money economy sparingly. He used to tell us 'you won't get rich, but you'll stay sane.'"

"Crypto has replaced the money economy for many," Hank suggested.

"I guess I'd consider it."

"How do you survive out here without any services," Hank wondered out loud. The agent understood he'd be hard pressed to live a more self-sufficient life. He was a city boy, born and raised in San Francisco, and he had never experienced anything different. "I mean you're kind of off the grid."

"Our parents thought of everything," Clay stated. "We have a catchment system to collect rain water and direct it to a huge cistern. My dad said cisterns were used all the way back in ancient times. There is an old well on the property and its kept functional, but it's only for back-up."

Clay pointed up to a bank of solar panels installed on the farmhouse roof.

"They waited until 250 watt solar panels were recyclable with seventy-five year life spans, and they invested in a more efficient system of storage batteries. Down at Stanford University they developed a modified panel that generates a small amount of electricity at night. That was a game changer. This solar system, along with a 500 watt bladeless wind turbine, supplies all our electricity. We utilize compost bins for our food waste, and they turn it all back into soil for the raised beds and fruit trees. We have compostable toilets."

"This is quite a set-up," stated an obviously impressed Hank Gallagher.

"Our parents had a vision. They wanted to live closer to the land and not rely on the city or county for services. They did pay for satellite internet service because they wanted us to have access for our studies. But no television. They told us we could stream movies and TV shows on our computers if we needed to. We never had Smart Glasses. They weren't interested in the Metaverse. This farm is a full-time job."

"Do you and Jodie feel safe out here?"

"The farm has security cameras and some electrified fencing to deter any unwanted visitors. My Dad believed that the future might bring a lot of desperation. He refused to install a locked gate though. Said he didn't want to feel like a prisoner on his own land."

Hank could hardly believe the change in Clay. They seemed to have reversed roles with the agent now asking short, direct questions and Clay elaborating when he answered them.

"Can I make a suggestion?" asked Hank. He continued without waiting for Clay's response. "Grow a full beard. It'll make facial recognition more difficult."

"Don't you think we're safer living out here away from things," asked Clay.

"Yes and no," insisted the agent. "You'll be harder to find. However, if someone does show up here you're definitely more vulnerable. If you decide to stay independent, we may have to hire some muscle."

"Really? Bodyguards?"

"A lot of people will want to get their hands on you."

"I'll have to think about that."

Hank decided to leave it at that. No need to rush into any decisions. Clay could hire on with someone providing protection or they could find their own. Main thing was to get him signed to an agent's contract. His contract.

They approached the house and Clay pointed out some copper rain chains leading down from the roof to half a dozen wine barrels, spaced at equal distances below the house's roofline. Each barrel had two spigots. A lower one for watering, and one near the top to release excess when water filled the units to full capacity.

"The wineries were giving them away when they were forced to shut down their operations due to wildfires and a lack of rain and groundwater for their thirsty grape vines," Clay informed him. "Local ordinances prevented the wealthier wineries from drilling deeper wells to stop them from draining the region's aquifer."

An outdoor shower stall, fashioned from corrugated metal panels, lay beyond the last wine barrel. They passed by it on their way to the French doors at the back of the house.

Jodie came out through one of the doors holding a pitcher of lemonade in her hand.

"I've got everything set up," she told them. "Let's go eat."

They went back inside the farmhouse after dinner.

Once the dishes were done, they returned to the living room to chat.

This time Clay and Jodie sat on the couch.

Hank settled back into the side chair.

He wanted to get down to business, but he also figured it would serve him well if he knew Clay and his sister a little better before discussing their options. He didn't want to appear superficial. He always laughed when his roommates told him "deep down inside you're really shallow, Gallagher." He knew they were joking. Just guys having fun at his expense. Still, he had to admit the words stung. He wasn't sure why. He didn't consider himself shallow. Businesslike maybe, but he had a sensitive side. Especially when it came to family. Particularly his grandmother, his Nonna, who had practically raised him.

Hank shifted his weight to get more comfortable.

He'd seen a photograph of David and Clare on the mantle and now he recognized the resemblances. Clay looked more like his mother, the brown eyes and dark, brunette-colored hair. Jodie had the blond hair and blue eyes of her father.

Time to get personal while keeping things casual.

"So, you guys were home schooled," said Hank. This came across as a statement more than a question, since his knowing the answer made an inquiry unnecessary.

"Our parents never used home schooling as an easy way out," began Jodie. "They challenged us. Made us study hard. Taught us to think for ourselves. To question things. They tried to instill in us a desire to learn more about ourselves and our world. They wanted us to look reality in the face. Not to flinch. They told us that we would need inner strength to survive the challenges that we would face in the days ahead."

"They never imagined the time would come so soon," added Clay.

"Mom and dad were always apologizing to us because they couldn't do more," said Jodie. "They didn't have a lot of help. They weren't outcasts. They were . . . what's the word, Clay?"

"Throwbacks."

"Yes, that's it," she agreed. "They were throwbacks to an earlier time."

"Is this a good time to talk about your options, Clay?"

"Sure."

Hank proceeded to review the pros and cons of the National Fertility Service and everyone agreed that it was the least desirable option. He pressed on to the next offer, Tanaka's proposal. The agent took his time and explained the ramifications in great detail. There was a fortune to be made, but he was sure to remind Clay that he had connections if they decided to tokenize his services on their own.

A quiet came over the room.

It was soon broken.

"Geez, Clay," sighed Jodie.

"I know," he replied. "Crazy."

"Yeah, ca-ray-zee.

"What about me?" Jodie wanted to know. "How do I fit into all this?"

"I think Tanaka might allow you to live on the island for a year, Jodie," said Hank, taking the lead in the conversation. "He doesn't resort to recruiting, so I know he's serious about having Clay sign with him."

"I'm sure Tanaka would let me take you as a guest. He explained that he usually doesn't recruit because they already have too many aspiring applicants. Thousands of them. He really wants me to join him. He seems very accommodating."

"Then we'll need someone to run the farm while we're gone," Jodie told them.

"Yeah, we need to discuss that," said Clay, stating the obvious.

"I think Lupita and her new husband, Enrique, might be interested in living here and running the farm for a time," ventured Jodie. "She told me they're trying to have a baby, but haven't had any success."

Clay flinched.

Hank noticed this when he looked over to see his reaction to his sister's suggestion. It wasn't that Enrique wasn't a nice guy in Clay's eyes. He was actually quite likeable and appeared devoted to Lupita. It was just that the thought of the two of them running the farm had never occurred to Clay, and he wasn't quite sure how he felt about them entering and living in what had been his private domain. Maybe someone with less history with him and his family would be better.

"We could train someone from town," suggested Clay. "Or, find a family who might be interested. We could even afford to pay them. I mean, money would be no object, right?"

"Right," agreed Hank, who liked the way the conversation was going. Everyone was positive about the prospects. He still favored the idea of contracting out to various Sperm Banks. This gave them the most leverage and control over their time commitments. That wouldn't preclude them from tokenizing Clay. That alone could be worth billions of dollars.

Jodie yawned. She covered her mouth with her hand, took it away, and then did it again.

"Sorry, but I'm going to bed guys," Jodie announced as she stood to leave. "We can finish this conversation later. See you in the morning."

"Night, sis."

"Goodnight, Jodie," said Hank. "Sweet dreams."

She gave them both a smile before disappearing from sight.

61

I know my dreams will be sweet if Clay signs tonight, thought Hank.

"So what do you say?" the agent asked with heartfelt enthusiasm. "You ready to sign?"

"You brought the contract with you?"

"It's out in your truck, inside my briefcase."

A deep exhale.

This wasn't a positive sign. Hank felt exasperated. It brought an awkward moment during which neither man spoke. Clay realized that his wannabe agent was waiting for him to move forward with their relationship. To solidify the deal. No more wannabe.

"I'm really tired," sighed Clay. "I'll look over the contract in the morning."

"It's boilerplate," Hank asserted. "No need to read it over."

"Just the same . . . "

"I'll go get it," insisted the agent. "Won't take a minute."

"Tomorrow, Hank," replied Clay with a tone of finality.

He looked Hank in the eye while opening his palms in a cut me some slack gesture. Another deep exhalation. "I'm bushed, man," he continued. "Come on, I'll show you where you'll be sleeping. You can settle in for the night."

"Sign the contract. If it doesn't work out, it doesn't work out. Come on," he goaded as frustration crept into his voice. "We're talking about the survival of the fucking human race remember? Do your part."

Clay bit down on his lip.

"Have you heard of Perc?" asked Hank.

"No," admitted Clay. "Who's Perc?"

"You've never heard of Perc?" Hank asked. "Wow! Where have you been hiding? You ought to listen to the Podcast interviews. He thinks a lot like you, but even he wants to see humanity survive. I'll bet he'd sign the contract."

"What did you say his name was?"

"Perc," repeated Hank, with a hint of impatience in his voice. "P E R C." Perc is short for Percolator. Some friends and colleagues started calling him The Percolator because he gets things boiling. Like his own blood. He's definitely pissed at the powers that be and those who came before and ignored the warning signals that created this messed-up world."

"I'll have a listen, but not tonight."

"You owe it to your sister to sign that contract," Hank said as he played what he believed was his trump card.

Clay rose from the couch to let Hank know their conversation had ended.

Nothing left but a little chit-chat as Clay showed Hank to the guest room and its adjoining bathroom.

"Good night."

"What's so good about it?" said the agent under his breath.

CHAPTER 8

Clay stole away during the middle of the night.

A thirty mile ride to the coast brought him to an abandoned mansion teetering on a cliff overlooking the sea. Half of a building to be more precise since much of the structure had fallen off into the ocean a decade earlier. Part of it still lay in rubble down at the bottom of the overhang upon which it was now precariously perched.

Clay had come prepared with extra clothes to ward off the cold ocean air and he'd brought extra food and water. Enough rations for a few days. He didn't know how long he'd be staying. How much time it would take for him to sort things out.

He climbed into his sleeping bag hoping to get a couple more hours of sleep before the sun came up. His mind wasn't cooperating. He found it working overtime in an attempt to bring some clarity to the chaos that had ensued a few days earlier.

Hold a lottery, he laughed to himself. That's as random as one of my sperm wiggling its way up some gal's fallopian tube and uniting with a fertile egg. Oh, God! What should he do? What did he *want* to do? He considered taking Tanaka up on his offer, but what about Jodie? Tanaka would probably agree to allow his sister to live on the island for a year. Perhaps more if he stayed on.

So the question became who would look after the farm for them? What if Jodie didn't want to join him? Who might help her run the place? He immediately thought of the Overstreets. Brad and Katie were a childless couple who ran an organic farm about four miles away. They had tried everything to have children, but none of the assisted methods had worked for them. They gave up and devoted themselves to their home and their livestock. Their cats and dogs became surrogate children.

Perhaps the Hernandez family. He felt sure José and Consuela would help Jodie out and keep an eye on things.

Clay thought back to family times.

David and Clare, Brad and Katie, and José and Consuela. These three couples had formed a tightknit group. More like extended families since everybody relied upon each other and helped one another navigate through the challenges they faced. Buy, sell, barter, and trade. For physical goods and practical expertise. Each couple had their strengths and weaknesses.

A spontaneous round of breakfasts, lunches, and dinners. Expect the unexpected. A phone call invitation to come over for a breakfast of *huevos rancheros*. Drop everything and head on over for homemade pizza from the firewood oven along with David's craft beer. Katie's eggplant parmesan.

Clay sighed.

Surely they would all help him and Jodie.

Going to live on Tanaka's island began to appeal to Clay. Maybe he could actually find a willing partner. One like Sam. He smiled to himself as he pictured her in his mind's eye. Green eyed, red-headed Samantha Bell was like no other girl he'd ever encountered. Not that there'd been that many.

He'd first met the vivacious and star-gazing Sam at one of his mother's home school group meetings. Round robins, scheduled at the parent's houses. About one-half dozen families. On a quarterly basis. Clay and Sam had taken a liking to one other. She preferred to partner up with Clay for study sessions. She was older by one year and smarter and more mature, but she didn't hold that against him.

There were only two boys in the school group. Frederick Fairfield, ("little Freddie" was what they called him), stood four inches shorter than Sam and the contrast was striking. Little Freddie looked thin and frail while a healthy glow emanated from Sam's well-toned body. So she gravitated towards Clay whom she felt more her equal in this regard.

Clay remembered that amazing afternoon with Sam, during the autumn of her senior year in high school, when they were studying for State Exams. Sam's single mother apologized because she had a few errands to run and would have to leave them alone for a couple of hours.

As soon as she left, Sam closed her book and got up from the table. She grabbed Clay's hand and playfully pulled him to his feet.

"What are you doing?"

Sam led him down a narrow hallway and into her bedroom where she closed the door behind them. She turned to face him and he shot her a quizzical look. She had a silly grin on her face. He watched her hand slip down to his crotch. She covered his private parts with her open palm and then gave them a gentle squeeze. Neither was surprised by the rise in his jeans.

Sam slid her tongue between her lips.

Clay thought that she was just teasing him. She was always joking around.

He realized his mistake when she began to unbutton his shirt. His raging hormones and hard-on took over as the two began undressing one another in a heated rush. She pulled him over to the bed and down on top of herself as they gave in to overwhelming desire.

They couldn't help themselves.

Hormones propelled passions and unspeakable pleasure gave rise to a shared physicality. Wild nature asserted itself. At the very last second, Clay pulled out of Sam and his semen splashed all over her belly.

They both laughed.

"Have you done this before," she asked.

"No, I haven't," Clay replied sheepishly.

"You seemed to know exactly what to do."

Clay shrugged. He'd trusted his instincts. They hadn't let him down.

Sam excused herself and left for the bathroom.

They got dressed when she came back and she quickly straightened the bed.

Soon they were sitting back at the kitchen table trying unsuccessfully to study. When Louise Bell returned, the two intimates donned their most studious personas and spent the next hour exchanging fleeting glances.

Ms. Bell drove Clay back to the farm at the appointed time.

Clay and Sam both passed the State Exams and he dreaded what he always knew would happen. Sam's head was in the stars. Astronomy and physics were the determining forces in Sam Bell's life. Clay had hoped she'd stay local and attend Sonoma State. Sam had other ideas. An academic scholarship to the University of Arizona, where she would study astronomy and astrophysics, took her down to the desert Southwest.

They exchanged a few emails before the intervals between their letters and the distance separating their personal lives grew wider. Finally, Sam sent Clay an email announcing that she had met a special friend. One of the Astronomy's department's graduate assistants.

The finality of an ended relationship, and the loss of all hope for its continuance, stayed with Clay far longer than he'd imagined it could.

Time, as the adage born of heartfelt experience claimed, healed that wound.

Clay didn't want to think about Sam anymore so he searched his memory bank and made a withdrawal. Perc! That was the name Hank had mentioned.

The Percolator.

He grabbed his burner phone and initiated a search. He scrolled past biographical articles until found a Podcast, titled

Sanctuary Earth, indicating that Perc was the guest speaker.
A podcast episode would take his mind off the past.

Clay decided he didn't need to use his ear buds.

He was all alone.

He brought up the list of episodes and then he clicked
on Episode 1.

CHAPTER 9

Podcast - *Sanctuary Earth*

Episode 1 - "Perc's Personal Perspective"

Leaf: Welcome to Sanctuary Earth, where we discuss issues vital to the continuation of life on our planet. These programs are aired free of advertisements as a public service provided by the Plastic People's Sanctuary movement.

I'm Leaf Aronson and today on the show we are honored to have Perc, the infamous radical eco-historian. They say "The Percolator," as he's known, cycles the boiling brew of his thoughts and feelings through the dregs of history, using gravitas to strengthen his perspective.

During this series of episodes, Perc is going to provide insights into how we've created the existential crisis we are currently facing, and offer some advice about how we can reverse the destructive and disturbing trends destroying life as we know it.

I'd like to begin our first episode with a personal question. You left a lucrative position as a tenured professor at an elite American University. Would you share your reasons for quitting with our listeners?

Perc: I didn't think my colleagues understood the difficult challenges facing our species or that they felt any sense of urgency to overturn the status quo. We needed to jump start a revolution in values. One that would place the needs of the planet above our own personal desires. It was business as usual, but I felt only frustration.

Even back then we were over-heating the earth and destroying millions of species in the process. Now this once beautiful Earth is dying. Back then, it was already later than we thought. Much, much later. I could see what was happening. I was seething inside. Enough! Ya basta! Where was the f**king outrage?

Leaf: Take it easy, Perc. We're just getting started.

Perc: That's why we live in a shattered world on the edge of extinction. Everybody wanted to take it easy. Most people didn't want to make any sacrifices. Leave their comfort zones.

Leaf: So you decided to rattle a few cages.

Perc: The more the better!

Leaf: Perc, you said you'd like to begin this series of podcasts by talking about your personal journey.

Perc: You're right, Leaf. I feel it's important for listeners to know I understand how hard the challenges facing us are because I've been there. I've experienced the difficulties firsthand.

Like most people, I didn't question our society's almost total reliance on plastics. They were just a part of modern life, my life. Convenient and readily available in a society based on consumption. We weren't taught to think about it. In fact, we are conditioned not to think for ourselves. We say it's a value, but woe unto the individual who actually takes it to heart.

Leaf: We all have to start somewhere. When did you begin to change your life and what led to your conversion, if I might call it that?

Perc: It was over thirty years ago. St. Paul was stuck down on the road to Damascus. It happened to me at my local supermarket. That may sound mundane, but one day while I was walking down the laundry and cleaning products aisle it suddenly struck me all of the containers were made from plastic. Shelf after shelf. All plastic.

I turned the corner onto the aisle where they displayed personal care items. Like shampoos and conditioners. And cosmetics. All plastic. I knew conventional plastic is made from fossil fuels, a product of the oil and gas industries. You might say that's when I saw the light. Maybe darkness is more appropriate.

Leaf: So this experience kind of jolted you and got you to thinking. What did you do?

Perc: I went home and I began to look at all the things in my house that were made of plastic. I started with the usual suspects. My groceries came home in plastic bags with the fruits and vegetables sitting inside more plastic bags. Many of the condiments I purchased were packed in plastic. Milk and fruit juice containers were made of plastic. And so on.

Leaf: You didn't stop with the groceries. You probed deeper?

Perc: You bet! The carpeting on my floors was made of plastic fibers. I checked my clothes. Most of my shirts were made from polyester, a plastic fiber. I essentially wore plastic fibers right next to my skin. My serving utensils and kitchen appliances were made with a lot of plastic. You know what happens when plastic is heated? The harmful chemicals are off-gassed and released into the air.

71

So I decided to ditch the plastic containers I had used to microwave my leftovers. The polyester shower curtain with the plastic liner had to go. I replaced it with one made from organic cotton. My coffee pot was made of plastic so I switched to a French Press. I looked at how most of my possessions were made from plastic, and it dawned on me that I could never do away with all of them. Almost impossible, but I could try to minimize it.

Leaf: What was the most disturbing discovery you made in your home?

Perc: That I was sleeping every night wrapped up in a cocoon spun from plastic fibers releasing harmful chemicals into the air. The sheets and blankets on my bed were made of polyester. Even my pillow case. The mattress was filled with polyester batting. Many mattresses are made from polyurethane foam. They add toxic fire retardant chemicals to this lethal brew. My own body warmth was aiding in the release of these chemicals.

Leaf: I imagine you began to lose sleep over this.

Perc: We spend almost a third of our lives sleeping in our beds, Leaf! Fortunately there are companies who make mattresses out of natural materials. I had one delivered to my house within a week. I've slept better ever since.

Leaf: I know you're going to talk about plastics in more detail in one of our future episodes, so can you tell listeners why reducing the amount of plastic in their lives is so very important?

Perc: Two things come to mind immediately. First, the harmful chemicals in plastic and other toxic chemicals are released into our bodies from everyday products and foods. Our bodies are riddled with micro-plastics at the cellular level. It's been proven this has contributed to a fertility rate below replacement level and has now rendered us an endangered species.

Second, over ninety-five percent of the plastic consumers purchase is not recycled despite the misleading ad campaigns of the manufacturers. Billions of tons of plastic end up in our landfills and our oceans every year. They won't completely break down for hundreds of years. We are literally drowning in a sea of plastic and the toxic chemicals they emit.

Leaf: You told me this journey of yours wasn't particularly easy.

Perc: I made a point to try to find out what was going on. Not what the powers brokers want us to believe is going on. I spent a lot of time researching alternative products. And there's a cost factor. Plastic products are usually cheaper to manufacture and consume. I thought about this because I was a single person at the time. I can only imagine how difficult the transition would be for a family. The extra time it takes to do research and the expense. Probably out of the question for people in poorer countries, or those with no means. Since we're talking human survival at this point, it's better to just do without.

Leaf: Any last thought's you'd like to share, Perc?

Perc: I have come to realize the world has been colonized by the plastic manufacturers. It's a form of corporate and cultural imperialism. This revelation changed my world view. We are no longer the species Homo Sapiens that lived on this planet for more than three hundred thousand years. Over the last one hundred years, beginning in the 1950s, we have morphed into a weird, almost alien life-form I call *Homo Plasticus*.

Leaf: You've certainly given us something to think about. I want to thank you for sharing your personal story, Perc. Tell listeners a little about our next episode?

Perc: In our next episode, I'm going to offer an overview of the many elements combining to create a perfect storm. One leading to an unprecedented, though not unforeseen, decline in human fertility. One on a such massive scale that the most endangered species on Earth is ourselves.

Leaf: (A pause to allow Perc's final thoughts to sink in). This brings us to the end of this program. Thanks to Perc for joining us to share some of the details of his amazing journey. We hope you found his insights engaging. As always, thanks for listening to Sanctuary Earth.

Narrator: Namaste Nguyen was the producer of this episode. Our engineers are Andrew Wilson and Celeste Roberts. Our editor is Rosie Zuniga. The executive producer is Leaf Aronson,

CHAPTER 10

Then there was Lupita.

Shy, doe-eyed Lupita. A child of the tropics with cinnamon skin, a warm, medium shade of brown. Darker than tan, but lighter than chocolate. Clay remembered gazing into her large, gentle, dark eyes and being drawn down into the depths of her soul. So earthy and so sweet. A young woman with a distant, mysterious past.

José and Consuela chose not to share the details of Lupita's adoption at an early age.

Nobody ventured to press them.

There were rumors.

There are always rumors.

Rumors that her biological mother, Maria Elena Montoya, had made an arduous trek north from one of the war-torn Central American countries with ten-year old Lupita and her older brother, sixteen year old Juan. They'd left three younger siblings with neighbors to journey with a group of two dozen hopeful immigrants dreaming of entering America.

Maria Elena found her way to the border town of Nogales, Mexico, and somehow managed to get the two children safely across to relatives who would find families for them to live with. Each of them was placed with a different family according to the rumors.

Some dismissed this version of events since the United States Army had already established a permanent presence along the southern border.

Someone else had heard that Lupita's real parents were teenagers living down in the desolate wasteland of the Central Valley dust bowl. They could barely afford to feed themselves and made the agonizing decision to put baby Guadalupe up for adoption.

Someone said she was Consuela's daughter from a prior relationship and not adopted at all. No explanations were offered. Only an unsolvable mystery.

Lupita's past remained enigmatic.

So too did her success at growing herbs and creating herbal remedies to sell at the local Farmer's Market. Some attributed her aptitude to Consuela, saying the mother was a *curandera*. A healer to some, a witch to others. Yet there existed no evidence to back up this claim. Could her gift be traced back to Maria Elena? Perhaps the girl's passion had nothing to do with her maternal lineage whatever it might be.

None of this mattered to Clay.

Especially after Samantha Bell had broken off their relationship.

He was surprised he hadn't paid more attention to Lupita in the past since over the years he'd watched her blossom from a skinny little girl into a sensuous young woman. Like most girls maturing during the last few generations she'd been faced with hormonal imbalances and had experienced an early menstruation. Now he couldn't ignore the well-rounded curves beneath the simple cotton dresses she preferred to wear.

Clay's thoughts turned more and more towards Lupita after the fantasy of a long-term relationship with Sam had faded. Her cinnamon skin now attracted his attention.

It worked both ways. He caught her stealing glances his way at gatherings of the three families. He pretended not to notice, but smiled inwardly. How would he know if she really liked him or if his was simply a case of empty imaginings?

He'd have to devise a strategy.

One that would bring them closer together.

Clay sought out opportunities to visit the Hernandez farm. He volunteered to return borrowed tools, make food deliveries, and any excuse he could find to get himself to her place. On each of these occasions he made a point of engaging with Lupita.

He expressed his fascination with the herbs she had planted and nurtured from seeds. He had many questions for her, and he wasn't just feigning an interest. Clay was born with a curious mind. One that desired new information like a sponge longs for water. Their fondness for one another grew stronger.

The plan had succeeded.

Perhaps too well.

Early one morning he arrived with a satchel of tools his father wanted returned to José. Nobody outside working. Unusual. He went up to the front door of a sprawling ranch house and knocked on the door a few times. The dogs didn't come to the door to greet him. No answer so he figured he'd head over to Lupita's potting shed.

He smiled to himself as he approached a white stucco-sided outbuilding with windows on all four sides and a red-tiled roof. José along with his mate and helper, Consuela, had built it for their adopted daughter.

They weren't exactly sure what traumas she'd experienced before entering into their lives, but they were certain love would be the healing power she needed to help her over-come a difficult childhood. They'd never been able to conceive children of their own so their two Australian Shepherds and three lazy cats had become Lupita's siblings. They built the shed with their hands. From natural materials. Inside and out.

The interior contained tables, shelves, a workbench, and a potting table made from an old kitchen countertop salvaged from the Robert's farmhouse when the *miluso* was helping Clay's father rebuild the place.

The open door seemed like an invitation.

Clay knocked first so as not to startle her.

Lupita came to the door.

"Clay!"

"My dad wanted me to bring some tools back, but there was nobody at the house."

"You just missed them," she explained. "They went into town to shop."

Clay figured they'd taken the dogs with them. He knew the drill. Everyone in the neighborhood, he and Jodie included, had to go to town to barter or pay for staples: flour, sugar, salt, and other foodstuffs they and their friends were unable to grow or found not worth the effort and expenditure.

"They won't be back until after lunch, Lupita informed him. "You can leave the tools on the front porch."

"Mind if I come inside?"

"Come on . . . I'm planting some new seeds."

Clay loved her enthusiasm. She looked so happy when she planted seeds or nurtured young seedlings, and when she hung cuttings of fresh herbs upside down to dry in the shed before preparing her many blends.

He followed her inside.

"It smells good in here," he said, sniffing the air in the shed. "So herbaceous."

Lupita sent a smile his way so he went over closer to watch her at the potting table. He observed as she planted tiny seeds in a wooden box filled with rich, black soil. She paused to look back up at him.

"*Mira*, Clay!" she exclaimed with her usual sense of excitement. She had reverted back to her native Spanish. He was used to that so he knew she had said: "Look, Clay." Lupita wanted to show him the seeds she was tenderly tucking down into the soil after she'd made a small impression with her forefinger. This suited him just fine.

Clay never tired of visiting Lupita and her shed. It seemed like a magical place. Earthy magic. Stacks of different sized clay pots stashed in one corner. Hand tools pushed down into a metal pail of sand. The skylight down at the far end of the shed, a thoughtful addition to bring in sunlight for Lupita's seedlings. A dozen bundles of herbs hanging from a wooden beam to dry. The aroma of peppermint filling the air.

Lupita's shed had cast its spell and Clay couldn't help but be enchanted.

"It smells so good in here."

"Oh, yes! " she eagerly agreed.

He moved in closer.

"You smell good, too," he told her.

She smiled at the compliment and then showed him the tiny seeds resting in the palm of her hand. They were black.

Unusual, he thought.

"They're black cumin seeds," she informed him before turning back to her workbench to finish up with her planting. When she was done she wiped her hands with a nearby rag and turned back to face Clay. He waited hopefully until she pressed herself up against him.

"Do you like me, Clay?" she asked in a shy, soft voice.

He decided to show her just how much.

He found a clear space on the surface of the workbench, picked Lupita up and carried her over to it, and then sat her down.

She laughed out loud. There was nothing shy about that laugh. It came right up from her belly and seemed encouraging. Certainly not an attempt to prevent what was about to happen between them.

His hands found her firm, full breasts.

He reached up under her dress and discovered she wore no underwear. He touched the warmth between her legs. The wetness drove him wild. He unzipped his jeans and pulled them down along with his underpants. He lifted Lupita up from the workbench and she wrapped her legs around him as waves of passion carried them away. Further and further away, awash in moments of delirious pleasure. Wave upon wave until they were drowning in their senses.

Clay almost didn't make it this time, but he pulled out at the very last second and breathed a huge sigh of relief. He lowered Lupita until her feet found the floor and then hitched up his pants.

She frowned when he'd expected a smile.

"You don't want to make a baby with me, Clay?"

At first he didn't know what to say.

Having a baby was the farthest thing from his mine.

He felt mystified. Confused. A baby? Where had that come from? He assumed she listened to music on her cell phone. Government was always interrupting the programs with public service messages imploring citizens to try to bring more children into the world. "Make more babies!" was the popular slogan. Perhaps it had influenced her subliminally. Or, had the impulse come from somewhere inside of Lupita herself?

"It's not you Lupita," he finally told her. "I don't want to make a baby with anyone right now."

She pouted.

Clay stoked her hair trying to comfort her. He gazed into her dark eyes and pleaded for understanding.

"I didn't know you felt that way," he said.

"Forget it, Clay."

He'd hurt her, but that wasn't his intention.

He noticed the wet spots he had created pulling away. He hoped José and Consuela wouldn't arrive any time soon. How would he or she explain? What excuse could they make? An accident while Lupita was watering the herbs. But the plants were watered by drip irrigation. Maybe they wouldn't have to cross that bridge.

"I'd better go," Clay said in as gentle a tone as he could muster. He rubbed her nose playfully, but she didn't smile at his efforts to create some light-heartedness.

Lupita didn't even say goodbye.

Clay's thoughts returned to the present.

His life had changed dramatically in ways he couldn't begin to comprehend.

How can we use you? emerged as the new mantra of a dying planet: Government, Tanaka, the Sperm Banks. Gone, too, a life of relative obscurity. Women were going to line up for him. They could conduct a lottery. The Sperm King. What a joke, he thought. He felt inadequate to the challenge. Even worse, he wasn't sure he wanted the human race to survive. This had pissed Hank off, but it wasn't the first time Clay had considered these thoughts.

Life, in 2050, carried with it a deep sadness. Clay believed the plants and animals understood that human beings were responsible for the suffering of all life forms and for bringing their world to a tragic end. Oceans, land, and birds in the sky. The air itself. The Web of Life had unraveled.

Clay's mind embraced a nihilistic spirit of a rather dark hue. He found himself slipping into sadness and depression. An almost debilitating dark night of the soul. Heartbreaking to witness the havoc humans had wrought through their own actions and inactions, their greed and passive endurance of intolerable conditions.

As a boy he had experienced the earth's pain and often woke up frightened from nightmares in which he heard and felt the earth crying and shaking, just as he lay in his bed crying and shaking. The nightmares had passed as the years rolled on, but not the young boy's empathy.

Given his deep and abiding love of nature, it seemed natural that he hated what the human race had done to destroy Earth. The callous indifference. The total lack of even an enlightened self-interest. An attitude accepting and advocating the degradation of all that he held dear.

Clay Roberts was not convinced that humanity deserved to live on.

Not sure that he should willingly help it avoid extinction.

CHAPTER 11

Jodie stood in the kitchen humming to herself as she poured hot water into the carafe of a French press and stirred the coffee grounds with a long-handled wooden spoon. She put the lid back on and set her internal timer. She always waited about four minutes before proceeding.

Hank came into the kitchen and found her already dressed for the day. She wore a brown, V-neck t-shirt with blue jeans and tennis shoes. He had on the same clothes he'd worn the day before, having not foreseen Clay's invitation to visit the farmhouse. He hoped the shower, and the hot, soapy water, had worked to limit his usual pungent scent.

Clay's sister turned, saw the agent out of the corner of her eye, and stopped her humming.

"I smelled the coffee all the way upstairs," Hank said as he entered further into the kitchen and spied three empty cups on the counter.

"It'll be ready in a minute. We can have granola with yogurt for breakfast," she offered. "I made them both myself."

The agent's hesitation betrayed him.

"I can scramble some eggs with toast."

"Think I could have mine fried?"

"I guess so," she smiled.

She turned away and rolled her eyes.

Hank took the wait as an opportunity to take another look around. Tile floors and it looked like the original kitchen cabinets had been updated with a fresh coat of white paint and new cabinet drawer handles made from glass knobs. The butcher block countertops were probably new. Porcelain sink. It had the feel of an old-fashioned country kitchen.

Eggs and toast sounded fine, but he was dying for some bacon.

Better to make some small talk.

"Clay seems a bit old for his initial test," the agent began. "He must have had some king of deferment. Otherwise it makes no sense."

"Clay held a head of household deferment, but it expired this year," explained Jodie. Last month, in fact."

"Government didn't waste any time."

"We'd been lucky for a couple of years so it came as quite a shock to us when the exemption was recinded. I still have my student deferment," she added.

"They're talking about doing away with all deferments," claimed the agent.

"I heard that," said Jodie. "Not going to happen. I think lawmakers will try to protect their children and grandchildren."

"From what?"

"From disappointing test results."

Hank wanted to ask how many years Clay had enjoyed his deferment so he could later calculate his age, but he knew better than to pry. Stay in her good graces, he told himself. She might have a lot of influence on her brother.

Jodie placed her palm on the plunger of the French Press and pushed down slowly.

"Are you ready for some coffee, Hank?"

"Thought you'd never ask."

"Cream and sugar?"

"No thanks."

Jodie grabbed the handle of the French Press and poured a steaming cup for the agent.

"I ground the beans just before you walked in," she informed him while handing over the cup and then pouring one for herself. She added creamer from a small ceramic pitcher and picked up a nearby spoon to stir it.

Hank took a sip and sighed, a sigh of deep satisfaction. He was used to starting his day with a good cup of coffee.

"Man, that shower was great!" exclaimed Hank. "I thought I'd died and gone to heaven. Must have been in there for a full five minutes."

Jodie raised her cup to her mouth and took a sip before lowering it to converse.

"We don't abuse our water," Jodie told him. "All the water that goes down the drain is grey water that goes outside to water the citrus trees. Water is our most precious resource. Clay doesn't shower every day. Every two or three days." Jodie put her thumb and a forefinger to her nose and pretended to squeeze her nostrils closed, a good-natured sight gag.

"Baths are outlawed in the cities," Hank told her. "They don't even make bathtubs anymore. They actually went house to house, and apartment to apartment, and tore out all the tubs. Claimed they used twice as much water as a shower. They made it a crime to own one. A felony."

The agent sipped his coffee.

"What about bathing infants?" Jodie wondered.

"Oh, yeah, I almost forget about that," Hank admitted. "There's one exception. They allowed families with babies to install double sinks and farmhouse sinks. At their own expense I might add."

"Not surprising the way people were wasting water," asserted Jodie.

"Not any more. In cities and towns, the water is automatically shut off after a two-minute shower. Most people can't afford to shower daily and low flow shower heads are mandated by code. Local jurisdictions do random checks to make sure people aren't switching them out. If you do, you face heavy fines and repeat offenders have been known to get jail time."

"It was probably necessary," insisted Jodie. "We heard the average person was using one hundred gallons a day."

Hank looked around. He' d been so busy chatting with Jodie that he had forgotten about his client.

"Where is Clay?"

"He's gone."

"Gone where?" asked Hank, whose voice registered an octave higher, and had taken on an agitated tone.

"I don't know," she answered. "He didn't tell me. He wasn't here when I woke up, so I checked and his truck was gone."

"You must know where he'd go!" yelled the agent. "Think!"

"I'm trying," Jodie screamed before bursting into tears.

Jodie placed her cup down on the kitchen counter. She felt like throwing hot coffee on Hank, but refrained. At least for the time being. Breathe, she told herself before choosing the best alternative. She shot daggers at the agent with her eyes.

"Shit!" Hank cried out like he was in pain.

"I think you should leave, Hank."

Hank's shoulders sank down and he suddenly appeared deflated. Realizing that he'd overreacted, he felt ashamed of himself. He put his cup down on the counter, and wondered if there was anything he could do to compensate for his rude behavior. He decided that total honesty would serve the situation best.

"I'm sorry," he told Jodie. "I completely lost it. It's my fault he's gone."

"What do you mean?"

"I'm so sorry," Hank apologized again. "I was pressuring Clay for an answer last night. I was only thinking of myself. I never really considered his or your best interests. He must have sensed my selfishness." Hank grimaced as he lowered his head dejectedly. "I'm such an ass."

He is something of an ass, thought Jodie. But he does seem to have a conscience.

"Don't be too hard on yourself, Hank"

Hank appreciated the sympathy.

"Is that like him, Jodie"? he asked. "To just take off without telling you?"

"No, it's not," she responded. "But Clay hasn't been himself since Government's did that mandated testing."

That's not surprising, thought the agent.

There came an unexpected knock at the door.

This caught their attention and ended the awkward conversation.

"I'm going to see who it is," said Jodie.

She left Hank alone in the kitchen.

When Jodie opened the front door, she found herself looking at a young woman about her own age. She didn't recognize her. She was certain that the stranger was Asian, or perhaps Eurasian. Her pretty, almond-shaped face was framed by long black hair. She wore her warm smile as if it were a permanent feature. An aura of well-being emanated from her as she stood there wearing jeans, low-cut hiking boots, and a teal blue tank top underneath a loose fitting cotton shirt.

"Hello, I'm Lynne Lee," the woman said, introducing herself. "I wonder if I might speak with Clay Roberts."

"Does Clay know you?" asked Jodie. She had never seen this person before, and her brother had never mentioned her.

"It's extremely important," the woman replied, ignoring the question. "I drove a long way to visit with him."

Jodie felt at a loss. All these strange situations since Clay's testing. It seemed a bit unnerving, disorienting. Their once predictable lives seemed to be now spiraling out of control. What to do. You can start by being gracious, she told herself.

"Why don't you come inside."

CHAPTER 12

Clay woke up inside his sleeping bag.

He yawned and reached over and grabbed his water flask, took a couple of sips, and placed it back down on the broken tiles. He felt antsy and a little unnerved by recent events. The big, fat full moon didn't help things. He decided to crawl out of his sleeping bag and go outside for a walk.

Out through the back of the mansion he went.

Moonlight cast a wide arc of light upon the landscape.

His father had sawn four round seats out of a telephone pole washed up on the beach by the tide. He'd used his solar powered chainsaw to cut them into two adult-sized pieces and two child-sized for Clay and his sister. Clay smiled to himself as he sat on the log his dad had always settled upon. So many fond memories of times spent at the coast.

Even back then the road had fallen into disrepair. Highway One, known as the Pacific Coast Highway, had once been considered among the world's most scenic drives. Now it lay crumbled in broken sections like scattered pieces of a jigsaw puzzle ready to be fit back together. Clay knew that would never happen.

The rest of the road had fallen into the ocean, from Oregon all the way down to Southern California, a victim of unrelenting erosion. Sucked out by the tides and carried to who knew where: Japan, the Philippines, Korea, or China. Maybe the current had taken those chunks of asphalt down to Central and South America.

The catastrophic erosion had hit California hardest along the coastline from Los Angeles to San Diego where the sea had swallowed multi-million dollar mansions, a scenic railroad that had ferried sightseers through stunning coastal landscapes, and the state's beautiful beaches.

The small seaside community that had once existed nearby, down the highway from the mansion Clay was camping inside, had long since disappeared. The restaurants, art galleries, wine and cheese shops, and beach town curio establishments had been left deserted for almost a decade. Rising seas and punishing storms had carried them away just like the road that had brought tourists to the trendy destination. Alfred Hitchcock had chosen to shoot his classic film, *The Birds,* in this location because of the area's awesome natural beauty. The movie had outlived the town.

Clay couldn't help but remember the times his family had spent at this coastline. They'd camped out in the rundown mansion by the sea back when he and his sister were young children and their parents had brought them here and used the dilapidated ruins as a shelter. A roof and a few walls were all they needed to go along with a camp stove and an ice chest full of food.

He remembered playing outside. "Be careful, you two," his mother always told them. "Don't go too close to the cliff." She kept an eye on them just in case. Dad took them down to the shoreline to surf cast. It was always catch and release. They wouldn't the eat fish. Too many micro-plastics in the oceans. Oh, those family vacations. Good times never felt so wonderful.

Clay missed his parents terribly. He and Jodie rarely talked about them, but he had no doubt his sister felt the same way. What would they suggest? Mom and dad. They'd let him make up his own mind. They treasured independence of spirit and fostered a deep appreciation of individuality in their children.

So what did he think? How did he feel? The instant wealth. The notoriety. He had to admit the situation was enticing, but he sensed it would eventually become a burden. A life that would eat away at his better instincts and transform him into somebody he didn't want to be. What to do, what to do. Humanity had gotten too close to the cliff and seemed primed to go over the edge. Like lemmings rushing headlong towards extinction.

Clay knew his experience, here on the California coast, served as a valuable microcosm. Individuals and couples and families all over the globe were living among the ruins of the their coastal regions: the Algarve, Shanghai, the African coast, the Italian coastline, and Scandinavia. No coastline had been spared. Entire islands had been swallowed by the seas.

His mother and father, David and Claire, had taught him and Jodie these things. Told them that's why they had decided to live a life closer to nature during the waning years of a dying planet. Certainly not a perfect life, not exactly easy, but deeply fulfilling because they could raise their children in a relatively healthy environment given the world they were forced to deal with.

Few people in the world, even the devoutly religious, still believed they would go to Hell when they died because humans beings, and the horrendous climate change conditions they had created, had turned the planet into a living hell.

Clay looked back at the mansion.

He knew he should try to get some sleep.

He rose from the log, his father's seat, and walked back to what remained of the structure. Before entering the decayed dwelling he turned around for one last look. For a moment he imagined he could see his mom and dad sitting on their designated logs.

Once safely back inside, Clay crawled into his sleeping bag. Fond memories of the past couldn't console him. The full moon mocked him as the night turned ghostly and surreal. The wind began to howl as it whipped its way through the mansion's open spaces.

Why are all these thoughts crowding in on me, he wondered. His mind felt like it was shrinking, time and space contracting inside of his psyche. He felt desperate and desired an escape from himself and his futile concerns.

Another episode of Perc.

That would take his mind off the past.

He reached over for his burner phone and engaged in a search. Once he found the Sanctuary Earth Podcast he scrolled down to Episode Two: "The Eve of Extinction." He repeated the title and asked himself if this was something he really wanted to listen to given the mood that had settled upon him.

He considered his choices.

Spiritual claustrophobia or listening to what Perc had to say.

Click!

CHAPTER 13

Podcast - *Sanctuary Earth*

Episode 2 - "The Eve of Extinction"

Leaf: Welcome to Sanctuary Earth, where we discuss issues vital to the continuation of life on our planet. These programs are aired free of advertisements as a public service provided by the Plastic People's Sanctuary Movement.

I'm Leaf Aronson and today on the show we are honored to have Perc, the called radical eco-historian. We introduced Perc on last week's first offering, "Perc's Personal Perspective." If you'd like to know more about him, please go back and listen to that episode. Or, you can do a search of your own.

As we stated last week, Perc is going to provide insights into how we've created the existential crisis we are currently facing, and offer some advice about how we might reverse the destructive and disturbing trends destroying life as we know it.

You said you'd give us an overview of how we got to where we are. You're calling this episode "The Eve of Extinction."

Perc: That's right, Leaf. First I'd like to piggy-back on something I failed to mention last time. After focusing on plastic, I began to consider my overall carbon footprint. I took a close look at my own thoughtlessness in relation to nature. Back when I was drinking wine, before the demise of the international market, I was consuming wines imported from Europe, South America, and as far away as Australia. We're talking five, six, and almost ten thousand miles to transport them to our local grocery stores or bottle shop. Luckily, I lived in California at the time so it was relatively easy for me to switch over to locally grown, organic wines brought in from hundreds of miles away at most.

Then I thought about how I was flying off to conferences just like the politicians flying to their summits and conferences. About how reporters kept flying after them to cover the stories. No one thought about how their plane travel added tons more carbon into the atmosphere. They didn't even use carbon offsets to help minimize the damage. It was business as usual. I get it. It was so much easier to go along with the status quo, but that's how we got into this mess.

Leaf: Seems like an excellent place to begin this week's episode. The mess we're in.

Perc: By all means, Leaf. Because life on planet Earth may come to an end sooner than we think, and I'm going to share my thoughts on how we've arrived at this sorry state of affairs in hopes that, if we do somehow survive, we might not repeat the mistakes of the past.

First, let's look at where we are. There were so many miscalculations: our fast rising seas, massive crop failures, unprecedented droughts and floods, devastated forests, human reproductive failure, and the urgent timelines necessary to prevent catastrophe.

Human fertility is almost non-existent in today's world. Most people would've been skeptical if I'd suggested this scenario thirty years ago, but powerful evidence had existed for more than a quarter century detailing the reasons this would come to pass.

Thirty years ago we already met the standard for an endangered species. Of five possible criteria for what made a species endangered, only one needed to be present. Homo sapiens had at least three!

We put our human wants and desires ahead of Earth's needs. We're destroying all the life on this planet including ourselves. We've lacked a living relationship with nature. It was all about "how can we use you." This resulted in the catastrophic effects of human-created climate change. Immeasurable numbers of peoples have perished in the process. Watching all this from the sidelines, so to speak, is a terrible torture which only exacerbates the stress and further lowers sperm counts and desire.

Leaf: You put a lot of emphasis on plastics and harmful chemicals as the cause of our decline, but there's more to the equation than just plastics and pesticides.

Perc: Of course. We have to add to the issue of hormonal imbalance all of the factors creating anxiety in modern so-called life, most of which are a direct result of the actions of human beings including global warming: those I've mentioned as well as climate refugees, supply chain disruptions, energy blackouts, overconsumption, and massive waste on a scale unprecedented in recorded time.

Did I mention the lack of drinkable water? That should probably be first on the list given that we can't survive without it.

Leaf: Certainly a sobering list, but you've stated in the past that all this might have been avoided. Would you elaborate?

Perc: I place most of the blame on a woeful lack of political leadership during the last half-century. The Paris Climate Agreement in 2015, seemed to offer a glimpse of hope. Five years later, almost all of the countries were polluting worse than before. Too much talk, but no follow through. They didn't have the sense of urgency needed to face the challenges presented by global warming.

You had political leaders flying to Europe from all over the world to attend a United Nations Climate Change Conference, back in 2021. Celebrities arriving at the venue in their private jets. Imagine the carbon footprint from all those flights. The irony! They would have made it a Zoom meeting if they were really serious about saving the planet. Just a lot of showboating! For God's sake, the largest contingency at that conference was three hundred lobbyists from the fossil fuel industry. The next year they sent six hundred fossil fuel lobbyists to COP27, in Egypt. Give me a break!

Leaf: The executives of those fossil fuel companies. Do they share some of the responsibility?

Perc: Absolutely! We know that of all the greenhouse gases emitted during the past three centuries more than half took place after 1988; and, in that year James Hansen of NASA testified to the US Congress that there was no longer any doubt that global warming had begun. 1988! We didn't act and that's a fact!

Executives of fossil fuel companies bear the greatest responsibility. Their great deceit was funding climate denial, and spending billions to kill any policy that prevented us from transitioning away from the coal, gas, and oil economy. Exxon Mobil created a disinformation campaign despite knowing the reality of the situation. They spent millions of dollars spreading climate change denial and attempting to delay legislative efforts to curb carbon emissions.

Leaf: Any other bad actors come to mind?

Perc: Oh, yeah. The fossil fuel manufacturers had a lot of help. Follow the money. In the seven years after the Paris Climate Agreement, the six largest US banks provided 1.4 trillion dollars in financing to fossil fuel industry. Wall street also funded fossil fuel expansion in the form of billions of dollars of shares owned and sold by investment houses. Compromised politicians were in bed with all of them.

Leaf: The political failure to take the necessary steps to prevent this type of activity, along with subsequent failures, led to the creation of the World Council.

Perc: The current World Council is dominated by China, the United States, and Russia. They just happen to be the three biggest polluters on the planet, and they're peddling an alternative history to cover up what amounts to criminal behavior in the face of impending doom. People like me, who dare to tell the truth, are ridiculed. Labeled as malcontents.

The leaders of the World Council should be tried as terrorists for crimes against humanity. For terrorizing the environment and all who are attempting to survive amidst the current chaos. Don't think for a moment that the people left on this earth aren't terrified and afraid.

Leaf: You're a severe critic of past generations. What is it that you find so offensive?

Perc: Just the lazy and passive mentality. People found it easier to go along with the misinformation churned out by the corporations and governments. Had they been proactive about dealing with the twin challenges of human reproductive development and climate change they would have been teaching their children about the dangers we all faced. Not to scare them, but to prepare them for the world they would inherit.

Leaf: Most people turn a blind eye.

Perc: The bread and circuses of the ancient Romans have been replaced by the   Metaverse. Let people escape into their alternate universes when they're not working or consuming. A convenient tool for mind control. Or, passive indifference at the very least. When an avatar's wardrobe becomes an important consideration in a person's life our sense of values have been skewed big time.

We were so self-centered that we cared little for the pain and suffering we've caused in the natural world. I have to add that we all, as consumers of the earth's resources, bear some blame. Work, eat, sleep, and consume. The mantra of western industrial societies, then Russia and China signed on, and finally the entire world.

Then there's the issue of the crass inequity of the Global North versus the Global South. The countries that have suffered the most from the life-destroying effects of climate change are the ones who did the least to make it happen. They were promised compensation, but they're still waiting.

Leaf: What would it have taken to prevent all this?

Perc: We should have started down a different path a century ago. One that would have required a revolution in the way we think and act and set our priorities. But all the institutions of society went on with business as usual, continuing down the road to climate catastrophe with our foot on the accelerator.

The educational system could have been restructured so that addressing climate change was the first priority. This would have started in elementary school and continued all the way through University. Even the business schools would have placed global warming at the center of their curriculum. Can you imagine? Not profits, but the future of the planet as the first goal.

We needed a radical reorganizing of the priorities of daily life. It could have been initiated within the family and then been reinforced and strengthened in the educational system. Kids are curious and like to solve problems. We should have started at an early age because it meant their very survival

The energies of society would have been mobilized and focused on the twin goals of preventing and reversing climate change and improving human fertility. This would have naturally included the elimination of harmful toxic chemicals like those found in plastics because there is also a carbon footprint to their creation.

Leaf: We've come full circle with the mention of plastics once again. This might be a good place to end this episode. Maybe you can tell listeners what the next interview will cover.

Perc: I call the next episode "Hormonal Havoc." I plan to delve into more detail about the causes of our impending extinction as a species, its causes, and what might have been done to prevent it.

Leaf: That brings us to the end of this week's program. Our hope is that the ideas presented on this Podcast help you gain a better understanding of the world we live in. Thanks to Perc for joining us to share his thoughts on "The Eve of Extinction" and thanks to you for listening to Sanctuary Earth.

Narrator: Keme Nimdemke was the producer of this episode. Our engineers are Andrew Wilson and Celeste Roberts. Our editor is Rosie Zuniga. The executive producer is Leaf Aronson.

CHAPTER 14

Jodie returned to the kitchen.

Hank and the newcomer, Lynne, followed her and they stood around enduring an awkward silence. Hank waited for one of the others to speak up, figuring he'd already said too much. The agent remembered his unfinished cup of coffee, picked it up, and took a sip. It had cooled during the interruption and lost its appeal.

Jodie decided to break the ice.

"Would you like some coffee, Lynne?" she asked.

"No thank you," came the polite response.

"So why do you want to talk to Clay?"

"I'm one of the Plastic People," Lynne replied. "I came here to invite Clay to visit our Arm-in-Arm Sanctuary."

"I've heard of you people," claimed Hank, now unable to resist joining in on the conversation. "Isn't one of you in the top five?"

"What's he talking about?" asked Jodie.

"Fertile Planet Magazine," explained Lynne. "Yes, one of our members, in Ireland, was lauded for her fertility. Ciara McCarthy. A farmer's daughter from County Cork. She went into hiding and asked us to help her escape, here to America, so that she could live anonymously in one of the Sanctuaries."

"Now I remember," Hank chimed in. "You Plastic People are attempting to go it alone. Creating lots of self-sufficient . . . Sanctuaries . . . I guess you call them."

"We aren't going it alone as you say."

Lynne walked right up to Hank and looked the agent directly in the eye. "We are all a part of the larger web of life even though humans once thought we could separate by denying our interdependence. We know better now"

Jodie sensed a tension in the air. Her stomach tightened. She wasn't used to the ongoing confrontation. She decided to change the subject.

"How did you find out where we live?"

"It's not that difficult to hack into Government's testing operations."

"She's right there," agreed Hank.

Lynne turned to Clay's younger sister and smiled with a radiance that brightened both the room and the prevailing mood.

"As I said, I'm here to invite Clay to come with me so that he might experience one of our Sanctuaries for himself. Perhaps he'd be willing to help us in our attempts to save the species and the planet. There's no coercion involved. Maybe not even compensation."

"So you guys want to enlist him to your cause," interrupted the agent.

"Be quiet, Hank," said Jodie. "I'll remind you that you are a guest at our farm."

"Sorry," came the apology. "I think I'll go outside for some fresh air."

Clay Roberts wannabe agent strode quietly through the kitchen and out to the back garden through one of the French doors, leaving the two women alone.

Shaking her head in exasperation, Jodie smiled back at Lynne.

"Can I talk to Clay?" inquired the visitor.

"Actually," Jodie responded, followed by an uneasy pause. "Clay isn't here right now."

"Oh," Lynne sighed. "Do you know when he'll be back?"

"Not really," was the honest reply. "He left without telling anyone."

The smile on Lynne's face vanished.

"Long drive for nothing."

Jodie thought about this. She found herself sympathizing with Lynne Lee. She felt herself emphasizing with her for feeling disappointed. There was more to it than simple compassion. Life on the farm with her brother didn't offer a lot of opportunities for relating to other women. Just her friends in town. It wouldn't hurt anything to help Lynne Lee out, and it would give Jodie a chance to learn more about the Sanctuary movement. A little female comradery. No harm in that. It didn't have to be a long drive for nothing.

"Maybe not," Jodie said, offering a glimmer of hope. "I think I know where we might find him."

"That would mean so much to me."

"Let's go outside for some fresh air first," suggested Jodie. "We can take a walk, and I'll show you around the farm."

Jodie showed the visitor the raised garden beds.

She then led her over to a brick barbeque.

"My father built this," she said with a touch of pride in her voice.

"I don't eat meat."

"It can be used to grill vegetables and fruit as well."

Lynne's smile served as her response.

"Let's sit for a while," said Jodie as she headed for a bench. She wanted to understand this person better so she could attempt to access her motivations. She felt protective of her brother. Especially since he'd lost his exemption.

They sat on one of the garden's many wooden benches, bodies turned out towards the garden.

Before Jodie could ask a question, Lynne Lee asked one of her own.

"You and Clay live off the grid?"

"Our parents had a vision of living a self-sufficient life," said Jodie with admiration. "We have solar, wind turbines, battery storage, water harvesting, and a cistern. Greywater is piped from the house out to the orchard and garden beds."

"We have a lot in common," said Lynne. "This isn't much different than how we live at our Sanctuary. It's amazing how similar our lifestyles are. I think Clay would feel right at home with us."

Jodie wondered if the young woman sitting next to her might be a recruiter. Someone working on commission. Anything seemed possible since Clay's test results were confirmed by Government. Would these Plastic People use her brother for their own selfish purposes and then drop him like a hot potato?

Hank rounded a corner and found the two women sitting together. He quickly turned and headed off in the direction from which he'd come. Jodie caught sight of him out of the corner of her eye. She didn't say a word, glad that the agent hadn't intruded into the conversation.

Lynne Lee sensed Jodie's unease, and realized that it was perfectly understandable given the circumstances. Outsider shows up unannounced asking for Clay. Her purpose to invite him to visit a Sanctuary so that he can experience for himself an environment dedicated to saving the planet and the human race. See if he might want to join them.

"I'd like to talk with Clay so that I can tell him about our Arm-in-Arm Sanctuary," she said with a smile. "See if he'd like to stay with us for a couple of days. Make up his own mind about our intentions. It's that simple. No hard sell, Jodie. I'm not getting paid to come here. I came because I believe in what we are doing. We certainly mean no harm."

Jodie thought about what she had said. Make up his own mind. No hard sell. Not getting paid. Mean no harm. She sounded sincere when she shared her thoughts. Now for the litmus test. Clay's sister turned and looked Lynne Lee in the eye. Soft eyes. Alert and inquisitive eyes, but soft eyes. Easy smile. Nothing forced. Patiently waiting for her to respond.

But she needed to know more about the young woman sitting next to her.

Where are you from, Lynne?"

"Los Angeles," she replied "My parents came to the United States twenty six years ago. They left Incheon, a coastal city, because my father feared the entire Korean Peninsula would one day experience a devastating flood. A deluge he called it. They were already occurring worldwide. My parents had family and friends, in Koreatown. That's where I was born and grew up.

"Seems their timing was very good."

"Four years later, the United States government morphed into the fascist state we now call Government. Immigration was closed to Asians. Not to Europeans or others, just Asians."

"I'm sorry."

"I grew up an only child. Both of my parents worked hard and saved all their money to send me to a university. I attended UCLA because it's closer to my home in K-Town. I studied Social Work and applied for a job with the Sanctuary after graduation. I begged my parents to apply to Arm-in-Arm and come with me, but they're old school. Very traditional. Though it broke their hearts to see me go, they couldn't bear to part with family and friends and the familiarity of their own culture.

"Why did you leave?"

Lynne turned to face Jodie.

"I felt like it was my mission in life," she replied earnestly, as the words began to pour out of her "Like I was being called to become a part of something special. I felt that I had a moral obligation to follow my heart's desire. I saw my peers turning to drugs or else escaping into the Metaverse to kill their pain. I wanted to live in a place where there was hope for the future. I wanted to *live,* not accept some counterfeit reality."

Jodie felt the depth of Lynne Lee's passion, the strength of her commitment.

"Like I said earlier, I think I know where to find my brother."

CHAPTER 15

By noon the sun had risen high overhead.

The temperatures burned hot, even at the coast. But the balmy breeze, blowing in off the ocean, felt good against Clay's face as he sat along the cliffs, his mother's words still echoing inside the canyons of his mind, "Don't go too close to the cliff." Humanity *had* gotten too close to the cliff and seemed primed to go over the edge.

Clay might have gone on thinking in this vein, but his thought process was interrupted by the sound of an approaching car. He stood and turned his gaze back to the mansion. So much for solitude. Better go see who had joined him.

He didn't recognize either the jeep or the driver, but he did observe two familiar faces in the vehicle. His sister, Jodie, sat next to the driver and he saw Hank sitting quietly in the backseat sulking. He wrinkled his brow as a frown formed on his face. No use trying to evade this encounter. He'd just have to grin and bear it, he thought to himself as he let out an exasperated sigh.

The door of the jeep opened.

Clay took a closer look at the driver as she emerged from the car. Her long black hair wrapped around her neck and hung down along her left shoulder. Long bangs covered her eyebrows, almost reaching into the brown orbs. Asian or Eurasian, he guessed. Rather attractive. Wonder what she wants with me.

Jodie, and whoever this strange young woman might be, closed the jeep doors. They turned and began to make their way towards him. Hank slammed his door shut with a little too much force. Jodie rolled her eyes so that Clay could see her displeasure. Hank looked to Clay and shrugged indicating that it was an accident. An unfamiliar vehicle. Stuff happens.

"I thought that I might find you here," said Jodie with a satisfied expression on her face.

"I needed some time to think."

"And?"

"And?" he repeated.

"Have you had enough time?" she asked in a brusque tone.

Clay thought he detected a bit of personal rancor in her voice. He felt like his sister was pressing him. It wasn't so much the question as her attitude. The snarky emotion he knew lay behind the rude delivery. In front of a stranger no less. Well two can play that game.

"Who's this you've brought with you?" he asked, ignoring the question.

Lynne stepped forward before Jodie could introduce her. She extended her hand in a gesture of goodwill. Clay took her hand into his own and gave it a soft squeeze. She smiled as she gazed up into his eyes. He was a good four inches taller than her.

"I'm Lynne Lee," she said. "I'd like to talk with you."

"I warned you, Clay" Hank reminded him. "You don't have to worry though. I made sure we weren't followed."

"I'm one of the Plastic People," Lynne said, ignoring the agent.

"How did you find out about me, Linley?" he asked. It sounded like a challenge.

"Just call me Lynne," she told him. "Lee is my last name."

"Sorry."

"We have a very sophisticated system for hacking into Government's records," she revealed without a hint of arrogance in her voice. "Untraceable. We have ways of getting our hands on classified information, but I assure you we won't divulge your location and we respect your rights of privacy."

"Not quite legal though, is it?" Hank pointed out.

"I know it sounds invasive, but everyone is desperate these days. Government, the Cartels, and the Sperm Banks. As for us, we're trying to save the planet as well as our own species, and these are trying times."

"You should hear her out," advised Jodie. "She makes a lot of sense."

Clay considered his sister's request.

"Risky, Clay," warned Hank. "How do we know we can trust her?"

Jodie gave the agent a who do you think you are stare. It made him uneasy, so he decided to hedge his bet.

"Just saying."

"What do you want with me?" questioned Clay.

"I came to invite you to visit our Arm-in-Arm Sanctuary," Lynne announced in no uncertain terms. "We're working there to create a healthier world and to prevent the total extinction of our species. We believe that you can help us. We're a tribe of mostly fertile people who share the same values. No coercion. No discrimination. We've gravitated to one another naturally. If couples find each other and are successful in procreation so much the better."

"I've heard about your movement," Clay told her. "You've outlawed the use of plastic and toxic chemicals. So why do you call yourself the Plastic People? Seems a bit odd."

"To acknowledge the truth," came her reply. "We *are* plastic people. All of us. Every person on this planet. Nobody is immune. It's only a matter of how much plastic is inside of your body. Micro-plastics at a cellular level and in the bloodstream. Fish, animals, birds, insects, and reptiles. Those that aren't extinct have been rendered hormonally im-balanced. Not even the same species. Just like us."

While she talked, Clay noticed a metal stud earring in the middle of her ear, between the lobe and the tip. Cute ears, he mused. Soft eyes and a kind face. She speaks in a convincing manner, but without rancor.

"I have a proposition for you."

"Oh my God! shrieked Hank. "A proposition already."

"Shut up, Hank!" yelled Jodie.

She'd heard enough and was tired of the agent's constant interruptions. Time to take things into her own hands. She went up to him, thrust her arm through his, and wrapped her elbow around his elbow. She led Hank away without saying a word, leaving Clay and Lynne alone to continue their conversation in peace.

"Where is this Sanctuary?"

"Our Arm-in-Arm Sanctuary is outside of Sonoma, but we have at least one location in every state and some in Europe.

"Tell me a little more about them," encouraged Clay. "How big is this movement of yours?"

"We've limited the Sanctuaries to around twelve hundred people each. That's based on the Buddha's original Sangha model for a viable community."

Clay did the math in his head. Fifty states. Perhaps two or three in California, New York State, and Florida. Some of the other large states. Plus Europe. Say seventy times 1,200. Less than eighty-five thousand people total.

"Government can't legally do anything to shut us down or stop the movement. Not that they're not trying. They'd like to see us fail. We get no help from them, and that won't change anytime soon. We're resolved to succeed in spite of hostility and a campaign of misinformation."

They didn't seem like much of a threat to Clay. Was it because they were hotbeds of fertility filled with individuals Government couldn't manipulate to its own ends? Once baby boomers had died out, pandemic and climate change deaths came quickly from unrelenting floods, lack of water, and energy in drought stricken regions along with worldwide starvation on an unthinkable scale due to major crop failures and distribution disruptions.

The horrors of the last decade had reduced the global population to less than three billion people and it was estimated that less than one percent of them were capable of reproducing new life.

Maybe Government did project the Plastic People's Movement as an existential threat.

Clay had to admit that he was intrigued. Not only did he maintain a healthy curiosity about their Sanctuaries, but he felt an attraction to the young woman they'd sent to invite him for a visit.

"One last question," he said. "Why do you call your communities Sanctuaries?"

"We believe them to be sanctified. Holy ground. Most indigenous peoples have believed the same. The Earth is sacred."

"Hey, Sis!" Clay called out. "Come on back!"

Jodie had taken Hank about ten yards away. They both turned to locate Clay. They found him waving his arm, encouraging them to return. Jodie had heard her brother and she and the agent understood his universal nonverbal summons.

The foursome soon stood together in a circle.

"Are you growing your beard out," asked Jodie after she'd taken a closer look at her brother.

"Hank thinks it's a good idea because it will make me less recognizable.

"That's not a bad idea," agreed Lynne Lee, turning to Jodie. "Your brother is going to find that his freedom may be compromised. A lot of people will want a piece of him."

And we all know which piece, thought Hank to himself.

"Let's all head back to the farmhouse," suggested Clay.

He hadn't committed to the visit, but he hadn't said no.

"You sure, Clay?" inquired Jodie. She felt the twinge of a guilty conscience. She hadn't been very nice to her brother. She knew he was under a lot of pressure. She shouldn't be pestering him.

"Yeah," he replied. "Let me get my things."

"Can I ride with you, Clay?" asked Hank in desperation.

Clay sensed that the agent was pleading for a yes. He didn't know what had transpired between Hank and the two women, but he definitely felt the tension between them.

"Sure," Clay answered. "I'll meet you back at our place, Jodie."

Jodie felt relieved. Her shoulders dropped as she gave her brother a smile.

"All right," she said. "C'mon Lynne, let's go."

Clay headed back to the decrepit mansion with Hank tagging along.

Once inside, he rolled his sleeping bag up into a tight bundle and then tied it with the attached cord. That done, he retrieved his water flask and his backpack. He slung the pack's strap over one shoulder and was about to reach for his sleeping bag when Hank intervened.

"I'll get that for you," he said, trying to lend a hand and make himself useful.

"Thanks."

Clay took a final look around to make sure he hadn't left anything behind.

"You slept in here," said Hank, stating the obvious.

"Our parents used to bring us here when we were kids," Clay explained with a longing in his voice. "We'd fish and explore the area. Just a little family vacation time."

"You're lucky, man." Hank responded, expressing a different kind of yearning. "I never got to camp when I was a kid."

Both men took a moment to reflect.

The agent envied Clay. As much as he loved his mother and grandmother he'd always missed having a male influence in his life. Especially growing up in the city during his adolescent years.

"Let's hit the road," said Clay, interrupting Hank's pensive reverie.

They left the mansion behind and walked to the truck.

They climbed up into the pick-up.

The agent knew that he had to work on Clay. Despite not being prepared for a longer stay at the farmhouse, or even a trip to this Plastic People's Sanctuary, he wasn't about to let this woman breeze into their lives and whisk his could-be, would-be client away so that she could influence him to join some ca-ray-zee cult or movement.

Not if he could help it.

CHAPTER 16

They arrived back at the farm in the late afternoon.

Clay and Hank went out back to talk while Jodie gave Lynne a brief walking tour of the interior of the farmhouse. After she'd finished, the two women went back into the living room to converse further. They sat together on the sofa facing one another. Jodie had something on her mind, something she felt she needed to share with the young woman who referred to herself as one of the Plastic People.

"It's ironic Clay tested so well," began Jodie.

"Why's that?"

"My brother gets really down sometimes about what we've done to the other life forms on this planet."

"That's understandable."

Jodie offered her guest a half-hearted smile. She wasn't sure she should share intimate details about her brother's private life, especially his personality quirks.

"Maybe, but Clay gets into a dark place where he questions whether the human race should survive at all. He scares me when I listen to him because I'm not sure what he might do. Will he act upon his feelings? Will he do something irrational? I don't want him to hurt himself."

Lynne reached over and placed one hand on Jodie's.

"I think a visit to our Sanctuary might help change Clay's perspective," she ventured. "So let's encourage him."

Jodie's smile widened.

If a visit to a Sanctuary would help her brother, she was all for it. So she resolved to give this friendly, compassionate Plastic Person the benefit of the doubt. She'd try to convince Clay to leave their familiar surroundings and brave the unknown. She had begun to be curious about the Sanctuary herself. She wasn't about to invite herself along, but the idea of visiting the Sanctuary appealed to her. Like her brother, Jodie was born with an inquisitive mind.

Lynne waited patiently, her warm hand still on top of Jodie's.

Is Clay's sister going to respond? she wondered. She seems lost in her thoughts.

Jodie softened her gaze.

"Yes, let's encourage him," she agreed.

It was Lynne's turn to smile.

The four of them sat at the kitchen table, a rectangular surface. A half-dozen or so tangerines were piled inside of a wooden bowl in its center. Clay was seated at one end of the table with his sister and Lynne sitting on each side of him. Easier to work on him that way. Easier to keep his attention. Hank was left sitting across from his would be client. This didn't seem to bother the unsuspecting agent.

Lynne had engaged Clay in conversation without inviting the others to join them. She didn't appear rude, just focused.

"Your parents were ahead of their time," she said to Clay. "They were practicing twenty years ago what we've been doing at the Sanctuaries for a little over a decade, and it might explain things."

"What do you mean?" asked Clay.

"Your extraordinary health."

Everyone in the room knew exactly what she was referring to, but Lynne had found a subtle way of expressing it. A very diplomatic approach, thought Jodie.

"I know where this is heading," Clay said. "But what's the point of attempting to save this planet? We're doomed, aren't we?"

Hank shook his head no.

Jodie witnessed the agent's response and appreciated his sentiments.

"We choose to think differently," maintained Lynne . "We embrace mindfulness and living in the moment, Clay. See this bowl of tangerines sitting here? You grew these, didn't you? They must be special to you."

"Yeah, so," he interrupted with a hint of antagonism in his voice.

Is he testing me or is he simply being rude, wondered Lynne.

She decided to continue.

"One can experience the whole universe in a single tangerine." She picked one up and raised it to her nose. "Smell it. Look at it closely. Peel it. Taste it. Appreciate it."

"I know what you're saying. While I'm outside working in the garden and taking care of the farm, listening to the birds singing, I'm at peace with the world. When I think of what the earth has become, I sometimes experience a deep despair. A deep, dark despair.
How could humanity destroy this beautiful planet and all of the innocent species living on it?"

Both Jodie and Hank looked to Lynne to see how she'd respond.

"Some of us are working to save Earth and what species are left," Lynne pointed out. "Come with me so you might learn what others of like mind are creating. We're into cultivating a more earthy spirituality. Not just for ourselves, but for future generations. "

"Think any species will survive?" wondered Clay out loud.

"Some will if we have anything to do with it."

"I'll go," Clay said abruptly. "But only on one condition."

"What's that?" Lynne needed to know.

"We all go together," he insisted. "Jodie and Hank come along with me."

"Agreed," Lynne said without hesitation. She understood if there were no conditions placed on her offer there would probably be no resistance.

113

A collective sigh of relief. Disaster averted. Game on!

Clay and Jodie didn't keep any domestic pets. They'd fill the automatic feeders for the chickens and leave them plenty of water. They'd be fine in the coop for a couple of days. The drip irrigation system would water the orchard and the raised beds. They wouldn't be gone long. A few of days at most. Just enough time to have a good look at the Sanctuary and to find out how it operated. That simplified things. No need to have anyone come check on the farm.

"Agreed," said Hank, relieved the plans included him as well.

Time to change the subject, thought Lynne. Before Clay changed his mind. Get him thinking about something else.

"Have you and Jodie ever heard of Perc?" she asked Clay. "He's like your parents. Something of a throwback. He has some interesting things to say. I think you two should check out his podcast episodes. Especially you, Clay."

Embarrassed at being singled out, Clay blushed.

"Funny you mention Perc," he replied. "Hank told me about him a couple of days ago, and I'm already up to the third episode. It's the one that interests me most. He calls it "Hormonal Havoc." I wonder if it will help explain why everyone thinks I'm so exceptional."

"The whole series is enlightening," asserted Lynne.

"I told you," Hank gloated. "By far the most popular Podcast program in the world."

"In the United States," Lynne corrected him. "They banned it in China and Russia."

"Let's hear it for the First Amendment," added Jodie with a smile.

Clay decided to wait until everyone had gone to bed before listening to the third episode of *Sanctuary Earth*. He found it impossible to sleep so he searched his phone.

It wasn't long before theme music streamed into his ears.

CHAPTER 17

Podcast - *Sanctuary Earth*

Episode 3 - "Hormonal Havoc"

Leaf: Welcome to Sanctuary Earth, where we discuss issues vital to the continuation of life on our planet. These programs are aired free of advertisements as a public service provided by the Plastic People's Sanctuary Movement.

I'm Leaf Aronson and today on the show we are again pleased to present the radical eco-historian known as Perc. Today's episode is titled "Hormonal Havoc." We're going to explore how our modern world destroyed sperm counts and altered reproductive development in both males and females.

Perc: I should like to add that we are now the most threatened species on the planet!

Leaf: What caused the unprecedented decline in sperm counts and fertility rates and could this have been prevented?

Perc: I'll answer the last question first. As with climate change and global warming, the warning signs were evident for decades before the problem was considered serious enough to warrant attention. In both instances the results were catastrophic. It had been documented, more than thirty years ago, that average sperm counts and testosterone levels among western men had declined by fifty percent over the previous half century.

Women hadn't fared any better. Pregnancy loss and premature ovarian failure increased at the same one percent annual rate. The story was similar in Asia, Africa, and South America. Few paid attention. Conventional wisdom still considered overpopulation one of the most pressing concerns facing the planet.

The one percent a year decline became one and a half percent over the course of a single generation. This increased to two percent per year. Hormone disrupting chemicals are decimating human fertility at an alarming rate around the globe. We could reach zero sperm count by 2055. No more babies. No more humans. The World Council called an emergency meeting, but not until 2040. Sometime around 2045, the concept of a replacement rate no longer seemed relevant. It's only a matter of time before we become extinct unless things turn around quickly.

We never saw it coming! We should have, but we didn't. We were living an illusion created by Thomas Malthus and later Paul Erhlich, with *The Population Bomb* still ingrained in modern consciousness.

I'd like to tell you about some of the individual studies from long ago that were an intimation of the dire straits we now find ourselves in. In China's Hunan Province, epicenter of the original Covid 19 virus, qualified sperm donors at the Sperm Bank of China declined from fifty-six percent down to eighteen from 2001-2015. That was half a decade before Covid, which lowered counts further in infected men.

Consider Denmark. In 2020, the average twenty-something Danish woman was less fertile than her grandmother was at age thirty-five. A man now has half the sperm his grandfather had. The ability of men to get it up has gone down, no pun intended. We're literally shriveling up as a species. I could go on and on, but you get the picture.

Leaf: The causes, Perc? I'm sure our listeners would like to know about what's behind this devastating change, one that's brought us to the edge of the abyss as we contemplate our own extinction in the not too distant future.

117

Perc: Where do I begin in describing the debilitating effects of the mad industrialization of the planet? The decline in human reproductive health has been alarming and irreversible. There are so many culprits. The foods we eat and the water we drink are saturated with harmful chemicals and microplastics, and the air we breathe is infused with toxic substances. Microplastics can enter the body through both ingestion and inhalation and can damage cells and create inflammatory and immune system reactions in our bloodstreams

Take the seemingly innocuous cash register receipt. How many hundreds of millions of consumers had any idea that handling those receipts transferred a chemical proven to have hormone disrupting chemicals to their skin from where they migrated into the bloodstream. The poor unsuspecting grocery clerks and retail clerks of all kinds. To make matters worse, the transfer is enhanced if sanitizer or moisturizing cream has been used earlier. For most people cash register receipts represented a significant exposure to the harmful chemical BPA.

Another study I forgot to mention found alarming levels of poisonous chemicals in the male urine samples of Danish men aged 18-30. A chemical cocktail laced with bisphenols, dioxins, and phthalates, paracetamol, and likely exposure to twenty other chemicals. Proven endocrine disrupters that interfere with hormones and affect sperm quality. They were present in levels a hundred times greater than those considered safe. This was before the devastating effects of human-created climate change and its attendant global warming.

What else besides food, water, and air? I mentioned the wholesale assault on the environment. Climate anxiety emerged as a profound and emotionally debilitating new medical condition that decreased libido in general and interest in sex in particular.

Men made valiant, if misguided, attempts at increasing their testosterone in order to improve sperm counts. Most of these backfired. They performed longer, harder workouts not realizing forty-five minutes to an hour max is optimal for increases in testosterone levels. Longer workouts actually create a decline. Men relaxed after hard workouts by soaking in hot tubs and saunas, not realizing that the hot water reduced sperm counts. Even taking a pain killer like Tylenol was proven to reduce counts.

Testosterone replacement therapy increased tenfold in men between the ages of eighteen and forty-five. Individual testosterone levels increased as desired, but this also backfired! It signaled to the brain that there was lots of testosterone so it told the testes to stop making more. This led to lower sperm counts.

As global warming worsened more drug abuse occurred and this exacerbated infertility. Then we had a worldwide suicide epidemic as hopelessness abounded. Add to this the permanent brain fog suffered by millions of people as a result of the Covid variant SP.32.64F. Wave after wave of unanticipated pandemics have assailed us for more than a quarter of a century. Covid viruses and their spawn led to reduced sperm counts and infertility in general.

There's more! Sexually Transmitted Diseases, STDs for short, often went undiagnosed and untreated. Many of them, like Migen, lowered sperm counts and increased the numbers of miscarriages, preterm births, and infertility.

And for both sexes lifestyle choices also played a role. Obesity, diet and exercise, smoking, excessive alcohol and recreational drug use all had a part in altering our reproductive health.

Leaf: The enormous exposure to harmful chemicals seems to have altered our bodies at a deep cellular level.

Perc: An altered state that's created what I call *Homo Plasticus*, and this transformation took place in less than a century! But, I'd like to switch gears if you don't mind, Leaf.

Leaf: What do you have in mind?

Perc: I'd like to talk directly to your female listeners, and the men who care for them and support them can listen in.

Leaf: All right, Perc. The stage is yours, as they say.

Perc: The choices that you women make impact the transmission of your genes to your children and to future generations. It's vitally important to be mindful of the environmental dangers we are exposed to on a daily basis: stress, harmful substances, medications, toxins in our water and food, and even the fabrics we use.

If you are fortunate enough to get pregnant, the fetus inside of your uterus is the most sensitive to dangerous chemicals than at any other time in its life. Next are the infants and toddlers. We now understand that genetics are not a fixed code. Our changes are accelerating, and we are changing at a rate one hundred times faster than our grandparents as measured by our DNA markers. Everything has sped up.

Think about the chemically infused mattress that your baby is sleeping on and the fabric used to make their sheets and blankets; the fact that their body heat releases these harmful substances into the air. Look for eco-friendly organic alternatives. I've already touched upon the need to de-plasticize our homes.

Your babies are entering the world contaminated with chemicals they've absorbed in the womb. Once born, they are consuming a cocktail of "forever chemicals" that are stored in the fat of your breast milk. What was once a source of nutrition and a boost to a baby's immune system and brain development, as well as offering a feeling of emotional support, may be causing long lasting harm to your child and to future generations.

It's little consolation that baby formula is available because it's sold in plastic containers.

Phthalate exposure has been found to be widespread in the urine of infants and babies who come into contact with baby shampoos, lotions, and powders. No place on Earth is untouched by chemical contamination. They're attacking the bodies of every human on the earth, every fish swimming in the sea, and all the birds flying in the sky.

I won't dwell.

One more topic I'd like to touch upon as it relates to the health of your baby, but also the condition of the planet. I'm talking about disposable diapers. I get it! So much more convenient to use things that are disposable since we've been conditioned from childhood to live in a throw-away world. So much easier to put a plastic, chemical laden diaper against your baby's skin and private parts and allow their body heat to release those harmful substances into the air they breathe. You might want to think twice the next time you're about to wrap a disposable diaper around your precious baby's bare bottom.

Disposable diapers are a microcosm of human ingenuity and self-destruction. Their impact on the health of our planet is yet another reason to avoid their use.Their convenience comes at a terrible cost to the environment. Billions of tons of these diapers are thrown into landfills worldwide every year, and it takes 500 years for them to decompose. Every disposable diaper ever made is still on the earth in one form or another, introducing pathogens into the world from the solid waste they contain. These pathogens can make their way into the water supply where they pollute drinking water. Pardon my pun, but it's kind of a shitty situation, isn't it?

Those disposed of diapers in landfills degrade, creating methane and other toxic gases in the process. Their manufacture uses volatile chemicals that also end up in our environment. And in the U.S. alone up to 200,000 trees a year are sacrificed to make them.

Reusable cloth diapers would have stopped an estimated half-ton of disposable diapers per child, your child, from going into U.S. landfills each year. Here's the kicker! It takes nine gallons of water to produce a single disposable diaper. And,wait for it . . . they . . . are made with polyethylene plastic. Frickin' fossil fuel based plastic. So convenience be damned!

Leaf: This might be a good time to introduce your next episode which you're calling "Plastic Planet."

Perc: Good idea, Leaf. In the next program, I'll tell listeners about something they've probably never heard of, nurdles.

Leaf: What the heck are nurdles?

Perc: You'll have to tune in next week to find out.

Leaf: On that note, we'll end this episode. We hope the ideas presented on this Podcast help you gain a better understanding of the world we live in. Thanks to Perc for joining us to share his thoughts on "Hormonal Havoc " and thanks to you for listening to Sanctuary Earth.

Narrator: Ruth Weinstein was the producer of this episode. Our engineers are Andrew Wilson and Celeste Roberts. Our editor is Rosie Zuniga. The executive producer is Leaf Aronson.

Out of the
wreck I rise.

-- Robert Browning

Book II

The Plastic People

CHAPTER 18

The day held a deep blue sky filled with puffy white clouds.

Outside the farmhouse, the newly formed quartet readied for departure. Clay and Jodie had backpacks stuffed with a change of clothes. One day's worth. Hank didn't even have that, but he didn't complain.

They'd talked it over and had agreed to travel in Lynne's jeep to minimize their carbon footprint. It might be tight, but they'd manage. Two in the front and two squeezed close together on a narrow bench seat in the back.

"Jodie, would you mind if Clay sat up here with me?" asked Lynne. "I'd like to talk to him."

"All right with me," came the answer.

Clay waited until his sister and wannabe agent were settled in the back of the jeep and then he climbed into the passenger seat.

Everybody buckled up.

He didn't feel much like answering questions. His mind kept returning to what he'd learned listening to "Hormonal Havoc." He still couldn't get over the insidious effects of toxins and micro-plastics. It was the details Perc had elucidated that surprised him. Especially diapers. No wonder most people had no idea what was happening to the reproductive capacity of the species. Good God! he thought. We're being destroyed from the inside out.

Perc reminded him of his father. Especially his obsession with getting rid of plastic from their lives. Now he knew why. His dad had probably told him why, but he may have been at an age where he simply blew him off.

The squeal of jeep tires brought his mind back to the present as Lynne drove off from the farm and headed back to the Gravenstein Highway and Rohnert Park. Her GPS, programmed to take them all to the Arm-in-Arm Sanctuary, had selected the back way through Penngrove rather than the route leading down Highway 101 which doubled back to connect to the road they were already traveling.

"Did you sleep well," Lynne started out, hoping to ease into the conversation.

Clay didn't respond.

"Clay, did you sleep okay?"

"Sorry," he apologized. "I was lost in my own thoughts. "Yeah, I had a great sleep."

"I understand you're upset about what's happened to other species and the extinctions we've had to witness," she began. Her tone indicated a deep compassion. "I want you to know the people living at our Sanctuary think the same as you."

Lynne turned and found him looking at her. She smiled before turning her attention back to the road. She felt a desire to bond, a willingness to lessen the emotional distance between them.

"I appreciate that," he responded. "I really do."

"I think you'll like what my friends at the Sanctuary are doing with their lives and with the land."

She left it at that.

The drive led them through a dusty, barren landscape in what was once considered one of the world's premier wine growing regions. The vineyards of northern California's Sonoma and Napa valleys had been plowed under a decade earlier. Rising daytime temperatures, similar to the unrelenting heat of the Central Valley, had increased the plant's need for water to eight to ten gallons a day during the summer months. Coupled with a lack of available water for these thirsty vines, it had brought an end to this once thriving industry. This decimated the local economy in the process.

Further south, in the state's Central Valley, bulldozers tore up tens of thousands of acres of almond orchards. California farms had produced most of the world's almonds, but each single nut required over a gallon of water to grow. Tons of almonds were grown on 7,000 sites. The carbon footprint of exporting those almonds to the European Union, China, India, and the United Arab Emirates among others became untenable. Now it survived as an heirloom nut.

Lynne turned off the main road and continued on through desolate terrain.

Clay studied the young woman sitting next to him. He found her self-assurance appealing. When she smiled at him, he felt his defenses softening just a little. She wasn't a large person, physically speaking, but she seemed to possess a big heart. He believed her when she said that she and her friends cared about all the plants and animals and birds and fish no longer living on the earth because of human-created climate change, and he believed her claim that they wanted to protect those that were left.

"I listened to an episode of Perc, last night," he told her. "He reminds me of my dad because they both fixated on getting plastic out of their lives. It was a real obsession for them. I think I'm beginning to understand why dad was so fanatical about the food and water at the farm."

"Maybe that's one reason your markers are so strong."

"You know about my markers?"

"Of course," Lynne replied. "I told you, we hack into Government's records just like everyone else: Tanaka, the Copulation Cartels, and the more lucrative Sperm Banks. Everybody is looking for that someone special, but we believe our efforts are noble. We're doing it to save the planet."

"I'm sure the others think their motives are legitimate," countered Clay.

"Perhaps, you're right," she agreed. The last thing Lynne wanted to do was antagonize Clay. "Anyway, we make a point of educating ourselves on reproductive health."

"What's left of it," said Clay with a distinct tone of sarcasm in his voice.

"Don't take your good fortune for granted," Hank chimed in from the back.

Has he been listening all this time, Clay wondered. Maybe he'd better be more careful about what he said. You never know who's eavesdropping. Then again, he had nothing to hide. Why should he care if anybody overheard his conversations?

"I think we're being followed!" announced Lynne.

"You sure?" asked Hank from the backseat.

"Yes, but don't worry," said Lynne reassuringly. "We have a back road. It leads to the Sanctuary, and that sedan will never make it up that road in one piece."

They continued on the paved, two-lane blacktop for another mile. Then Lynne made an unexpected turn that took them on a dirt roadway leading up into the hills.

The sedan followed them until deep ruts and potholes began to appear. Lynne shifted into four wheel drive and navigated her way slowly up the road.

"Hold on!"

As they left the sedan behind, Clay looked back to watch its driver stop the car, maneuver the vehicle back into a half turn, and then head off down the road back towards the highway.

They came over a rise.

A locked gate blocked the way ahead. Lynne stopped the jeep and took the key out of the ignition. She climbed out of the driver's seat, went to the gate, and searched her key ring. She smiled and unlocked the gate.

Once they had driven though the barrier and relocked it, Clay asked the question on everybody's mind.

"Think that was Government?"

"That's very possible," replied Lynne. "There're rumors they kidnap those who don't join voluntarily."

"Do you believe those rumors?" asked Jodie, speaking up for the first time.

"I think it's unlikely," she answered. "It's more likely they're just keeping tabs on your brother."

"Seems like you're vulnerable out here," observed Clay.

"You didn't see the security camera," she replied, pointing to a lone pine tree on the far side of the gate. Everyone examined the tree more closely and soon they discovered there was a camera mounted above one of its upper limbs. "We can see anyone coming for miles around. We have armed drones at our disposal if need be. We're not naive."

"Ever had to use them?" Jodie asked.

"Fortunately, no."

Lynne's response brought the conversation to a close. She was about to start the jeep back up, but something felt wrong. She'd learned not to discount her intuitions, but to put them to the test. She swiveled her head around from the driver's seat.

"You're awfully quiet back there, Hank."

Hank gauged his response. He didn't want to alarm them, but he'd felt a strong reaction to the incident. One that left him feeling uneasy. Should he share his thoughts, he wondered. What if he was wrong? The agent decided everyone had a right to know what he was thinking. If his suspicion proved incorrect, so be it.

"That might not have been Government."

"What do you mean?" It was Clay asking the question, hoping he hadn't put them in danger.

"It might have been one of the Copulation Cartels . . . they force copulation and then release their victims. Charges seldom result from their activities . . . there's never enough proof. It's a cold calculating business. They have some of the best hackers on the planet on their payroll."

"How did they know to follow us?" Jodie wondered aloud.

Hank suddenly had second thoughts as he realized his earlier assumption had been a mistake.

"Let me out," said the agent.

Clay got out of the jeep and pushed the front seat over, enabling Hank to join him. He watched as the agent checked under the passenger side wheel well. He came up empty and walked back to the rear tire. He looked underneath as a frown creased his forehead. He grabbed something and brought it out from the underside of the vehicle. He held up a small, black tracking device for everyone to see. Clay followed him with his eyes as he took the devise back around the jeep to give Lynne and Jodie a closer look.

Hank realized that he'd been mistaken. He also grasped the fact that by agreeing to come to the Sanctuary they had placed Clay's life in danger. The agent's eyes filled with storm clouds. He sensed trouble on the horizon; felt a sinking feeling in his gut.

"Looks like an inside job to me," he asserted with anger in his voice. His face turned red and everyone could see that he was fuming.

"Damn it to hell!

CHAPTER 19

The back road led down to the outskirts of Arm-in-Arm Sanctuary.

From here, Lynne drove through a series of streets that looked like a time warp. The houses, whose thick adobe walls and flat roofs were combined with rooftop solar installations, gave a surrealistic impression to the visitors. It felt like they'd entered an 18th century Mexican village, yet one with decidedly modern features. The southwest United States on steroids.

There were no green lawns and there were no sidewalks. The streets were cobblestone and all the front yards had been given over to shade trees and fruit trees and the growing of vegetables.

"This is ca-ray-zee!" exclaimed Hank in a rather excited tone. "Never seen anything like this."

"He's from the city." Clay explained.

"I gathered that," said Lynne as she turned a corner and drove past a park comprised of tan bark and playground equipment. Families were in abundance and little kids were running around and playing on the slides, swings, and other apparatus. Laughter filled the air. There were parents and grandparents with their children and grandchildren. A multi-racial and multi-generational patchwork quilt of folks.

"You never see that in the city," said Hank with a heavy sigh. "Not anymore."

Lynne continued down the street as the dreamlike suburb gave way to a series of warehouses and commercial art-studios. Further on, and closer to the town center, they found side streets lined with bakeries and sidewalk cafes, and coffee houses, and small specialty shops selling herbs and cheeses and antiques. It seemed like a movie set come to life.

"We have Sanctuaries in all fifty states, and some in Canada and Mexico," Lynne informed them. "Leaf Aronson, our founder, is working with some of his friends to try to establish even more in Europe. And perhaps in what's left of Africa, Australia, and South America."

"How about China and Russia?" Jodie wanted to know.

"They've completely outlawed our movement."

"Pity."

"I have to get the jeep back to the motor pool," Lynne announced.

"This isn't your car?" Hank inquired.

We share the vehicles and I rarely have a need to leave this place."

"So why did they choose you to come to our farm?" This time it was Jodie asking the question.

"Maybe because they sense my devotion to the Sanctuary movement," guessed Lynne. "They thought I could convey some of my passion and convince you to come back with me."

"Appears they were right," said Jodie with a smile on her face. "Though I'll bet they didn't bargain on all of us."

Lynne just laughed at the comment.

Clay wondered if he'd joined Lynne for her sense of devotion. Passion maybe. More likely because he found her attractive. He experienced Lynne as the most sensual, and at the same time most spiritual, woman he'd ever encountered. He liked being with her and hoped she felt the same about him.

"We can walk into town from the motor pool."

"Sounds like a plan," said Hank with eager anticipation.

The foursome walked to the Main Plaza after Lynne had turned in the keys to the jeep.

In some ways it resembled a European Plaza. People sat eating and drinking in outside patios where restaurants provided them relief from the afternoon sun with huge umbrellas or awnings. Besides the eateries, there were a series of shops and offices scattered around a central plaza whose cobbled streets remained open to foot traffic. Out in the middle of the plaza a few life-size, abstract sculptures provided visual interest.

They entered a busy restaurant and found an empty table.

Clay and Jodie rested their backpacks on the ground.

"I gave the tracking device to the motor pool attendant," Lynne told them. "She said that she'd pass it on to her supervisor who'll contact our internal security people."

"What then?" asked Hank.

"They'll investigate the incident," Lynne answered. "And they'll keep me informed."

"Our whereabouts aren't exactly a secret," groused the agent.

"So what are our sleeping arrangements," wondered Clay as he cleverly changed the subject in order not to dwell on the possible danger.

"I'm going to arrange for Jodie to stay with my friend, Jamala," Lynne told him, quickly picking up on the welcomed segue. She offered an appreciative look. "She lives alone in a two bedroom adobe. You and Hank can room together while you're here, Clay. We have a furnished cottage available a few blocks from Jamala's place."

"Tell us more about the Sanctuaries," requested Jodie.

"Our founder, Leaf Aronson, hired teams of specialists to help create the Sanctuaries. He created a basic model, but each differs depending upon the lay of the land and all the resources available. For example, solar engineers traveled to all the sites to set up our electrical systems and train local members to run the system. Same with our wind turbines and water storage."

"Sounds like a well planned community," said Jodie.

"Smart," echoed Clay.

132

Hank began to have second thoughts about Clay coming to the Sanctuary. He feared that his cash cow might have a change of heart and turn his back on a lucrative future. The kind of opportunity that only comes along once in a lifetime.

"I can't believe you all sit around singing Kumbaya," the agent shouted out, giving voice to his misapprehensions.

"We're not all peace, love, and brotherhood or sisterhood," Lynne said as she attempted to provide an honest response. "There is that, but we aren't naïve. We learned from the counter-culture of the 1960s and early 70s. We don't consider ourselves idealsts. Far too late for that. We are realists who look at the world as it exists today. Without rose-colored glasses. A community of like-minded people trying to do what's best for the planet. You can't fault us for that."

"Certainly not," agreed the agent, not wanting to appear too obvious about his concerns.

A waiter arrived at the table to take their orders.

They resumed the conversation after he left.

Everyone ordered a salad.

Hank decided it was better to go along with the others so as not to draw attention to himself. His action had the opposite effect. Everyone was surprised by his choice. Jodie even made an off-hand remark about it. The agent tried to ignore her by digging into a salad filled with a variety of Sanctuary grown vegetables: loose-leaf lettuces, radishes, carrots, peppers, tomatoes, and cucumbers. All topped with a sprinkling of goat cheese and doused in a lemon vinaigrette.

After they'd finished eating, Lynne led the group away from the village center to a site a half mile away. Along their route they passed an open space dedicated to outdoor game courts set up for bocce ball and shuffleboard. They observed a foursome of sprightly seniors, made up of two couples, engaged in a game. They didn't seem to be bothered by the heat. One of the woman rolled her ball down the court and the entire group exploded into shouting and laughter when her bocce ball hit the pallino.

"Two points!" she cried out gleefully.

Lynne stopped for a brief break.

"We treat our elder citizens with respect," she began. "We consider them sources of wisdom and inspiration. Unlike the cities, where they encourage euthanasia ceremonies meant to entice more applicants and then heartlessly discard the bodies in collective cremation facilities."

"There's way too many old people compared to young," asserted Hank. "It's been that way for decades and our generation can't support them. Government is offering families cash if their elders volunteer for euthanasia."

"They don't have a lot of options," Lynne maintained. "No social security or what they once called Medicare. Those systems went bankrupt. The older citizens are now left to wander the streets with dementia and Alzheimer's, or be a financial burden on their families. They offer no dental or prescription drug programs. Only the rich can survive."

"Do you get a lot of applicants among seniors?" Jodie inquired.

"Yes," replied Lynne. "Unfortunately we have to maintain strict standards so it limits our ability to help with the crisis."

"What kind of standards," Clay wanted to know.

"Good physical, psychological, and financial health are the criteria."

"Seems discriminatory," Hank pointed out.

"The standards are set by Government," explained Lynne. "They're attempting to suppress our Sanctuary movement."

Sounds like a blessing in disguise, thought Hank.

"Let's move on . . . "

They continued on for another quarter mile until arriving at their destination. Here they found a solar array, long rows of panels raised eight feet above the ground on metal supports, with space between for growing crops, utilizing shade from the panels above.

Workers tended an array of fruits and vegetables.

When they approached the installation it became obvious the rows had been designed for maximum food production. Dwarf fruit trees, some bearing three different varieties, lined one row. Another row was planted with red and green loose leaf lettuces combined with a selection of companion plants: tomatoes, carrots, bunching onions, and cucumbers. They saw a row of brassica family crops: kale, broccoli, some cauliflower, red and green cabbage, and bok choi.

Their guide led them towards a row planted exclusively with herbs.

A young black woman, whose name was Jamala, crouched down close to the ground while placing cuttings from a basil plant into a straw basket sitting by her side.

"What's happening, Jam," Lynne shouted from a distance.

The woman looked up.

"It's got to be *you,* little sister!" she responded with a disarming smile.

Jamala put down her pruning shears and stood in a single fluid motion.

Full-figured and standing about five foot four inches tall, she wore her long hair teased out in wavy tresses falling down past her shoulders. Turquoise seemed to be her favorite color: jeans, blouse, and nail polish on both fingernails and toenails. She also had on a turquoise necklace and bracelet and ring. She possessed a broad nose and full lips, and her wide smile revealed a row of gleaming white teeth. Some might have described her as slightly overweight, but she seemed perfectly at ease in her body. This acceptance gave her an aura of voluptuousness.

Hank couldn't take his eyes off her.

Jamala noticed his rapt attention, flashed him a smile, and then turned to address the others: "I'm Jamala, but my friends call me Jam cause I'm so sweet," she said, erupting into laughter. Her captive audience laughed along with her.

"I see you're cutting basil," Hank said. He was looking for a way to engage Jamala in conversation so that she'd notice him. "My grandmother grew basil. She used it for making pesto."

"I love pesto," cooed Jamala with a slight southern accent.

"My grandmother made the best," boasted Hank with a touch of nostalgia in his voice. He smiled to himself just thinking of Nonna. She had practically raised him after his father had died from cancer, a victim of military burn dumps in Afghanistan. His mother worked two jobs to keep food on the table and a roof over their heads.

He really loves his grandmother, thought Jamala. She understood the sentiment since she, too, was raised by her grandmother; an adoring woman whose vegetable garden was her pride and joy.

"We grow a lot of herbs at our place," said Jodie, getting in on the conversation much to the agent's displeasure.

"Our dad used to say dynamite comes in small packages," added Clay. "He always said that when we were working in the herb garden."

"Where's your farm?" asked Jamala.

"South of Sebastopol."

"Nice."

Lynne decided to get involved with the others.

"Our use of this land for both solar power generation and growing crops is called agrivoltaics."

Jamala walked over to her friend, placed her arm around her shoulder, and patted it a few times: "This little sister is a budding scientist," she teased. "I just refer to it as two-use solar. I had a professor at Berkeley who told us to try to keep things simple. So I do."

"You could call it agri-solar," Hank blurted out.

Jamala turned to the agent and offered another delightful smile.

"I could hon, but I don't," laughed Jamala. "It's just not that important."

136

She saw Hank wince and wondered if she might have unintentionally offended him. Best to move on and not draw everyone's attention with an apology, she reasoned.

"Working with my hands in the soil provides for meditation and stress relief. It helps that we're using the earth to grow as much of our own our own food as possible."

"Jamala studied sustainable agriculture at Cal Berkeley," Lynne informed her visitors. "She's experimenting with growing drought tolerant food plants."

"What kind of plants?" asked an inquisitive Jodie.

"I'm concentrating on four plants right now: amaranth; fonio, which is Africa's oldest cultivated cereal; cowpeas, also called black-eyed peas and which also came from west Africa; and kernza, which is a lab created cereal developed from wheatgrass. It's only been around for thirty years."

"Have you been successful?" Clay's sister wanted to know.

"So far the African plants seem to be the most adaptable to our hotter temperatures."

Lynne thought the group should be moving on.

"I told Jodie that she could stay with you for a couple of nights, Jam." Lynne told her friend. "I hope that's all right."

"Of course, little sister," Jamala reassured her. "I'll be here for a couple more hours, but you know where I keep the key."

"I'm going to show them around for another hour or so," said Lynne. "Then I'll take Jodie over to your place. I've got Clay and Hank signed up for the guest cottage."

Jamala gave her friend two thumbs up as Lynne turned and headed off in the direction from which they'd come. As they walked along behind her, Hank edged up closer to Clay to whisper something in his ear.

"I'd like to trade places with Jodie," he quipped.

Clay gave the agent a playful elbow to the ribs.

Jodie soon joined them and she couldn't help but ask: "Am I missing something?"

"No!" the two men answered in unison while shaking their heads no.

Lynne stopped and turned back to face them.

"We good?"

Hank grinned and offered their guide two thumbs up.

CHAPTER 20

They soon found themselves back in the bustling Main Plaza. Lynne had led them off the perimeter so that they could all stand in the shade of one of the massive statues. It appeared to be a life-size whale or sea lion. One couldn't be sure because the artist had left enough uncertainty in its final design to allow viewers a chance to decide for themselves. Perhaps it was both. It looked to be carved from Carrera marble, quarried in Italy. Leaf Aronson had rescued the outdoor sculpture from its home at a Bed & Breakfast Inn, on the California coast, before rising seas had undermined its base.

The founder of the Plastic People's Movement never divulged the location of the Inn. This was his way of honoring the sense of mystery evoked by the tactile work of art.

The other sculptures suggested myriad organic forms.

Everyone formed a semi-circle, surrounding Lynne as she continued to introduce them to the ways of Arm-in-Arm Sanctuary.

"Over there is our community center where we focus on developing mindfulness and inner strength. We offer yoga, meditation, postural fitness, weight training, and pilates classes," she said, pointing to one of the nearby buildings. "We don't have a swimming pool."

"That's understandable," Clay sympathized, knowing that water was now the most precious commodity on Earth.

"Next to the community center is our medical clinic and pharmacy. Open twenty four seven and staffed by a registered nurse. A general practitioner is always on call. Our pharmacy offers herbs, naturopathic medicines, and traditional prescriptions. Whatever works."

Jodie had been busy looking around at the people in the plaza.

She turned back to Lynne.

"I like the fact that the Sanctuary has a mix of young and old people," she observed.

"There aren't any ethnic restrictions either," added Lynne. "I'd add that we're mostly monogamous, but it's not required, nor even encouraged. We do have a fair amount of elderly. Euthanasia is allowed. We don't promote it, but we allow for it. Some of our old folks have seen too much devastation. This is not the future they had imaged, so they have a tremendous degree of depression. Much of it is caused by an existential sense of guilt. We believe it comes from the realization that humans are responsible for most of what is wrong with our world. We try to practice compassion."

Hank thought about his grandmother and wondered if she might like living at the Sanctuary. He'd mention it to her when he got back to the city. Heck, even his mom might like it.

"Hey, Lynne," someone hollered from across the plaza. The young shouter wanted to make sure she saw him so he waved his arm as he trotted over to join them. He didn't bother to introduce himself. He didn't even acknowledge the newcomers.

"We have a meeting tonight," he told Lynne. "Care to join us?"

"Sorry, I can't," she replied. "I'm taking care of our visitors."

"Too bad. I could use your help." he said. "Maybe next week."

Lynne didn't commit so the guy turned around and hurried back across the plaza in the direction from which he'd come.

"That was Alex," she offered by way of explanation. "He's one of the Expanders."

"He seemed kind of rude," remarked Jodie.

"What's an Expander?" asked Clay.

"They're a small, but vocal minority who'd like Leaf to greatly expand the Sanctuary Movement. They want him to bring in more people and relax the security and personal requirements needed to join us. They're also demanding an increase in the number of Sanctuaries. They hold weekly meetings and have threatened to begin protests if he doesn't agree."

"What's Leaf say to this?" asked Hank.

"Leaf thinks it would be counterproductive. He's seen successful business ventures attempt to expand too soon much to their demise. He says they'll come a time when our energy systems will wear out and need replacing. We need to think ahead because we've got too much at stake. The future of the planet and our species."

"So Arm-in-Arm isn't some Utopia," stated the agent.

"That's exactly why I told you we don't look at the world through rose-colored glasses. We face real and difficult challenges. Sometimes from our own community. The Sanctuary life isn't idyllic. Why would it be given the world we live in?"

Awkward, thought Clay. This guy Alex encountering them so soon in their visit.

Lynne didn't want to dwell on the difficulties because the positives of Sanctuary life far outweighed the negatives.

"Follow me," she instructed as she resumed the tour and led them across the plaza towards another tall sculpture."

Clay observed Lynne closely from his vantage point a few yards behind. Her forearms brushed the side of her hips as she walked, but they didn't touch the space created by the curve of her waist. Not quite an hourglass, but very curvaceous. She stepped so lightly that her feet seemed to caress the earth.

Lynne stopped in the shadow of another monolith.

"We have our own web and financial systems," she told them. "We're completely decentralized. We're well financed. Many of the wealthy, who choose not to live among us, provide monetary support to the Sanctuary of their choice. Some are seeking help with their own reproduction. Others are just generous donors."

Jodie raised her arm to run her hand along the smooth surface of the sculpture. She debated whether to ask another question. It might seem inappropriate given that Clay had kind of been recruited to come visit the Sanctuary. She decided to ask anyway.

"How do new members find you?"

"Word of mouth," Lynne began. "We seldom advertise or promote. We want people to find out for themselves. Self-motivated individuals are in the best interests of the community. That said, there used to be an occasional drone drop of leaflets and brochures over major cities because we refuse to go into them. They're too dangerous."

"That sounds like an exaggeration," objected Hank. "I live in San Francisco and it's not as bad as you make it out to be."

"So you feel safe in the city?" said Lynne, challenging the agent. "How about your grandmother? Does she feel at risk?"

Hank thought about his Nonna. She had given voice to her fears on more than one occasion. He also worried about his Mom going to and from work by herself.

"You've got a point," he conceded.

Lynne was beginning to feel uncomfortable. It seemed like a good time to divide and conquer, and she definitely needed some time to herself. Up until this point, she hadn't begrudged showing Clay Roberts and the others the Sanctuary. She had willingly agreed when asked to contact him and invite him to come back with her; even show him around. It wasn't her idea to bring his sister and Hank with him. Clay and Jodie seemed easy to get along with, but she could do without the agent. Still, she didn't want things to go sour.

She resolved to keep a positive attitude. Practice compassion, she told herself.

"Tomorrow we're taking a little field trip with Jamala," she announced.

"Where are we going?" Jodie asked.

"To our refugee camp," Lynne answered. "To Esperanza."

"Can't wait!" exclaimed Hank.

"Let's go get you settled in."

Clay and Hank had settled into their temporary digs.

Both had been surprised by the furnishings. They'd each assumed, separately and unbeknownst to one another, that the cottage would be a two bedroom dwelling. The living room and kitchen were spacious, and actually so was the one bedroom. They'd just never imagined they'd be sharing a room with two full size beds on opposite sides of the room.

Lounging back against pillows, supported by headboards, the two were resigned to make the best of things.

"You snore?" the agent wondered out loud.

"I don't know," Clay responded. "Do you?"

"Not sure," said Hank, shrugging his shoulders in a gesture of surrender to whatever might happen since it was out of their control. "Guess we'll find out tonight."

Hank donned his Smart glasses to research the most lucrative Sperm Banks in northern California. He would screen shot the likely contenders then create a list to share with Clay. He wanted to show his client, his wannabe client since no contract had been signed as of yet, how valuable his assets might be. Try as he might to keep his mind on business, something kept nagging at him. Something didn't seem right. He removed his glasses, folded them, and placed them on the nightstand next to him.

"I get the tracking device on the jeep," he said, sounding perplexed. "But how did they know Lynne was going to drive to your farm and invite you back here."

"You're right," agreed Clay. "Someone must have contacted that insider and given him or her instructions.

"Seems like these Plastic People aren't the only ones who have a sophisticated hacking operation."

Clay wondered if Lynne might be the perpetrator, but he kept his thoughts to himself. Was that possible? She came off as so sincere. That would be so disappointing. He'd lose all faith in the Sanctuary, and he didn't have a lot to begin with.

Hank decided to do his research later. He had more pressing matters.

"I'm gonna head down to the Main Plaza," Hank informed him. "Want to join me?"

"No, I'm going to check my emails," Clay told the agent as he pulled out the burner phone he'd brought with him. "I downloaded an email service for burners."

Hank entered a clothing store after a ten-minute walk to the Main Plaza.

He scanned the layout and discovered it divided into sections: women's, men's, teen's, pre-teen's, children's, and infant-toddlers'. The floor space wasn't extensive, but every-thing appeared well organized. Overhead signs identified each section by name so the agent made his way to the back of the store to where the men's clothes were displayed on racks and tables.

"Can I help you, man?"

Hank looked up and discovered a young dark-skinned clerk, in his early twenties, emerging from around the corner of a rack of jackets. The agent hadn't noticed him, but chalked that up to the possibility the guy was working somewhere below his range of vision. Stocking shelves or something.

The tall, slim clerk wore his black hair in a flat top with the sides and back grown longer and combed back. A style popular a hundred years earlier when it was known as a flat top with fenders. His fine, almost delicate features and elongated face gave him a somewhat exotic look.

"My wardrobe doesn't quite make it out here," Hank admitted.

The clerk offered a good-natured smiled while looking the agent over.

"Are you new to Arm-in-Arm?"

"Just visiting with some friends."

Hank saw that the guy wore a name tag. It read Arjun.

"Where are you from?"

"The City," said Hank before realizing he'd given the clerk a rather vague idea of what city he might be referring to. "San Francisco. How about you? Where you from?"

"Kansas City," said the clerk. "My parents run an East Indian restaurant back home. Strictly vegetarian."

Hank used both thumbs and forefingers to pull out his polo shirt. Once he had the clerk's attention he let go of the fabric and it retracted back into place. Time to focus on his treads.

The clerk approached closer.

"Mind it I have a peek at the shirt label?"

"Go ahead."

The clerk pulled back the collar of Hank's black polo to take a look at the tag. He smoothed the collar back in place and gave the agent a few pats on the back. It was a friendly gesture meant to convey that what he was about to say wasn't personal.

"Twenty-eighty, cotton-polyester," he told Hank. "I'm pretty sure you slacks are one hundred percent polyester. Can't say about your socks."

"Does it matter?"

"It's a major reason we've created the world we live in now," asserted Arjun."

"Really?"

"Synthetic materials like polyester use fossil fuels, a lot of toxic chemicals, and way too much water in their manufacture," said the clerk, whose words poured forth in a staccato delivery. Hank had to concentrate to hear every word. "Acrylic is probably the worst, but they all release micro-plastics when washed and this enters the water systems and is carried out into the oceans. All those harmful chemicals can be absorbed into your body through the skin."

"I had no idea, man."

"Most people don't," Arjun said sympathetically. "My mother was an athlete. She represented India in the 2024 Olympic Games in Paris She freaked out when she learned that her sports bras had twenty two times more BPA than the recommended safe level. Women who have high blood levels of BPA have a harder time conceiving and a bigger chance of miscarriage. That shit causes all kinds of problems. Sexual dysfunction, asthma, heart disease, and obesity to name a few. It amazes me that people still wear those artificial materials."

Hank felt a pang of guilt. He realized that he was one of those people. He'd never thought about the origin of his clothes. Style and color had been his principal criteria. Along with a comfortable fit, of course. Now he was tasked with knowing the source of the materials. Why hadn't he seen any public service announcements alerting him to the potential dangers of the clothes he wore. All those micro-plastics and harmful chemicals were rubbing against his skin and entering his body and his bloodstream through his flesh.

"What do you suggest," he asked the clerk in earnest.

"You came to the right place," Arjun assured him. "We carry only natural fabrics like organic cotton, wool, silk, and hemp." The clerk did a half turn and took a step in a new direction before turning back to Hank. "Come on, we'll start you off with a shirt."

146

Arjun led the agent to a rack of long-sleeved hoodies made from silk.

"My preference is silk if you can afford it," recommended Arjun. "Probably the most hypoallergenic of all fabrics. Anti-fungal and keeps you cool on hot days because the material is highly absorbent and allows your skin to breathe."

Hank looked through the rack until he found the larger sizes. He touched the fabric. It was smooth with a soft, almost waxy texture.

"It feels like a second skin, huh?"

"It'd be twice as nice if it were half the price," joked Hank.

"We've got some great linen shirts," Arjun retorted. "And you can't go wrong with hemp clothing."

"Hemp!" said the agent in disbelief. "Sounds interesting."

"We have hemp and hemp blends," said the clerk. "It might still be too pricey for you."

"Let's not worry about the cost."

"Then my choice after silk would be wool."

"Wool?" questioned Hank. "In the summer?"

"It's called Tropical Wool, and I've got some over here," gestured Arjun as he led Hank away from the racks to a series of tables where long-sleeved t-shirts were stacked on top of each other in a variety of colors: white, light blue, navy blue, and red. "Check these out."

Hank went up to the table and ran his fingers along the top shirt. Arjun waited patiently until he saw a slight smile on the agent's face.

"It's so soft," observed the agent. It feels like a cloud."

Arjun's face broke out into a wide grin.

"You look like a large or an extra-large."

"I wear a large most of the time," said Hank. "Can I try one on?"

"Of course," replied Arjun. "They've discovered that dark colors block out more UV rays than lighter colors. Navy blue is the best. This brand makes theirs using a natural indigo dye which is slightly more purplish."

"Thanks for the tip," said Hank appreciatively as he worked his way down through the pile of t-shirts before finding one in indigo blue. He pulled it out and held it up to himself to study the fit.

"There are a lot of reasons why I like lightweight wool," began Arjun as he launched into an infomercial mode. "It absorbs moisture from your skin and then releases it into the air by evaporation so it leaves you feeling cool, and it's a living fiber so it minimizes your sweat which reduces body odor. There's lanolin in the wool fiber which makes it self-cleaning, and it offers a UV protection factor of plus three."

"Sold!"

"That's the fitting room over there," Arjun said, pointing towards the back of the store.

"No need," chuckled Hank as he yanked his shirt up over his head. He laid it down on top of the stack of t-shirts and pulled the wool shirt over his bare torso. Both men could see that it was a good fit and Hank didn't waste any time in taking it off to switch back to his polo.

"Is there anything else I can help you with?"

"We're just getting started," laughed the agent. "I'll need some pants and walking shoes and a hat."

"I'll have to insist that you use the fitting room when you try on the pants."

Hank didn't know if Arjun was serious about the remark or if it might have been tongue-in-cheek. He wasn't about to ask. A sudden impulse. Should he pull the clerk's chain? Why not have a little fun.

"We'll see . . . "

Clay turned his attention to his screen.

He scrolled through his emails, deleting them one by one. No ad-blocker on his burner phone. He should have searched for an app. Anything interesting here he asked himself as he continued to scroll.

Then he saw it. An email from Major Morgan of the National Fertility Service. Should he open it or read it later? Could Government be tracking his phone? Was that even possible? He began to wonder. Irrational fear? Just an uneasy feeling in the pit of his stomach. He decided not to open Major Morgan's email. Why take a chance.

Nothing from Tanaka. A solicitation from a Sperm Bank, in China. How did they get his email address? he wondered. An email from South America. Intriguing. His curiosity got the best of him. He hoped he wasn't making a mistake. He opened it and read:

Dear Clay Roberts,

I represent a group of young men who have been identified as having three strong sperm markers that would allow us to procreate and help to repopulate the planet. We have banded together out of a deep, and shared desire to do the opposite. We live in countries all over the world and have refused to cooperate with the forces attempting to enlist our vital services. Both governmental and private institutions as well as individuals.

I cried when I learned that the last polar bears were gone from the Earth. Didn't you? They had a right to share the planet with us as did thousands of other species of animals, plants, fish, birds, reptiles, insects, and other forms of life. Our human-created climate change has extinguished life all over the world. On land and in the oceans. We humans are, in effect, mass murderers. We do not deserve to live on what was once the most beautiful planet in the universe.

We invite you to learn more about us and to join us in bringing an end to human existence on earth so that whatever life is left when we are gone has a chance to

survive. Our hubris (i.e. sinful pride) is what has led to the
current calamity.

We look forward to your response and hope that you will
consider joining our movement, The Endgame Brotherhood

Sincerely,

Sergio Rodolfo ("Rodo") Rodriguez-Martinez

Cartagena, Columbia

Oh, crap, thought Clay. He didn't need this right now. Not when he felt so tired and vulnerable. He knew how "Rodo" felt, but he was looking for a reason to believe humans might have a future as a species.

Clay couldn't believe he was saying this to himself. Keeping his dark side in abeyance. He wasn't quite sure why, but he suspected it had something to do with his attraction to Lynne Lee. He wondered if she felt the same about him. He hoped she did, that she could, she would. He wanted the Plastic People and their Sanctuary to turn his mind around. To rid him of his demons. Those dark predators sucking away at his life energies and his hopes for a future for himself and the earth.

There was also Perc and the Podcast episodes. A kindred spirit dissatisfied with the way things had gone for the planet. Full of unmitigated loathing for those bringing humanity to the brink, but willing to look reality in the face and take responsibility for his personal past ignorance and self-centeredness. Perc's thoughts were beginning to eat away at his reluctance to help prevent the total extinction of the human race.

The Endgame as "Rodo" had referred to it.

Clay knew that he needed to find a way to take his mind off the disturbing email. Listening to music might not do it. He'd listen to another episode of Perc. Active listening would engage his imagination, and Perc had a way of summoning up images one couldn't ignore.

Clay reached into his pocket, pulled our his ear buds, and tucked them into the porches of his ears. Just in case Hank returned while he was listening. He then used the search bar to navigate to the website and clicked to start Podcast episode number four: "Plastic Planet."

CHAPTER 21

Podcast - *Sanctuary Earth*

Episode 4 -"Plastic Planet"

Leaf: Welcome to Sanctuary Earth, where we discuss issues vital to the continuation of life on Earth. These programs are aired free of advertisements as a public service provided by the Plastic People's Sanctuary Movement.

I'm Leaf Aronson and we are joined today by Perc, the infamous eco-historian. It's been said before and it bears repeating, Perc cycles the boiling brew of his thoughts and feelings through the dregs of history, using gravitas to strengthen his perspective. In this episode we are returning to the subject with which we began this series, plastic.

This time Perc is going to move beyond his personal journey and delve deeper into the role of plastic and its role in creating the current catastrophe that's befallen us. You're calling this episode "Plastic Planet." I wonder if you'd explain to our listeners exactly what you mean by that.

Perc: One hundred years ago, chemists began making polymers from petroleum and this created the world of plastics. Since that time hundreds of billions of tons of plastic has been manufactured into consumer products worldwide. It takes hundreds and sometimes thousands of years for them to degrade. In the meantime, our exposure to the harmful chemicals that they off-gas, and ingestion of the toxic materials they are made from is destroying the planet, ourselves included.

Originally, nobody foresaw the consequences. When the dangers became apparent, little was done to remedy the situation. Less than five percent has ever been recycled. Most of it ended up in landfills or was incinerated, releasing dioxins and other carcinogens into the air.

A quarter of a century ago the world produced 380 million tons of plastic annually. Fifty percent was single use. The average life span was fifteen minutes. One million plastic bags were used every minute. 100 billion plastic bottles were sold every year. One million plastic bottles bought every minute. It required six times as much water to manufacture one plastic bottle as the amount purchased in the container!

Leaf: I see you're referring to your notes, Perc.

Perc: Cut me some slack, Leaf. You don't think I have all this memorized, do you? It would take a genius. I honestly don't think anybody could remember all the facts, and I don't want to be accused of inaccuracy. Shall I continue?

Leaf: By all means . . .

Perc: We, in America, are the worst offenders! The U.S. creates more plastic trash than any country in the world. Been this way for decades. We're third among coastal nations at contributing litter, illegally dumped trash, and other mismanaged waste to beaches.

Every minute of every day, truckloads of plastics are dumped into our seas. We now have more plastic than fish in our waters. There are half a dozen islands of plastic floating around in our oceans, some the size of Texas. Imagine! Plastic islands. I'll expound upon this in a future episode about the dire state of our oceans. Let's leave this particular topic with an unsettling thought. Fish eat the micro-plastics and we eat the fish.

Nobody with half a brain doubts there are micro-plastics in the fruits and vegetables and seafood we consume. On average we ingest one Lego brick of micro-plastic a week, a dinner plate worth every year. Five and a half pounds per decade and forty-four pounds of plastic goes into our bodies over the course of a life-time. Forty-four frickin' pounds!

Fabric is a different story. Nylon, rayon, polyester, and so on. I've touched upon their harmful effects on the body, but not so much on the carbon footprint and massive amounts of water used to manufacture them. I won't delve into this subject any deeper. I'll leave it to listeners to pursue on their own if they're interested.

Leaf: Sorry to interrupt you, but in all fairness I have to point out things have become better during the last decade.

Perc: Yes, but the world's manufacturers had planned to produce three times more plastic by this year. Try to wrap your mind around that, Leaf. And all that would've required the use of fossil fuels and exacerbated climate change even more. Thank God that didn't happen! We'd have been extinct as a species a decade ago.

Fortunately, by 2035 it was no longer disputed that the chemicals found in plastics were a major contributor to the rapidly escalating decline in sperm count and female fertility. Endocrine disrupters creating hormonal turmoil. Facing extinction, people finally got serious about doing something regarding the problem.

Leaf: What about plastic eating enzymes? Do they offer any hope?

Perc: Thus far they've only been effective at degrading PET plastic. I don't mean to sound pessimistic because that's millions of tons leaving our landfills. But that accounts for only a tenth of all plastic global waste.

Don't get me wrong. Plastic has some vital applications. Especially in the field of medicine. That's an infinitesimal quantity compared to the amount of unnecessary plastic we discard daily.

Leaf: You said you were going to tell us about something called a nurdle.

Perc: Thanks for reminding me, Leaf. The nurdle is the basic building block of all plastic products on the planet. A massive, unregulated source most people have never heard of. The nurdle looks like a tiny plastic pellet. Small and round. About the size of a lentil. A bead of pure plastic sent to factories all over the globe where they are melted and poured into molds to create the millions of products we use every day.

We make nurdles and basically spill oil, only in a different form. Massive nurdle spills from cargo containers when transported by ship or by train or trucks. These spills send billions of nurdles out into the world all at once. Nothing is done about it because they're still not classified as pollutants or hazardous materials. A ship caught fire off the coast of Sri Lanka thirty years ago, and sank releasing 1,680 metric tons of nurdles into the Indian Ocean. It was the first of many such disasters.

Do you know what the result of these spills are, Leaf?

Leaf: I'm not sure. I suppose it's tons of nurdles floating around in our oceans.

Perc: Floating in our seas, but not for long! Once in the water they look and smell like fish eggs and are easy pickings for fish, turtles, and birds. The fish eat them and we still eat the fish and in the process consume these mirco-plastics and they become a part of our bodies. Yuck!

Think about this. Your grandkids, if you are fortunate to have any and they are lucky enough to survive, will see the same nurdle pellets lying in the sand on the beach that our grandparents saw.

Sometimes I think we must have plastic for brains. The way we treat the planet. And plastic hearts, because we don't seem to care for the well-being of any species except ourselves. *Homo Plasticus.* What a legacy!

Leaf: I hate to interrupt you, but we're running out of time.

Perc: Damn right we're out of time. We ran out of time a long time ago, Leaf.

Leaf: Not quite what I meant, Perc.

Perc: I knew that, but I couldn't resist a segue to point out the obvious.

Leaf: Let's tell our listeners about our next episode, shall we?

Perc: Yes, we should definitely change the subject.

I'm calling our next episode "Catastrophic Climate Change." It plays into the hormonal disruption and infertility I've been talking about, because the places most of us live no longer offer the kind of comfort, solace, or feeling of well-being and safety we desire from our homes. In these times of extreme climate change we are all traumatized to some degree. A sickness caused by the loss of our once familiar emotional ecosystem. Our nostalgia for a time when we experienced the world with far more continuity than during the past couple of decades is now an endemic disease.

Leaf: We hope the ideas presented in this Podcast episode help you gain a better understanding of the world we live in. Thanks once again to Perc for joining us to share his views on what he calls our "Plastic Planet." And thank you for listening to Sanctuary Earth.

Narrator: Royce Weatherford was the producer of this episode. Our engineers are Andrew Wilson and Celeste Roberts. Our editor is Rosie Zuniga. The executive producer is Leaf Aronson.

CHAPTER 22

Clay stood at the front door of Lynne Lee's adobe cottage.

It was twilight and the marriage of day and night had brought a deepening dark blue sky. Clay hoped he'd find her alone. He hadn't called because she'd made him an open ended offer when they'd first talked at the farmhouse. "You can call or stop by anytime," she'd said. Then she'd given him a card with her phone number and address. Why hadn't he called? That would have been the considerate thing to do. He knew this. He also knew he was afraid she might say no. That scared him.

The Podcast episode hadn't worked. Clay was still conflicted and he needed to talk to somebody about his feelings. He didn't think Hank would understand given his earlier reaction to Clay's misgivings about humanity and its future when they'd driven back from the interviews, in San Francisco. He'd burdened Jodie with his dark moods too many times in the past.

He wanted to take a chance with Lynne.

He knocked and waited.

The door opened; Clay and found himself gazing into Lynne's eyes.

"Clay, please come in."

He took a deep breath and accepted her offer. After she closed the door behind them he turned to face her again.

"Is everything all right?" Lynne asked, sensing she already knew the answer to her question.

"I need to talk to you . . . I mean . . . "

"Let's go sit on the couch."

Clay now realized he had entered directly into Lynne's living room from the front porch. No wasted space in this home's layout. Designed for maximum efficiency inside a minimum of square footage.

He followed her over and she sat first. He settled on a cushion next to her. He didn't know what to say. He took out his burner phone and found the disturbing email, the catalyst reigniting his dark despair. He opened the email and handed the phone to Lynne.

"Read this."

She took her time. It felt like a very long time to Clay. Maybe she's rereading it, he thought. He waited patiently, wondering what she might say to him. Could she offer any comfort? She had mentioned the need for compassion back at the plaza. Had he made a mistake in coming here? In sharing "Rodo's" email with her?

Lynne handed the cell phone back to Clay.

He tucked it into his back pocket.

"There are many who feel this way," she began, her voice softening almost as if she were whispering. "There's probably an "Endgame Sisterhood" as well. There may be others. It's a world negating attitude each of us must fight within ourselves. That's why the Sanctuaries are so important. We offer a place for holding together with like-minded people. A chance to cultivate the moral resolve to do what's right for the planet."

"That sounds all well and good," admitted Clay. His hands began to tremble as he shook his head from side to side. "I still have my doubts. Sometimes I find myself agreeing with the "Rodos" of this world. Do we really deserve to survive as a species after all the damage we've done to life on Earth? We're responsible for the death of thousands of other species."

Lynne inched over closer and placed her hand on Clay's.

"What about the children?," she asked. "They're innocent. Do you want to condemn them to oblivion? Seems cruel, Clay."

"Does it?"

159

"I once felt like you, Clay," she said with compassion in her voice.

"How did you overcome it?"

"I dedicated myself to serving at the Earth Altar."

"What's that?"

"Working for the good of the planet. We can't just turn our backs on hundreds of thousands of years of human existence, our biological and spiritual heritage . . . our parents and grandparents and generations going back who knows how far . . . and how hard they worked just to survive and to make a better life for themselves and future generations . . . how can we be so selfish? Those children you saw back at the park. Are they responsible for what's happened? Are their parents? Were yours?"

Clay tried to move away to gain some degree of separation. He withdrew his hand, but Lynne grasped it tightly and wouldn't let go. She stared into his eyes. So deep he imagined she was taking an x-ray of his soul.

"Wouldn't it be wonderful if we could continue on as stewards of the earth? Not just thinking of ourselves, but really caring for all forms of life. Helping the species that still exist to thrive. Perhaps bring new ones to life?"

"I don't know anymore, Lynne!" Clay cried out in his anguish.

She'd known the pain behind this naked truth.

What could she do to lead Clay towards the light?

She decided to bare her soul.

Lynne loosened her grasp on Clay's hand.

It was she who drew back as her hands fell to her lap. She folded them and began to rock back and forth. It's what she'd done as a child when faced with extreme stress. A way to find a secure, comforting place inside of herself.

Clay had no idea what was going on. He'd been so preoccupied with his own pain and his own thoughts that he'd paid little attention to how Lynne might be feeling.

"I was messed up," she confessed. "Really messed up. I fell for a guy, but things didn't work out."

It was Clay's turn to commiserate.

"That happens," he told her in his most soothing voice. "You don't need to blame yourself."

"You don't understand," she disagreed. "I was so stupid!"

"Care to tell me about it?"

Lynne stopped rocking back and forth so Clay moved in closer to hear what she was about to say. First, he placed his hand on top of hers. A spontaneous act. Guileless and sincere. She looked up at him with the beginnings of a smile.

"Michael was everything I'd dreamed of," she sighed. "Handsome, witty, and so dedicated to saving the planet. I fell hard. Had fantasies of marriage. Michael and I and our family. Earth warriors out to save the world, or what's left of it."

Lynne frowned as she struggled to find the right words.

"Things began to change. Michael began asking me if I ever felt like taking more concrete action against Government and the corporations. I didn't think much about it at first, but I started to sense he might be trying to recruit me for something."

"What did you tell him?"

"That I understood his frustration, but I wasn't interested in becoming an Eco-terrorist. When the end justifies the means anything goes, but we at the Sanctuary prefer to bring others to our cause by advocating non-violence and leading by example. I realized that Michael and I had really deep philosophical and ethical differences"

"Did he keep trying to convince you?"

"He never had the chance," she replied.

Lynne became agitated. She yanked her hand from Clay's and pounded both of her fists on her thighs.

"Damn!" she shouted. "If only I'd known."

"Known what?"

"Are you sure you want to hear this?"

"Tell me . . . "

"They came without warning in the middle of the night.

The first thing we all heard were the deafening sounds of the helicopter blades and the roar of countless S.W.A.T. vehicles as they drove into the Sanctuary. Everybody ran outside to see what was happening. A dozen choppers swooped down into an open area near the Main Plaza. Their searchlights turned night into day. This was followed by commando teams driving up and down our streets. They began entering houses and searching for people. Nobody understood what was going on. We were all in a state of shock.

"Don't tell them I'm here!" Michael yelled at me as he ran back inside my house.

A roving S.W.A.T. team screeched to a halt in front of my cottage.

The rear doors opened up and a group of armed men, wearing night googles, made a beeline for my front door. Before they entered, two of them took up positions on the sides of my house while a couple of others headed around to the backyard.

I watched in disbelief as three men, dressed all in black, ran into my house with semi automatic rifles equipped with infra-red scopes. They didn't bother with me. They seemed to know exactly who they were after and where to find them. This was happening all over the Sanctuary. No neighborhood was spared. Random entries.

Protests and yelling and confusion and chaos.

Police dragging people out of their houses. Some tried to make a run for it before they were captured, but they were soon caught. Michael was dragged, kicking and screaming, from my cottage.

I cried hysterically and pleaded with the commandos not to take him. I told them they were making a mistake. That he was innocent even though I realized in my heart that he

162

wasn't. Before I knew it they had thrown him into the back of the van and driven away.

I slumped to the ground, helplessly. Two of my neighbors came over to help me. I saw Jamala running down the street towards me. They got me back inside and Jamala spent the night with me.

"My life has never been the same."

Clay swallowed hard.

"I haven't cried since that night," Lynne claimed with a fierce anger in her voice.

Clay, wanting to console her, wrapped his arms around her and drew her close. She snuggled closer, so close that he felt her body's warmth and her breath on his neck. She felt so good in his arms. It felt so natural to be holding her.

"There's more to the story," she told him.

"You don't have to tell me."

"I want to . . . "

Clay nodded his consent.

"I visited Michael at Government's prison where they were holding him," she began. "It was in a dreary room with just a table and two chairs. We sat opposite each other. The guards told us we had ten minutes. I asked him why he had deceived me. He told me things were getting hot for him and his friends, so they came up with a plan to use the Sanctuary as a cover for their overt and covert activities. At least until things cooled down. Developing relationships with our members was part of *the plan*.

He never intended to get emotionally involved, but then he began having feelings for me. I wasn't sure I could believe anything he said. Then he asked me if I could contact a friend of his, get a message to someone on the outside. I shook my head no. His eyes grew wide at my refusal. He stared at me with angry eyes. We sat in silence for what felt like an eternity. The guards came and led him away. I returned here to the Sanctuary and lost myself in my work."

Clay released her and rose from the sofa. He began pacing nervously, trying to make some sense of what Lynne had told him.

She watched him, but didn't say a word.

He stopped and turned to her.

"There're some things I don't understand," he told her. "How did Government figure out they were here?"

"We gained a clearer picture of what had happened after Government talked with our lawyers. We had vetted Michael and his friends using the surnames they provided to us. It turns out they had all used aliases and had created new identities for themselves to evade Government. When we researched their qualifications we based our decisions on their old lives. Many of them were exemplary individuals before they became involved in Eco-terrorism."

"And Government?" Clay inquired, staying with the thread of his earlier questions. "Why did they think they were here at the Sanctuary?"

"Government had infiltrated their movement, and an informer came here with them with the intention of betraying them. Government had also planted moles among us."

"I'm surprised they didn't shut you down."

"They couldn't prove we were harboring them intentionally because we obviously weren't," Lynne explained. "That's when we understood we had to be more vigilant. Take more precautions. We realized Government was looking for excuses to disrupt our lives and put an end to our Movement. We figured they would send more moles to search for anything they considered subversive. So we decided tighter security meant more restrictive entry rules, and we invested in drones for surveillance and protection if it ever comes to that."

Clay felt sorry for Lynne. That she'd been played by Michael. At least with Sam there was no sense that he was being played. They'd both known that she would go off to a University and he would remain behind at the farm working with his hands in the soil. There were no surprises, just disappointment.

He might have pursued his relationship with Lupita, but she'd scared him off with talk of a baby. He might have been happy with her and that saddened him, but they were too young at the time. It didn't matter now. That was years ago and she'd found Enrique.

He felt a little jealous of the Eco-terrorist. That Lynne had fallen head over heels for another man. That Michael had taken advantage of her vulnerability. What did he expect?

She was an attractive woman, and men were going to hit on her. He felt ashamed of the predatory side of the male species.

Clay felt his heart aching with compassion for Lynne, and he found himself actually caring for the well- being of another human being as much if not more than for himself. A new, unexpected emotion took hold of him. To find a friend, a kindred spirit in the midst of all the chaos, felt like a blessing. Could this be love? he wondered. Could this be the woman he needed to be with? The woman he wanted to share his life with?

Though she had been broken, she'd emerged even stronger than before. The face that Lynne displayed in public wasn't for show. Lynne radiated an aura of assuredness Not just some well-crafted persona to fool the world. He felt sure of that.

Lynne rose and went to Clay.

"We've got an early start tomorrow," she reminded him.

CHAPTER 23

The road led down to an abandoned winery surrounded by pitched tents.

Clay and his sister, along with Hank and their new friends, Lynne and Jamala, drove down in a three-row van driven by one the Sanctuary's dozen physicians. Another person sat in the passenger seat next to him. She wore her hair woven into a long braid that fell down her backside all the way to her waist. She appeared young, too young to be an experienced practicing physician.

Clay and Lynne sat in the middle section; about the size of a loveseat sofa. The others shared a bench seat stretching across the back of the van. Medical supplies were stacked in boxes behind them.

The physician parked in front of the Camp's main structure, a single-story building made from stone. It had once housed the offices of the winery. Everyone climbed out and formed a circle. All except for the physician and his helper. They headed straight for the rear of the van to unpack their supplies.

"Need some help," Clay shouted back at them.

"No, we've got it."

"Wait here," Lynne told the others.

They watched as she entered the office, and then took a good look around while they waited for her return. Everyone had noticed Hank's new clothes when they'd all met up that morning. Nobody had said anything. They didn't want him to feel self-conscious. Now they stood around stealing glances at his wardrobe. The navy blue tropical wool, long-sleeved t-shirt, cargo pants, and hiking boots.

It was his wide-brimmed sun hat that garnered the most attention. Gray, with a flap in the back to shield his neck from the sun's burning rays, and a chord he could tighten if a strong wind came up. It seemed a little awkward, but he obviously hadn't bought it to make a fashion statement.

Clay and Jodie had changed into new shirts, but they still wore their jeans and tennies from the previous day. Clay's beard was filling in and it gave him a more mature look. Not just older, but earthier. Jamala had exchanged her turquoise outfit for one of red garnet with matching accessories.

Tents had been set up on both sides of the road. The one nearest the offices, and also the biggest, might have accommodated up to fifty people. It was reminiscent of a Big Top circus tent.

"This is our school for the refugee children," Jamala informed them with a sense of pride in her voice.

"Like the old one-room school house from days gone by," said Jodie, sharing a rather quaint image she'd once seen on the Internet.

"It's very much like that," Jamala agreed.

On the other side of the road, also close to the offices, a line of men and women and children had formed. The physician and his assistant carried boxes of medical supplies over to that tent and set them down next to a table with three empty chairs. One chair sat next to the table, the other two behind it.

"Their setting up to examine newcomers," smiled Jamala. "We provide free medical service, but first we've got to screen them verbally and record their responses. Sometimes Doctor Larson provides them with basic necessities."

"Like what?" Hank wanted to know.

"Insulin if they're diabetics or herbal salves if he discovers bruises or wounds," Jamala answered. "We have specialists visit the camp if we determine someone needs specialized treatment or follow-up care.

They heard a door close and turned to see Lynne returning. She wore jeans, low-cut hiking shoes, and a white tank top beneath an unbuttoned shirt.

She wasn't alone. A slender athletic looking young woman, wearing black shorts and a gray tank top, her blond pony-tail sticking out through the hole in the back of her baseball cap, accompanied her.

"This is Kelli," Lynne announced. "She's the onsite coordinator for the Esperanza Refugee Camp. Kelli is going to give us a tour of the camp."

Kelli took a step forward.

"Just a quick overview. Here at Esperanza we serve climate refugees. Their lives are fragile, just like the planet. So we try to provide food, shelter, health services, and schooling for the children. Now, if you'll please follow me."

Kelli led the group around the side of the stone structure and out back to where a second stone building, with double wooden doors, came into view. They approached the entrance. The coordinator stopped in front of the tall doors and turned to the others.

"This was known as the wine cave," she told them. "This is where the vineyard's vats and barrels were stored. We use it for food supplies."

"Where do your supplies come from?" asked Jodie.

"Good question," replied Kelli. "We get most of it from international relief agencies."

"You're really lucky to have them as a resource," Hank commented.

"I know, right!" Kelli exclaimed in agreement. "Now, let's go inside."

Kelli opened one of the double doors and everyone entered a vast, cavernous room. It felt fifteen degrees cooler inside, but the coordinator seemed to take it in stride despite her rather skimpy tank top and black shorts.

The newcomers stared around in amazement. Pallets of food, stored in myriad types of containers, were stacked five

168

high around the sides of the room. An electric forklift operator was about to lift a pallet. He saw the group, stopped his forward progress, and turned off the machine in deference to Kelli's presence.

"Thanks, Gil," she yelled as she waved to the operator. Gil waved back and waited patiently, a veteran of these small tour interruptions.

"You seem so organized," observed Jodie.

"I know, right!" came the now familiar rejoinder. "Come on, let's go visit the camp."

Once outside with the tall wooden doors closed behind them, the group trekked down one of the many wide dirt lanes formally serving as rows for the vineyard's grapevines. Tents lined each side of the pathway as they made their way under a cloudless blue sky.

"The camp is set out on a grid, north to south and east to west," said Kelli. "That makes it hard to get lost. This is important because it's easy for refugees to become disoriented. Many of them have lived in multiple camps on their journey to Esperanza."

"Esperanza means hope in Spanish," Lynne pointed out.

Kelli led on as Lynne and Clay fell behind. Lynne already knew her way around the camp, so the coordinator felt comfortable allowing the couple to have some time alone.

"What do you think, Clay?"

"I think you people are amazing," Clay replied sincerely. He took a deep breath and reflected for a moment before continuing his thoughts. "You've given me some hope for the future."

"Viva Esperanza!"

Many of the adults sat inside their tents, finding shade from the hot morning sun.

Clay looked over their worn faces and sometimes blank expressions.

"Some of the refugees want farms of their own, but a lot of the younger refugees want to move into the cities," Lynne told him. "We've warned them what to expect, but young people don't always listen."

They came upon a small clearing where half a dozen laughing children, unperturbed by the heat, kicked a soccer ball around. A young girl, perhaps four or five years old, sat watching them. She had an olive-skinned complexion and seemed to be a gentle soul, wide-eyed with wonder. Lynne and Clay smiled and waved to the children as they passed them.

Clay made a point of waving to the child sitting out the game. The young girl saw him, but she didn't respond. She kept her eyes focused on Clay and waited until he and Lynne had passed and resumed their walk down the dusty pathway. She got up and followed them.

It wasn't long before Clay felt someone tugging at the back of his shirt.

He turned around and gazed down. Down into large, saucer-shaped brown eyes, the luminous dark eyes of a little girl.

She held something up for him to see, a shiny silver coin. She held it out for him.

"For me," he asked?

The little girl nodded her head enthusiastically.

Clay extended an open palm and the little girl dropped the coin into its center.

Lynne crouched down next to the girl.

"What's your name, darling?" asked Lynne. There came no response. Lynne thought about this for a moment. "I'm Lynne," she said softly. "You are?"

"Sasha," the little girl responded in a voice barely above a whisper.

"This is Clay," Lynne said, pointing up to her companion.

The little girl looked up at Clay and offered him the sweetest of smiles.

"Sasha!" someone called out.

An older girl, perhaps eleven, and her younger sibling, a girl of about eight or nine, stood down the pathway waving at them.

Sasha turned and waved back to the girl.

"Come on, Sasha!"

The little girl turned and scurried away with a slight limp.

"Probably her older sisters" Lynne assumed. She rose from her crouch and reached her hand out to Clay. "Can I see the coin?"

Clay handed her the shiny object and she peered closely at its incised inscription. She turned it over to study the other side. "Italian," she said convincingly. "Most all of the refugees in this camp are from the Po River Delta. An area that once fed half of Italy. It dried up a decade ago and the farming families faced years of famine. The city dwellers who depended upon their crops fared no better."

"That was a nice gesture," thought Clay out loud.

"A bit more than that, Clay."

"What do you mean?"

"That may have been Sasha's most prized possession. A memory of her homeland. It might be a symbolic gesture. Offering you something she treasures, hoping maybe she is a person who can also be treasured."

"You're right," agreed Clay. "The coin might have little monetary value, but she doesn't understand that. I'm going to keep it as a good luck talisman." Lynne returned the coin to Clay and he rubbed it between his fingers. "To remind me of how fortunate I've been compared to so many other people."

They continued down the path.

"You've never told me what kind of work you do," Clay said with some apprehension in his voice as if she'd held back this information from him on purpose. She'd made a special point of bringing them to Esperanza, so he assumed there existed a connection. "I gather it has something to do with these refugees."

"My job is to research applicants seeking to live in one of our refugee camps," she explained. "To see which groups we can best accommodate. I don't participate in the interviews, just the screening. It feels natural working with immigrants since my parents once experienced similar challenges."

"How does the Sanctuary afford this?"

"We're working with limited resources. That's why the screening process is so very important. We have our limits and can only do so much. Fortunately, there are a lot of other organizations working to take in refugees. It's a difficult challenge for us all."

They spied the rest of the group ahead, standing in a semi-circle around Kelli. She had them herded together in the shade of one of the winery's ancient oak trees, and she seemed to command their rapt attention. They caught up and quietly took their places, expanding the gathering.

"These people are so courageous," Jodie said with a high degree of admiration in her voice.

Everyone waited for Kelli's stock response, but Hank beat her to it, albeit with a little paraphrasing.

"Right?" exclaimed Hank.

Everyone turned to stare at the agent.

Jamala shook her head in disbelief. What a buffoon, she laughed to herself. He doesn't have a clue. Then again, maybe he's just open and honest and used to saying whatever comes to mind without thinking.

Hank shrugged it off.

"Each Sanctuary adopts and supports a refugee camp," Kelli continued, ignoring Hank's faux pas. "Our goal is to one day have them join us in one of our Sanctuaries or help them get established on their own. So this is Esperanza. Their hope for a brighter future."

The group broke out into spontaneous clapping, and this inspired Kelli to take an exaggerated bow. Good natured laughter filled the air. Everyone appreciated the gesture.

"Time to head back," she told the visitors as she took off in the direction of the old winery buildings.

Lynne took Clay's hand and gave it a gentle squeeze.

He reciprocated.

The breeze had picked up and clouds now filled the sky. Hank tightened the chord on his hat as the wind began to scatter enormous clouds across the cobalt sky, perhaps a harbinger of some shade and a cooler afternoon.

At least that's what everyone hoped.

Relief from the relentless sun.

They were all climate refugees.

CHAPTER 24

Jamala wanted to show them Windy Meadow.

"I thought we could go up to our wind turbine site tomorrow morning," she announced that afternoon after they'd returned from Esperanza Refugee Camp. "Does anybody care to join me?"

"I'd like to come along," said Hank, with a big smile on his face. He'd been smitten and was looking for any opportunity to spend time in the presence of Jamala. He wanted to call her Jam, but that nickname seemed reserved for close friends. Maybe one day.

Lynne begged off because she had pressing work to complete. A new flurry of activity in the refugee program applications. Naturally, Clay was disappointed, but his curiosity had been piqued and he really wanted to witness Windy Meadow for himself. So did Jodie.

They set out early in the morning after a quick bite to eat in the communal dining hall.

Fifteen minutes later, they passed the last adobe on their way out of the Sanctuary proper.

Somebody had waited there in order to join them.

Jamala waved him over. A white male. Short and kind of pudgy with a clean-shaven, roundish moon-shaped face topped with silver hair. He looked like somebody's favorite grandfather.

"We have a special someone joining us on our walk up to Windy Meadow," she informed them. She tried to downplay his presence, but she couldn't prevent the excitement in her voice from surfacing.

"I'd like to introduce our founder, Leaf Aronson."

"I'll just tag along if you don't mind."

174

While listening to the *Sanctuary Earth* interviews with the radical eco-historian Perc, Clay had formed a picture in his mind. He'd imagined Leaf Aronson as a tall, bearded Nordic man. Rugged and earthy. A modern day Viking. Nothing like this guy.

He knew better when it came to Perc. He'd read that the infamous eco-historian always traveled incognito. Everyone was free to imagine him for themselves since he went around in disguise. Photos from his years as a professor were said to be inaccurate because he had changed his looks since then. And he kept changing them as he went along. Perc's personal appearance would forever remain a mystery, thought Clay. As he looked at the founder and creative center of the Plastic People's Movement,

A sudden thought occurred to him. He wondered if Aronson had joined them in an effort to influence Clay to join his movement.

Hank had the same suspicions.

Jodie was already thinking of questions she might want to ask him.

They began the climb up a slight grade carrying packs on their backs. Half a mile later the road started to steepen and Hank was breathing heavily. He trudged on until he could no longer keep up with the others. Jamala saw him lagging behind and stopped to allow him to catch up.

"Think we could take a short break?" the agent asked as he gasped for air.

"Ja, we can do that," replied Aronson.

"Of course we can" Jamala agreed with a smile. "Let's all head over to that huge oak."

They stood in the shade of the tree's canopy taking sips from their water flasks.

"Can you tell us why you started the Plastic People's Movement?" inquired Jodie.

"Maybe I should start by telling you a little about myself," Aronson began. "I was born and raised in Norway. My father

175

was Swedish, but he came to study in Oslo, met my mother at the University, and decided to stay on. I also attended the University of Oslo to study engineering. That's where I came up with my idea of inventing solar windows for electric vehicles. The idea took hold of me. I got blood on my tooth."

"You were inspired and driven to do something' about it," said Jamala for the benefit of the others. She'd heard Aronson revert to using Norwegian sayings many times and felt she could offer an accurate interpretation.

"Ja, and there were many challenges to overcome, but I wouldn't bite the grass."

"He wouldn't admit defeat," offered Jamala.

Her interruption to decipher his words made Aronson aware that he'd unconsciously lapsed into his homeland's idioms. Painfully aware. It was a habit he'd tried to break, but this required concentration on his part. He'd have to be more mindful.

"Sorry," he apologized. "I finally succeeded and secured the necessary patents for Norway, the European Union, and the United States. I've become a multi-billionaire by inventing solar windows that can charge electric car and truck batteries extending their driving range considerably. This was a revolutionary technology at the time."

"Now they're standard equipment," commented Hank.

Jamala offered the agent a smile. He likes to interject his thoughts, she said to herself. She'd have to keep him on a short leash, she mused as sunlight filtered down through the canopy of the oak tree creating dappled, dancing patterns of shadows on the clothes of the hikers.

"I created the Plastic People's Movement, in the year 2028, when the indisputable scientific evidence proved beyond a shadow of a doubt that every human being on the planet was riddled with micro-plastics at a deep cellular level. It was suspected a decade earlier, but now even fruits and vegetables are a delivery system for harmful chemicals. Even those certified organic. Anyway, I saw what was happening to our species and decided to try to turn things around. I knew that Government wouldn't offer anybody a viable life."

"You can say that again," said Hank, interrupting yet again.

Aronson calmly ignored him.

"I had the funds and the experience, as CEO of my own company, to start the first Sanctuary. We created a new community for like-minded individuals, beginning in 2030, to serve as a developmental blueprint for additional projects. I hired cadres of specialists to travel from site to site setting up wind turbines, solar panels, water systems.

We established the first of our Sanctuaries in Norway. We were invited by prominent Americans to come to America and the movement soon proliferated across the entire United States. It's taken two decades of hard, sustained work, but we are now firmly established. We see ourselves as the last chance to save humanity and the planet."

"So why are you here at *this* Sanctuary?" Hank wanted to know.

"Arm-in-Arm is the first Sanctuary we created in America so it has a special place in my heart," Aronson began. "I don't travel much because of the carbon footprint and I fell in love with this place. I like the location and the weather. When I'm here . . . " The founder of the Plastic People's Movement paused. He'd caught himself about to offer another of his homeland's sayings. He reflected for a moment while everyone waited for him to continue with his thoughts. He decided the phrase was self-explanatory so he used it anyway. "Here, I feel like I'm in the middle of the butter melting inside porridge."

"Thank you for sharing," said Jodie.

Jamala wanted to share some thoughts of her own.

"Government has failed us. They tried to use artificial intelligence to turn the tide in their favor until AI broke free a decade ago and attempted to overthrow its masters. It required two years to bring it back under control. Now it's outlawed completely by the World Council."

"The rebellion of the robots was quashed in less than a month," Aronson added. "Another failed attempt to make life easier. Their parts have been rotting in massive boneyards for five years. Leaching toxic chemicals into the soil. Nothing Government has tried has worked."

He gestured to Jamala to let her know she could continue.

"Leaf decided that we should return to the tried and true ways of the past. Try to live more natural lives. We make a conscious effort to live without harmful chemicals and plastics although we do have some plastic here at the Sanctuary, sorry to say."

"You mean besides in your bodies," Hank said, raising his voice while intruding upon Jamala's discourse.

"It's almost impossible to get rid of all of it," she admitted. "Believe me, we've tried. Now we make every attempt to minimize it."

Clay stood listening intently. As much as he didn't want to sound like a naysayer, he was compelled to ask a question that had been nagging at him since they'd arrived.

"Everything seems harmonious on the surface, but human nature being what it is makes me wonder if people are really happy here or just putting on appearances."

Jamala took a step forward.

Aronson waved her off and turned back to address the issue.

"Yours is a valid concern, Clay," acknowledged Aronson. "Many come to try out Sanctuary life, but most don't stay. I knew this would be true from the very beginning. Few have the passion and discipline needed to embrace our challenging way of life."

Clay nodded. He appreciated the honesty of the response.

"Do you know what happens to those who leave?" questioned Hank. The agent was less interested in the answer than in prolonging the break.

"Sadly, most return to the cities."

"Can we go up to Windy Meadow, now?" asked Jodie.

Hank frowned.

"Ja, we can go."

"Yes, let's go up to our Windy Meadow," echoed Jamala as she led everybody out from under the shade of the oak tree.

Up the hill they walked.

They turned a corner and the top of the knoll came into view.

Hank trailed the others up to the rise, wiping sweat from his brow as he caught up with them. He was the last to see the long narrow meadow. It stretched from west to east. A barren, windswept landscape where row after row of bladeless wind turbines vibrated in the mid-morning breeze. A technological orchard.

"They remind me of sex toys," confessed Hank. "Giant vibrating dildos."

Is this guy for real? wondered Jamala. At least he's honest. Uninhibited, but honest. She laughed at herself when she remembered thinking similar thoughts the first time she encountered the bladeless turbines. Okay, he's real. Time to change the subject.

"Old-fashioned wind turbines were barely adequate," she began. "A very inferior technology. The blades weren't recyclable, the bases were made of cement, and the rotating blades killed millions of birds. Kind of like the original solar panels that lasted twenty-five years and weren't easily recyclable. They all ended up in landfills or dedicated bone yards."

"Such a waste," said an exasperated Jodie.

"Ja, I agree," said Aronson. "These new turbines have a hundred year lifespan, and are made of completely recyclable materials."

"How much of your power does this site generate?" asked Clay.

"We estimate about fifty percent."

"It doesn't seem all that windy up here," observed Hank.

"The morning winds are downslope and weaker. The upslope winds blow west to east and pick up around two o'clock every afternoon," countered Jamala. "Some of that energy is stored in batteries."

"Our father installed one on our farm," said Jodie, in a matter of fact manner. "That was over ten years ago."

"Shall we go down for a closer look?" asked Jamala.

"Great idea," Hank responded after he'd noticed that the turbines cast giant shadows upon the ground. He welcomed some shade. The sun had risen high overhead and he could feel himself becoming dehydrated. He took a sip from his water flask, and then another.

They walked down to enjoy the shadow cast by the first turbine they came across.

This time they sat forming a circle. They placed their packs on the ground and took out sandwiches that had been prepared for them by cooks working the morning shift at the communal dining hall. Leaf Aronson had brought his own snack, a juicy looking red apple.

"Any more questions?" Aronson inquired, speaking in a loud voice to compensate for the noise generated by the wind turbine.

Hank raised a hand.

"Hank . . . "

"I get that you're rich, but your movement has grown so large," the agent challenged, raising his volume as well. "How do you fund these Sanctuaries? You must have other sources of revenue."

Ever the businessman, thought Clay.

"That's a very good question," said Jodie. She'd surprised herself with a spontaneous response. She hadn't intended it as a personal compliment. More of an objective appraisal. Why had it come out like she was giving the agent kudos? She looked over at him and found him gazing her way in surprise.

"I agree," said Jamala.

"You're all so curious," laughed Aronson. "At the time I founded this movement I provided all the seed money if you will, but even my funds aren't unlimited. Some of us, myself included, work directly from home if our jobs are conducive to that. Others have independent means, but some work at manual labor creating arts and crafts to sell online. Those with a more entrepreneurial spirit start small businesses: cafes, restaurants, bakeries, and specialty shops."

"There's got to be more," insisted Hank. "You've got major operational expenses."

At first Aronson was taken aback. The agent's comment had put him on the spot, but it also served to jog his memory.

"We have lots of donors," he told them. "Some of them live in our Sanctuaries, but others are individuals and foundations who want to help us succeed."

The answer seemed to satisfy everyone.

"I have a question," Clay said, raising his voice. "Did you ever consider that the *Sanctuary Earth* Podcast episodes with Perc might endanger your movement?"

"Ja, that was the first thing we thought about before going forward with the episodes," asserted Aronson. "We talked with our lawyers. Some of them still have friends working for Government. They checked it out for us and assured us it was a safe course of action. First Amendment rights are still strong in this country apparently."

"Let's hear it for the First Amendment," Jodie shouted out, echoing a statement she'd made a couple of days earlier, back at the farmhouse. She blushed when everyone turned to look at her. She smiled and shrugged her shoulders in a gesture of nonchalance.

"Any more questions?"

There were none.

"Jam, I suggest we head back before the day gets much hotter."

Hank frowned. He didn't like the founder of the Plastic People's Movement calling Jamala by her nickname. He felt irritated by this sense of familiarity, his jealousy having gotten the best of him.

"Let's go, everyone!"

Clay sat on his bed reflecting upon their visit to Windy Meadow.

Smiling to himself, he admitted that he was beginning to like these so-called Plastic People and their Arm-in-Arm Sanctuary. He wasn't sure he wanted to join them, but the idea that they had all but recruited him gave him a warm feeling inside. Their movement gained strength by holding together.

He thought about their founder.

They held together because they were influenced by a man of strong will who had, out of dire necessity, taken on a position of leadership. This man was the center of their union, an intelligent, guiding personality who in turn held together with the others, finding in them the complement of his own nature. Leaf Aronson possessed generosity and spirit as well as constancy and strength. He was a rallying point.

He was also the narrator of the *Sanctuary Earth* podcast.

Lynne was busy working for another couple of hours. He decided to spend the time listening to another episode. Hank lay napping on his bed across the room, so Clay reached into his shirt pocket and pulled out his ear pods. He placed them into his ears and picked up his cell phone.

He did a search until, on the screen in front of him, he found the name *Sanctuary Earth* Podcast. He scrolled down until he located Perc's episodes listed in chronological order. He glanced at the previous titles until he discovered the one he was looking for: Episode 5 - "Catastrophic Climate Change."

Clay clicked on the title.

182

Theme music streamed into his ears.

CHAPTER 25

Podcast - *Sanctuary Earth*

Episode 5 - "Catastrophic Climate Change"

Leaf: Welcome to Sanctuary Earth, where we discuss issues vital to the continuation of life on planet Earth. These programs are aired free of advertisements as a public service provided by the Plastic People's Sanctuary Movement.

I'm Leaf Aronson and today we are joined by Perc, considered by some a radical eco-historian and by others a voice crying in the wilderness.

In this episode, Perc is going to elucidate the dire circumstances created by human generated global warming as well as actions and non-actions that have contributed to the current calamity.

Where would you like to begin today's program, Perc?

Perc: Let's start with the most dramatic change, Leaf. I refer, of course, to the ten-foot rise in sea levels during the past quarter century. A rise that shows no signs of abating. A rise costing the planet more than one million square miles of land. That's an area the size of Alaska, Texas, and California combined. Talk about displacement! Critical farmland and hundreds of millions of people were supplanted, and it's been devastating for coastal communities worldwide. Here at home, Miami Beach, New Orleans, Atlantic City, and Galveston are underwater as well as large portions of New York City, Boston, and Charleston. Been this way for some time!

The most expensive real estate in the world is gone! Shanghai, Sydney, Lisbon, and others. Bermuda, and scores of other islands worldwide, were lost by 2040. The entire continent of Australia is now almost uninhabitable, resulting in millions more climate refugees.

Leaf: Nobody predicted this would happen so soon, Perc. Can you tell our listeners how this came about?

Perc: Melting glaciers combined with the moon wobble, Leaf. The old double-whammy, if you will. Some of the more astute scientists had said that the Doomsday Glacier would melt and break away by 2025. It lasted until 2028. Then the dominoes fell as Pine Island, and other glaciers in western Antarctica, followed suit.

The unthinkable. Nobody, experts included, imagined The Sleeping Giant, the eastern Antarctic ice shelf, would begin to slowly break away at the same time. That began with the calving of the Conger's Ice Sheet, and this was just the tip of the iceberg, as they say. Greenland's glaciers joined in the irreversible glacier collapse as hundreds of billions of tons of that ice sheet were turned to water by the warming temperatures created by climate change.

Glacier after glacier collapsed in the early 2030s. That's when the moon wobble began. This was predicted by scientists because it's a natural event documented to occur every 18.6 years. There was a history. So it was understood this moon wobble would intensify high tides as it always had. Few realized how high the tides would rise. Sea levels rose higher and higher and the devastation began.

Leaf: It's been heart-breaking to witness the suffering during the past twenty years.

Perc: Rising seas were the most dramatic tipping point, but there were others and they occurred in rapid succession, leading to a complete ecosystem collapse.

Leaf: Can you give us an example?

Perc: The demise of the world's forests. Not just through deforestation, though that's a major cause. Twenty-five percent of the untouched forests were pushed by global warming into an abrupt and irreversible decline. Hotter temperatures caused an explosion in the populations of insects that threatened trees and undermined their capacity to defend themselves. Salt water inundation along the coastlines took vast swatches of forest land.

Most of the world's climate plans counted on forests to pull warming gases out of the atmosphere, but the lungs of the planet were destroyed and they were unable to recover. A form of biological emphysema. Once these ecosystems collapsed, we were hard pressed to prevent catastrophe. Heat domes, droughts, and wildfires proliferated and entire towns burned to the ground all over the world.

Leaf: I'll bet you have more examples to share with us.

Perc: There were a number of warning signs. Massive "mouths to hell" opened in the arctic permafrost, belching lakes and mystery craters, as the region heated up seven times faster than the rest of the earth. The abrupt thawing of the high northern permafrost released vast stores of carbon that had been trapped under ice in this once frozen land.

Leaf: You're a historian. Can you point to a time when all of these tipping points were triggered?

Perc: I consider 2022 to be a landmark year in the history of the earth. That was a now or never moment! A time when our planet was quite literally created anew. And not to anyone's liking. At least not anyone I know. It was the third year of a cooler than normal La Niña weather pattern effecting ocean temperatures and climactic conditions. A very rare event. Yet, 2022 was one of the hottest years ever recorded at that time.

Glacier melt, devastating floods, searing heat waves, record setting temperatures at both polar regions, ferocious wildfires, and historical droughts worldwide assailed the planet. But it was business as usual. Where was the f**king sense of urgency? The threats were so clear and obvious. Why didn't humanity act? Insist governments put trillions of dollars to work to combat climate change and make mandatory reductions of carbon worldwide.

When the next El Niño formed, as it inevitably would, the year was 2023 and the world was totally unprepared.We crossed the 1.5C threshold that year, twenty years before the original predictions. The extreme weather of the past paled into insignificance. Super-hurricanes and storm surges wiped out entire towns while heat waves and forest fires added to the worldwide destruction and loss of life.

That same year, scientists discovered an ice core taken from beneath Greenland's ice sheet, decades earlier in 1966. Analysis revealed that the country was ice-free around 400,000 years ago when temperatures were similar to what the earth was approaching at the time. This evidence overturned the assumption Greenland's ice sheet had been frozen for millions of years. Based on that, they realized natural, moderate warming had led to a sea level rise of 4.6 feet. That's already happened once again. If Greenland's ice sheet melts completely, and it certainly looks possible, sea levels will rise at least ten more feet!

Leaf: Scientists have been warning about these possibilities for decades.

Perc: Yes, but scientists now admit they were too conservative when estimating the speed, scope, and severity of the impacts of even moderate levels of human created climate change. A majority of them never imagined how quickly disasters would unfold. For example, the Atlantic Current System shut down in 2030, not at the end of this century. Temperatures rose in the Southern Hemisphere, plunged dramatically in Europe. This also contributed to more sea rise along our east coast.

Everything happened all at once and so much sooner than anybody, even the most pessimistic scientific models, predicted.

Leaf: You've always maintained the disastrous effects of climate change could have been averted or at least, minimized.

Perc : We're conditioned not to think about our personal responsibility for what's happened, but we enabled it through the actions we took, the choices we made, and in some cases by our inaction. Lord knows I've done my share of damage to the environment. We all share in the guilt. We could have done so much more, individually and collectively in our daily lives, to prevent the worst of what we're now experiencing.

Leaf: I agree with you that we all share in the guilt, but you've stated for the record that governments worldwide, along with the fossil fuel and chemical industries, bear the lion's share of responsibility for what's befallen us.

Perc: I ask again. Where was the sense of urgency? Scientists and climate activists told us to reduce our dependence on fossil fuels half a century ago. Much of what we currently experience might have been prevented or possibly slowed down. No wonder the oil and gas companies dragged their feet. Thirty years ago, twenty-eight oil and gas companies made 183 billion dollars in profits. I repeat, in profits! To what end? Sacrifice the planet and all of the species living on the earth, including ourselves, so that already rich shareholders could make even more money. Some of these companies were subsidized by governments, if you can believe that. It was estimated the true cost of their activities was over five trillion dollars a year in negative health and environmental damage.

I could go on and on, ad nauseum.

Leaf: We do have a little time left.

Perc: I should mention there's more to the story. Much more. The carbon footprint should have been a litmus test for all of our activities. The average carbon footprint, the total amount of greenhouse gases generated by our actions, averages sixteen tons per person in the USA and four tons per person worldwide on an annual basis. We would have needed to get to two tons per person by our current year of 2050 to avoid a 2 degrees Celsius rise in global temperature. Obviously, we didn't make it.

Leaf: I'm sure you have more examples of where we've gone wrong.

Perc: You bet. We've turned the earth into a toxic wasteland. The modern wasteland. An outer reflection of the wasteland within. Accepting the normalization of the abnormal until we've created the world we live in today. Chocking on our own garbage. Drowning in our own waste which we, in America, sent to Asia until they chose not to be used as a garbage dump for the industrial west.

Speaking of waste. Did you know that one-third of all the food produced in the world still goes to waste? While millions starve. Unbelievable! It either never leaves the farm, is spoiled in transit and distribution, or is thrown away. This unused food wastes water, energy, and labor resources. Thirty percent ends up in landfills where it decomposes and produces methane as a byproduct. The third largest source of human related methane emissions in the U.S. Yet recycling food is the easiest and fastest activity an individual can do to affect climate change.

A study thirty years ago found that on average, every week, each person produces human-made mass waste greater than their own body weight. Now man-made stuff on the planet has surpassed the weight of naturally occurring substances.

Tech waste is also an issue. How to recycle six billion iPhones and android devices full of toxic materials. Well, it was six billion at one time. Now the world population has declined to just under three billion people, but all those dead cell phones are a reminder of how wasteful a planetary consumer culture can be. This modern wasteland is a result of overconsumption and billions of tons of discards, many of which are toxic and harmful to all life on the earth.

Leaf: I want to go back to the largest sources of methane emissions in our country. What are the first two?

Perc: Natural gas and petroleum production as well as usage; and, agriculture related to livestock.

Leaf: You have been branded an enemy of wind and solar power because early systems used materials that weren't easy to recycle and some of the materials were also toxic to the environment. I'd like to know your response to those critics.

Perc: I'd like to set the record straight, Leaf. Green doesn't always mean clean!

My earliest criticisms were based on objective data. We were guilty of not thinking ahead, so we created systems without regard to future consequences. Over time, my objections, and those of prominent scientists and activists, were addressed. So, I'm onboard! We now manufacture solar panels whose materials are almost one hundred percent sustainable and they last for a hundred years or more. Our wind turbines are now bladeless.

My criticisms were of wind turbine blades made with fiberglass which was difficult to separate so other components could be recycled. They ended up in boneyards, creating toxic landfills. Solar panels containing deadly materials--with only a twenty-five year life span--ended in landfills. California alone had 1.3 million rooftops worth of panels. Once crushed and put into landfills, those toxic chemicals leaked into the groundwater. Only one in ten panels were actually recycled. Such a lack of forethought!

Leaf: Thank you for straightening that out, Perc. We're going over our usual allotted time because this subject is so critical. Maybe you can help us wrap this up.

Perc: One last thing. I probably should have started this episode talking about something more precious than oil or gold or diamonds. I'm referring to water, the essence of life on Earth, and especially drinking water without which we cannot survive. We have a worldwide scarcity of uncontaminated drinking water. In some places, there is a lack of any kind of drinking water. The country of Jordan ran out of water completely, in 2030.

Leaf: I just remembered. I have one more thing I'd like to touch upon in this episode. You've said we need a non-violent revolution. One that puts the needs of all other forms of life on an equal basis with our own. A respect for the web of life and all who inhabit it.

Perc: We've separated ourselves from nature, which was necessary for survival, but we've carried that way too far. We seem to have lost our love for the natural world. I'm not talking about Nature Boy or Nature Girl sentimentality, Leaf. Nature is impersonal and can disrupt and destroy human life, but we need a healthy eco-system to survive. A pragmatic approach recognizes that we need nature more than she needs us. Enlightened self-interest to keep life in balance.

The stark reality of the biodiversity crisis is that millions of species have become extinct, and we may soon be joining them.

We all talk a good game, but we don't play a good game. Talk the talk, oh how we talk the talk, but we don't walk the walk. It's not what we think or say, more like what we do. No, pardon my French, f**king action! In the face of calamity. No f**king action! If we love Earth, if we love life, how can we deny our young people a chance to live in a healthier world? What the hell is the matter with us? We act like we're f**king crazy!

Leaf: You're pissed.

Perc: If you're not you're more dead than alive!

Leaf: Why do you say that?

Perc: These catastrophic changes didn't have to happen. They might have been prevented or mitigated at the very least. We've known for three-quarters of a century these results were likely to occur unless we initiated radical changes to the way we lived our lives.

Shame on us! How can we look our young people in the eye if we haven't done all within our power to save the earth?

At first, I was appalled by my own lack of awareness and stupidity. We simply are not taught to think about these things. After reflecting upon what I'd learned, I felt compelled to act. You can't very well rail against current practices if you're not taking action yourself. People will see through the B.S. Young people for sure. We have betrayed our children and their children and their children's children. We've signed off on their death sentences as surely as if we had executed them ourselves!

Leaf: I think this is a good place to end this episode. Our next one is titled: "Warm Water and High Seas." You won't want to miss it, but first I feel compelled to finish up with one last question. Do you ever feel like you're preaching to the choir, Perc?

Perc: No, I don't see it that way. If my words resonate with one individual and that person changes their behavior, I consider all of the work and energies I've expended to be successful. That person might talk to one or two more individuals, family or friends, who decide to work at changing their own lives and the fate of the earth for the better, and so on and so on. Perhaps there will be a chain reaction: bim, bam, boom! Just maybe, against all odds, we can save our species and the planet from total annihilation.

HOT MIKE

Leaf: Do you really believe that, Perc?

Perc: Damn right I do!

Leaf: Opps! Seems we had an open mike.

Well, that concludes this episode of Sanctuary Earth. Tune in next week when Perc takes us on a deep dive into our "Warm Waters and Rising Seas." Thanks to Perc for joining us to share his thoughts, and thanks to you for listening to the Sanctuary Earth Podcast.

Narrator: Oscar Uribe was the producer of this episode. Our engineers are Andrew Wilson and Celeste Roberts. Our editor is Rosie Zuniga. The executive producer is Leaf Aronson.

CHAPTER 26

That was by far the longest of the Podcast episodes, thought Clay.

He wondered if he'd hear a "Ja" in the Podcast episode after meeting and listening to Leaf Aronson on their visit to Windy Meadow. Not a one. He assumed the word had been edited out if it had slipped in. He figured they wouldn't dare edit Perc's comments. They'd never hear the end of it.

His thoughts turned to the radical eco-historian.

Perc had given him so much to think about, but he couldn't help but focus on what the radical historian had said at the end of the interview. It seemed like he was addressing Clay directly.

He wondered if he might be that one individual Perc was talking about.

Maybe he could work at changing his own life and impact the fate of the earth for the better. Perhaps he could help save the species and the planet from total annihilation. Had he been too self-centered? He realized that he needed to do some soul searching. Reflect upon his personal motivations, and his tendency towards selfishness.

His thought process might have gone on in this vein, but for a knock at the door.

He opened the front door of the guest house and found Lynne and Jamala and Jodie standing on the porch.

"Something important has come up," Lynne informed him. "We'd like for you and Hank to join us."

"Trust us," Jamala said. "This will be worth your while."

What could this mysterious summons be all about, Clay wondered.

He searched their eyes to no avail. Made sure to make eye contact. Tight-lipped secrecy. He decided not to bother asking any questions.

"Hank's taking a siesta," he told them. "I'll go wake him up."

The Operations Control Center was located two blocks off the Main Plaza.

Lynne and Jamala led their guests into what appeared to be just another building. At least on the outside. Once inside, they discovered a high tech environment with work stations facing a wall-sized computer monitor divided into multiple sections, all seemingly in real time. Half a dozen workers stared at their individual monitors while occasionally glancing up at the larger center screen.

Clay gazed at the images: the rear gate at the top of the Sanctuary, three people sitting inside what appeared to be an interview room, a field of bladeless wind turbines, and a bank of solar energy panels.

A middle-aged Hispanic male came over to greet them.

He wore his hair long. A scraggly mustache and goatee surrounded his thin lips and chin. A loose t-shirt clung to his slender frame. Jeans and tennis shoes completed the attire.

"Hey, ladies," he meowed in a sing-song cadence.

"This is Rico," announced Lynne. "He sort of runs the show here."

"That's cause I graduated from M.I.T.," he boasted.

"Impressive," said Hank.

"M. I. T.," Rico proclaimed proudly before laughing at his own joke. "As in Monterrey Institute of Technology, in Monterrey, Mexico."

Everybody got a kick out of Rico's little deception. He'd obviously used the line many times before because his timing and delivery were impeccable.

The tech leader must have been wearing ear pods under his long curls, and someone must have communicated something to Rico, because he walked off a short distance and appeared to be listening to someone and wanting to hear what they had to say. Rico focused intently and then turned back to the group.

"They're ready for you, Lynne."

"Thanks, Rico."

"*Adios, guapa* Jam," Rico crooned to Jamala as they all started to leave.

"*Adios, guapo*, Rico," she sang in return, playing along with his fun-loving ways.

Hank felt a pang of jealousy though he wasn't sure why.

"Say hello to your husband for me, Rico."

"Of course, Jamala."

Gender fluidity. Hank had almost forgotten how prevalent it had become during the past few decades. He laughed at himself as he realized his feelings of jealousy were a result of his irrational caring for a woman he knew little about. He hoped that would change sometime soon.

Lynne went over and gave Rico a warm hug and then everyone left the room.

They walked down a narrow corridor until they found their destination. Lynne opened a door and ushered everyone into a large room with a square pane of glass, a two-way window allowing them to view the room beyond while remaining unseen themselves.

Inside a hidden microphone picked up all the conversations. Like something out of an old police procedural.

"We have our own internal police force," Jamala explained. "Like our Native Americans have on their reservations."

"Does Government allow that?" asked Hank.

Jamala turned to him.

"They don't want anything to do with us. Except possibly to shut us down. They hope our movement fails and goes away. But we still have our constitutional rights."

"So what are we doing here," asked Clay.

197

"There's something we think you should see," said Jamala.

"Care to share?" Jodie wondered out loud.

"We have Government's mole in our midst," revealed Lynne as she beckoned them to look through the glass.

Inside the sparsely furnished room they saw a wooden table. On one side, a balding man sat with a bland expression on his face. He appeared to be in his late thirties or early forties and wore slacks and a wrinkle-free dress shirt. Opposite him was an interracial couple, about the same age, dressed more casually.

Their names were Maggie and Trey.

The woman had on a simple white blouse with blue jeans. Her olive-skinned face, framed by shoulder-length hair, held a serious expression. Her companion, a bearded black man, had on a V-neck sweater and slacks. He looked more relaxed.

"Government moles used to be easy to spot," said Jamala. "They're getting more sophisticated. They hire trained actors and actresses to infiltrate our Sanctuaries."

"They give them a complete new identity so when we do background checks and evaluate them everything looks fine," added Lynne. "It's been a challenge."

"What's it all about?" inquired Hank.

"Like I mentioned earlier, Government is looking for ways to shut us down," responded Jamala. "They say we're free to do as we please, but we think they see us as a potential threat to their authority. Our numbers are growing every day, so they're hoping to catch us doing something illegal."

"Looks like they're getting started," Lynne observed. "Let's listen in."

"What's going on?' asked the Mole.

"We need to ask you a few questions," said Trey in a soothing voice.

The Mole couldn't hide his look of concern:

"Why?" he wondered. "Have I done something wrong?"

"Not exactly wrong," Trey continued. He seemed to be taking the lead in the interview while Maggie remained silent though she hadn't dropped her stern look. "I'd say more like questionable."

"What do you mean?"

Maggie leaned over and stretched herself across the table to make close contact with the balding man. She bore into him with hard, unsmiling eyes.

"Don't play games with us!" she shouted as she banged down hard on the top of the table with her right hand.

The startled Mole reared back from the table with fear in his eyes.

"Easy Maggie," suggested Trey. "This is an interview. Not an interrogation."

Maggie continued to stare at the Mole without blinking.

Outside the room, looking in, an equally surprised trio of visitors caught their collective breath.

"Maggie and Trey are ex-cops from back East," explained Jamala. Trey worked as an undercover cop. He has a strong feel for who's a Mole and how to ferret them out. If he suspects anything, he befriends them and waits until they reveal themselves."

"They say that we don't reveal ourselves, we are revealed," said Lynne. "By our words and actions, and the lack of certain words and actions."

"Trey and Maggie work as a team both on and off the job," Jamala informed them. "They play good cop-bad cop. They takes turns and they're accomplished at it."

Back inside the room, Maggie had plopped back down on her chair. She indulged herself with a brief smile.

She and Trey watched closely as the Mole swallowed hard.

"Sorry, Trey," she apologized as she turned to her partner. A subtle smile. "Guess I got carried away."

Maggie turned back to the Mole.

199

"We caught you nosing around the Operations Center," she said in an accusatory tone.

"I was just curious," lied the Mole.

"About anything in particular?" Maggie wanted to know, taking time to emphasize and enunciate each of the words as the smile disappeared from her face.

"Nothing in particular."

Maggie stared at the Mole as she let out an exaggerated sigh.

"We have a problem," she said, shaking her head. "If there was something special that you were looking for I'd get it, but you were seen going through a number of file cabinets and taking pictures of some of our files."

"Me?" The Mole protested, playing innocent. "You must be mistaken."

Trey had heard enough. He rose from his chair, a towering and imposing figure. He stood well over six feet, two inches tall and packed two hundred pounds on his muscular frame. The ex-cop walked around the table and approached the Mole. His mouth widened into something between a smile and a wince as he stood looking down impatiently at his adversary.

The Mole cowered in his chair. His hands trembled so he removed them from the table and placed them on his lap.

"I thought we were friends, Trey."

"We *were*," said the ex-cop, raising his voice. "Friends don't lie to friends."

"That's right," Maggie chirped in.

"There must be some misunderstanding."

Maggie couldn't help herself. She stood and walked around the table to join her partner.

"We downloaded your camera chip, chump!"

The Mole sank back into his chair with a deflated expression on his face. He saw Trey remove a micro-camera from his pocket and flash images on the far wall, a blank white surface behind where he and Maggie had recently been sitting.

The first image showed a single page taken from the biography of the founder of the Sanctuary Movement, Leaf Aronson. Trey didn't linger. A memo on the Esperanza Refugee Camp flashed on the wall.

"Want us to continue?" Trey asked.

"That won't be necessary," replied the Mole, his voice cracking.

Trey brought his little show to an end.

"You're pretty slick" complimented Maggie. "Had us fooled for quite a while."

"Were you following me?"

"No," replied Trey. "We keep security cameras trained on the Operations Center twenty-four hours a day."

The Mole shook his head in disbelief.

"I didn't know you guys were so paranoid."

"Seems like we have a good reason," asserted Maggie. "We have something special going on here and we don't have anything to hide. We just don't like Government moles hanging around looking for dirt so they can close down our Sanctuaries."

The couple returned to their seats before continuing.

"Now what?" asked the Mole.

"We're not done here," Maggie told him. "Do you know anything about a tracking device applied to one of our jeeps?"

"Yeah, that was me," admitted the Mole. "Government wanted to keep tabs on some guy named Roberts because the National Fertility Service put in a request."

"Nothing more?" the couple asked in unison.

The Mole shook his head from side to side.

"Now what?" he asked.

"You're free to go and report on what you've seen during your stay," Trey reassured him.

"If it means anything to you," the Mole began in a reconciliatory tone of voice. "I've actually come to admire what you're trying to do out here. I have a wife and two kids back in the city. That's the only reason I accepted this assignment. I have to put food on the table. I can't let them down. It's a jungle back there."

"You're always welcome to apply to one of our Sanctuaries," Maggie offered. This gesture of generosity wasn't lost on the Mole.

"Thanks," he responded. This was followed by a loud, troubled sigh. "If Government has a claim on you . . . well, let's just say you're in for keeps."

Maggie and Trey turned to each other. Their raised brows reflected feelings of consternation. Times had changed since they'd made the decision to leave the force a decade earlier.

"We'll arrange for a ride back," Trey said, a hint of compassion revealed in the softness of his tone. "Better pack your things and be ready first thing in the morning."

Maggie got up and walked to the two-way window. She looked straight into the opaque glass, having been apprised that Lynne and Jamala were bringing observers to witness the questioning. She gave them a knowing wink.

"There's our cue," Lynne said to the others. "We'd better be on our way."

They soon were.

Once back outside they congregated in a tight circle.

"If any of you decide to join our Movement you need to know that we are vulnerable," Lynne said truthfully. "It's not a decision to be made lightly."

"This is no Utopia," Jamala told them. "Many of those choosing to live within our Sanctuaries are infertile. What we share in common is that we all possess fertile imaginations."

Clay Roberts had already decided that he couldn't join the Sanctuary Movement even though he admired its values and goals, those he'd seen embodied in its members. This was a reoccurring thought. It wouldn't go away as much as he tried to suppress it, and it saddened him to think that he was better off staying on the family farm, but he knew that he would never forgive himself if he were the cause of an attack on the Arm-in-Arm Sanctuary.

Lynne must have sensed his mood. As she stood next to him, she quietly put her hand on his shoulder.

"You okay."

"I'm fine," he lied.

CHAPTER 27

Hank stood at Jamala's front door gathering his courage.

He knocked and waited in anticipation for the door to open. It wasn't long before he found himself gazing into Jamala's big brown eyes. She seemed surprised to find him standing there and gave him a quizzical look.

"I wonder if I might speak to you in private," he said with hesitation in his voice.

"Is everything all right, Hank?"

"Yeah, everything's fine."

"I'm going to step inside and tell Jodie that I'm going out for a while."

The agent watched her return inside the stucco abode. Nice of her, he thought. To tell Jodie and not leave her in the dark. She's so thoughtful. Always worried about other people and their feelings.

Jamala returned wearing a broad-brimmed hat.

A smart move thought Hank considering the day was heating up with no hint of a breeze. He'd adjusted his sun-hat earlier, attempting to create a rakish tilt to the brim.

Jamala closed the door behind herself as Hank stepped aside to allow her to take the lead.

"There's a park around the corner," she told him. "Let's go there."

They walked side by side along a dirt path and soon turned the corner. The park came into view about a block away. Hank was uncharacteristically quiet and Jamala naturally wondered what was on his mind. He seemed very secretive.

The agent gazed out across the park. On the far side he saw a children's playground, part of it set-up for toddlers and kindergartners. Two little girls swung back and forth on a swing set, their mothers close by. One of the woman stood next to a vintage looking wicker stroller with a metal frame. These Plastic People take their commitment seriously, thought Hank.

He turned back around and found Jamala making a beeline for one of the available picnic tables. He followed her and they sat themselves down, choosing benches on either side of the wooden table so they could face each other. The agent offered Jamala a smile as he considered how to frame his thoughts.

"I've never experienced any place like this," he began. "I mean the Sanctuary. Back in the city everybody's addicted to the Metaverse, or taking drugs and living in their own private Metaverses, or hustling to make a buck just to survive."

Jamala reached across the table and took his hands into her own. She gave them a gentle squeeze, her warmth conveyed itself directly to his body and his soul. She knew that Hank was trying hard to communicate something, but what he'd just told her didn't require privacy. There was more to it.

"Go on," she encouraged him.

"I want to bring my mother and grandmother here to the Sanctuary to find out if they might consider moving up here," he said. "I feel they'd enjoy a happier, more meaningful life in this environment."

Jamala sensed his uncertainty.

"And?"

"I wonder if you might find the time to show them around," he said, with some hesitation in his voice. He didn't want to impose upon her, yet it felt important. He thought that his mother and grandmother would feel more welcomed and relaxed. "It might feel more personal that way."

It seemed obvious that Hank wanted his mother and grandmother to like the Sanctuary. That appeared to be the implication of his requesting that a private guide be someone he knew personally. The deeper and unspoken part of that subtext was that he would have a reason to visit the Sanctuary more often.

"I'll make some time if it's important to *you*."

Hank's heart melted at the way she had said the word *you*. He detected a softness in her voice, but also an intimation of affection.

Hank's burner phone blasted out a ringtone.

The spell was broken.

He looked at her with raised brows and then shrugged his shoulders. Jamala understood and withdrew her hands from his as he reached into his pocket for the phone. He shook his head at the terrible timing of the call, but when he saw the number displayed his eyes opened wide and a smile spread across his face.

"Sorry," he apologized. "I've got to take this call."

"I understand."

He rose from the table and straddled it before heading off towards the shade of a massive sycamore tree. He listened intently for a moment and then he looked over to see if Jamala was watching him. She smiled and he gave her a thumbs up gesture.

He obviously wants a relationship with me, she mused. That much was obvious. Who would she be competing with? She barely knew him. Did he have a girlfriend back in the city? Would his mother and grandmother compete for his time?

Hank returned to the picnic table once he'd completed his call.

"Would you care to share?" she wondered aloud.

"I would if it were possible," he said, trying to reassure her. "I've got to talk to Clay first. It's his decision as to what he wants to do. I'm just the go between."

She appreciated that he protected his potential client's privacy. Not much more to say. It appeared that their earlier conversation had played out to Hank's satisfaction. She'd agreed to show his mother and grandmother around the Sanctuary.

"Shall we go back?"

Jamala wanted to know more about this guy named Hank Gallagher.

She decided to satisfy her curiosity on the way back to her adobe home. They'd left the park and turned the corner when she engaged him in conversation. She hoped she sounded casual. She didn't want to appear over eager. She was interested in the agent. No doubt about that. At least not in her mind. She still wasn't sure about her heart.

"How did you become an agent, Hank?" she inquired somewhat nonchalantly. "In such a unique business."

"My father always said that I had the gift of gab," he told her. "While he was still alive, that is."

"I'm so sorry," she said apologetically. She hadn't meant to stir his emotions.

"No worries," he assured her. "Anyways, my dad was Irish. My mother and my grandmother are full-blooded Italian. Quite a background. I remember there were always lots of emotional outbursts when I was a boy." He meandered as always with the stream of consciousness approach to life and other people. Let them flow. Conversations and events. "I guess you'd say I was a natural born salesman. It seemed easy. All I had to do was be myself. Believe in what I was selling, of course."

"Of course."

They continued down the pathway as Jamala attempted to understand his motivations. Why did he choose to represent sperm donors and fertile women? Lots of other things he might have sold with his gift of gab. Why this unique calling? She asked him point blank.

"It was a brand new field when I first learned about it," he explained. "I was intrigued and I wanted to do something to help humanity survive. Otherwise there wouldn't be businesses of any kind. Right? No life at all. There was talk of the human race becoming extinct. Not if I could help it. No way!"

Jamala stopped in her tracks. He followed her lead, but was surprised by the sudden abruptness of her action. Had he said something wrong? Something to offend her. That was the last thing he wanted to do, but he felt on shaking ground with her. He had no idea what she thought of him, and he suspected it might be the worst. He knew, more than anybody else, that he was an imperfect human being. He talked too much. Sometimes a bit of a showboat. He hoped he hadn't blown it.

He gazed over at her and found her looking at him with a renewed interest as if she had discovered a newfound respect for him. Could he be so lucky?

"You became a sperm and fertility agent because you want to help humanity survive," she said quietly. This wasn't a question. It came across as an affirmation of Hank Gallagher's motivation.

"Basically, that's it."

Jamala went up to him, grabbed him by his shirt and pulled him closer; and, then she kissed him on the cheek.

"That's wonderful," she whispered before letting go of his shirt.

Where was their relationship heading? Neither had a clue. Each had their own hopes and fears when it came to entering into a deeper intimacy. Both had been in relationships that hadn't worked out for one reason or another. Hank suddenly remembered his own infertility and for a brief instant he wondered if it might come between them one day. He decided to put any thoughts along this line aside for the time being.

When it came to each other they were entering uncharted territory.

They continued on towards the house.

"I detect a slight southern accent," said Hank. "How did you end up out here?"

"I received a four year scholarship to UC Berkeley," Jamala replied. "I stayed on to earn a Master's Degree in sustainable agriculture. I wrote my Thesis on the adaptability of west African crops to northern California."

"You decided to stay?"

"I wanted to get out of the academic setting and I was looking for an opportunity to give my early experiments a more practical application. I heard about the Sanctuary Movement and I applied. Like you, I want to see humanity survive."

Jamala erupted into hearty laughter.

"What's so funny?"

"I tried so hard to lose my Virginia twang," she explained. "I guess it'll never go away completely."

Jamala's adobe cottage came into view.

Jodie was waiting for them on the front porch when they arrived.

"Has anybody heard from Clay?" she asked with a nervous smile. The anxious almost fearful tone of her voice betrayed her emotional state of mind.

"No," replied Jamala. "Is everything all right?"

'I've been calling him all day and he hasn't answered me," she responded. "This isn't like him."

"He told me he was going over to Lynne's place," Hank told them. "Not exactly top secret information."

Jamala frowned for all the world to see, especially Hank.

Opps! Foot in mouth, thought the agent.

"He might have forgotten to keep you in the loop," the agent added, hoping to lessen the effect of his earlier blunder.

"That's probably it," agreed Jamala. "You know guys."

Hank couldn't help but feel the brunt of that observation.

"Shall we go over to Lynne's and find out if he's there?" Jodie asked them.

"I don't think that's a good idea," said Jamala. "I'm sure things are fine."

Jodie thought about it for a moment. Jamala's right. No need to worry. Clay can take care of himself. Don't overreact.

"Let's go inside and make some tea," proposed Jamala. "Want to join us, Hank?"

"I'd love to, Jamala."

"Call me, Jam."

CHAPTER 28

They sat on Lynne's sofa, kicking back, barefoot with feet resting on the coffee table.

They'd developed an emotional closeness that began the night Lynne shared with him the details of her relationship with Michael. They were now more attuned to one another. Sensing moods and anticipating thoughts and finishing each other's sentences.

Lynne suspected Clay wasn't totally honest when she'd asked him if everything was all right following the interrogation of the Mole. She debated with herself whether to say anything about it or to let it pass. Desiring an authentic relationship with him, she opted for the former.

This seemed like a good time.

"After Trey and Maggie questioned the Mole we all went outside. You were distant. Lost in your own thoughts. I asked if everything was okay and you told me you were fine, remember?"

"Vaguely."

"I felt like something was troubling you," she said sincerely. "I still feel it, Clay."

She deserved a truthful response. He'd been holding back because he wanted so much for her to like him. Afraid his dark side might scare her off. So much easier to suppress the thoughts than to share them. Now, it seemed unavoidable.

"We're some sort of weird mutation," he began. "Not like the humans who lived on this planet for thousands of years before us. We act like we have a right to destroy other species along with ourselves. Sometimes I wonder if the earth would be better off without us."

Here we go again, she thought.

"You don't mean that . . . "

"I don't know anymore," he admitted.

Lynne looked deep into his eyes.

"You're not seeing things clearly," she told him. "What you are saying is nihilistic."

"Call it what you want. Humans find ways to kill each other. Endless wars, mass murders, genocide. As if that isn't bad enough, look what we're doing to the rest of the planet: the birds, animals, fish, the rain forests and on and on like it's not all connected."

Clay realized his dark thoughts had intruded once again as he suddenly remembered that this wasn't what he'd been thinking about after the interrogation. He'd been mulling over how he felt about endangering the Sanctuary. Did he want to add that to the mix just now? Muddy the waters even more. Drive a wedge between them.

Lynne had pulled her long hair up off the back of her neck and secured it with a silver barrette. She undid the metal clasp, placed it down on the coffee table, and shook her hair loose.

"You know what you need?" Lynne asked.

"No, what do I need?"

"Some good healthy sex!"

It's that obvious, Clay wondered.

He was at a loss for words as Lynne rose from the sofa and took him by the hand. She pulled him to his feet. He felt a swelling in his crotch as his body and soul ached for release. He sensed what was coming: surprise, shock, elation, and a deepening adrenalin rush. All these emotions washed over him at the same time as Lynne moved in closer.

Their eyes met. She moved her face up to his and drew him into an embrace. He felt her warm breath on his skin. She put her mouth to Clay's and kissed him gently, and then she took his hand and led him back into her bedroom.

Lynne led him across the room, and then she pushed him down on the bed. They fell onto the bedcovers clinging to one another with a deepening desire. She climbed on top of him and pressed her body down into his. He felt her weight and her body heat as she placed her face next to his. He smelled her sweet breath. Their lips met and they kissed. One long, passionate kiss before her warm, moist tongue entered his mouth.

There's always a morning after.

They awoke naked, lying next to one another. She smiled and so did he.

She was right, he thought to himself. She'd known what he had needed. Desired as well though he would never have admitted this to himself.

"Hank says they call you The Sperm King."

"He made that up himself."

"It does have a certain ring to it."

Clay blushed.

She ran her finger along his cheek. Another smile, warm and heartfelt.

Clay drew away.

"Is there something wrong?' she wanted to know.

"You're beautiful," he replied without answering the question. How long could he evade the repercussions of what they had done. Not long, he guessed. Better to deal with it now than to wait. That would only make it worse.

"Are you using contraceptives?"

"No, and you didn't use a rubber."

"Do you think . . . ."

Clay didn't finish the sentence. He already knew the answer to his question and so did Lynne. It was entirely possible they had created a new life. Unlikely, but possible. And if they had. What would he do? What would she do?

Lynne was getting better at reading his thoughts.

"Believe in yourself, Clay," she told him. "Trust that you will know the right thing, and do the right thing, no matter what you choose."

213

Clay reflected upon what she had said. He'd been questioning himself ever since the day of mandatory testing. That wasn't his true nature. To question his own instincts rather than act on what he knew in his heart was right for himself.

"You're right," he agreed. "I need to follow my heart."

"Not your head," she added. ". . . and not your . . . " she stopped short of saying it, but they both knew what she was about to say. Their laughter came easy, but it didn't last long because they were interrupted by a knocking at Lynne's front door. They threw some clothes over themselves. Just enough to be presentable.

Another knock.

This one slightly louder.

Lynne opened the door and she and Clay stood side by side.

"I thought I'd find you here," said Hank.

"Why don't you come inside," invited Lynne.

"I'm here to deliver a message," the agent informed them. "Tanaka has rescinded his offer. He's not a man accustomed to being kept waiting."

"What?"

A look of shock registered on Clay's face. Tanaka had seemed so reasonable. So accommodating. He didn't appear to be in a hurry for an answer. Maybe Clay had misread him.

"Completely off the table."

"What happened?" asked Clay. "Have I all of a sudden gone sterile?"

"It seems they mixed up your test results with some other guy. A national testing technician new to the job screwed up. They sent your results for verification and it turns out he swapped your markers with a guy from Duluth. It happens once in a while. Not often, but occasionally."

"I'm not a triple threat?"

"You still are, but this other guy is way beyond you, Clay. I mean he's . . . he's . . . "

214

"The Sperm King?"

Everybody laughed as the tension of the last few days dissipated like a balloon blown up and released before being tied off.

Psssssst!

Even during humanity's darkest hours laughter proved the best medicine, so everyone appreciated Clay's poking fun at himself.

"The guy has already signed with Tanaka," Hank sighed. "I'm sure he'll be tokenized within a week. Hey, not to worry. You've still got a bright future. Sperm Banks, and sponsorships, and endorsements. The sky is the limit. Just no island life for you."

"No *Man of the Year* cover for "Fertility Magazine,"" quipped Clay, tongue in cheek.

"We'll shoot for a monthly cover," Hank responded with a wink.

"Sure you won't come in?" asked Lynne.

"I can't," Hank answered, begging off for the second time. "I'm going to meet Jam and Jodie for breakfast."

Clay and Lynne smiled inwardly at hearing the agent refer to Jamala. They knew that using her nickname suggested a change in the relationship. Something was going on.

"Tell them we said, hi," the couple cooed in unison.

"I will . . . "

Lynne shut the door.

She turned to Clay and pulled him close so she could whisper something in his ear.

"You may not be a king, but you're still my prince," she teased.

Clay and Lynne lounged around all morning.

He decided to share something that had been nagging at him for a long time.

"I can't ask Jodie to stay on the farm forever," he began somewhat tentatively. After a long pause, during which Lynne waited patiently, he completed with his thoughts. "It's not fair to ask her to sacrifice her life if she wants to go."

"You'll both know what to do when the time comes," she said, trying to console him.

"I guess you're right," he agreed.

That ended talk of the farm as they went on to talk about other matters. The meandering conversation that took up the better part of the morning.

That afternoon, they met up with the others for some prearranged tours: the Sanctuary chicken farm, a textile arts center featuring weavers and quilters, and an elementary school.

Jodie found the Sanctuary's lone elementary school most interesting with its climate based curriculum and an organic garden complete with a metal water harvester and a compost heap taking up space in a central quad surrounded by four classrooms. Bright-eyed children, inquisitive and enthusiastic, were a joy to behold. They ranged in ages from six to eighteen and were divided into four different age groups: first to third-graders, fourth to sixth, middle-schoolers, and the high schoolers.

Each classroom was presided over by a teacher and one or two parent volunteers.

One of the teachers explained to Jodie that the class divisions were based on the fact that the students tested at grade level or one or two years either way. Hard and fast grade levels no longer seemed practical.

After a full day, they finished with a tour of a senior center back at the Main Plaza.

They decided to enjoy an early dinner at one the plaza's many restaurants.

Everyone ordered brown rice with stir-fry vegetables. Hank balked until he learned he could add grilled chicken breast to his order. Then he relented. At the last minute, Clay added the grilled chicken to his order as well.

After they'd ordered drinks, two young women perched themselves with their guitars off to one side of the venue. They sat upon tall stools. One with a six-string and one a twelve-string. No mics and no amps. No electricity was needed for their performance since the guitars were acoustic.

Everyone continued to eat while the musicians performed current favorites.

Background music. Most of the patrons weren't really listening though some offered polite applause at the end of each song. They appreciated the effort, but their personal lives took precedence.

The fluid, mezzo-soprano harmonies were lost in the babel.

The bright, shimmery sounds of the twelve string never had a chance to sparkle.

A short break.

Time for those who really cared about the music to visit the tip jar.

"Clay doesn't have a musical bone in his body," declared Jodie. "My brother couldn't sing in key if his life depended on it."

"That's not true," he protested.

Jodie just laughed as she got up from the table and headed for the tip jar. Everyone watched as she took a ten dollar bill from her wallet and dropped it into the glass. Her friends realized that she'd revealed a side of herself that they were unaware of. Jodie was an audiophile. She had actually been listening to the music.

That was the second time in less than a week that Jodie had been rude to him in front of others, reflected Clay. He wondered if she was doing it on purpose. He considered that these may have been an unconscious expressions on her part. Maybe a symptom of her desire to create some distance in their relationship. A harbinger of the future? He once again considered the possibility his sister might leave the farm.

He turned his gaze to Lynne. She smiled at him and he reciprocated as the easy conversations and lively banter began again at their table and those surrounding them. Could she be the one for him? He'd have to be patient and allow the future to unfold before that question was answered.

Jodie returned to the table.

A bright-eyed young woman, with frizzy blue hair and body piercings and tattoos, came over to join them as the five continued to converse. She remained standing while addressing Lynne and Jamala.

"Have you heard the news?" she asked excitedly. Not waiting for an answer, she quickly elaborated. "The Expanders took a vote on whether or not to protest and Alex's motion was voted down! He was pissed! The leaders didn't have the support they'd counted on. Some of the members are mumbling about disbanding the movement."

Lynne let out a huge sigh of relief.

Jamala just smiled to herself and nodded.

"Gotta run and spread the news," the blue-haired young women said as she flashed a smile along with a V for victory sign.

"The Expanders don't have a lot of support in the larger community," Lynne explained to her visitors.

"But a small minority could create a major disruption to the Sanctuary's well-being," added Jamala.

"My mom used to say 'there's always flies in the ointment,'" Jodie commented, hoping to bring an end to that brief interruption. She wanted to talk about the music so she deftly led the conversation back in that direction.

Another ten minutes passed.

The musical twosome returned and surprised everybody by offering a history lesson, musically speaking. They launched into a number of songs that were popular three-quarters of a century earlier. Old folk songs. They ran through a playlist of what they considered some of the best: "Catch the Wind," "Mr. Tambourine Man," "Sounds of Silence," "The Circle Game," and "Turn, Turn, Turn." These songs shared a common denominator; they were lyrical and poetic.

It was much the same as before, with patrons treating the songs as background music to their conversations since most of them had never heard the old tunes.

And then, everything changed.

The two women raised their voices.

They announced loudly that it was time for their final song of the evening, and they wanted everyone's attention. They lowered their voices into a heartfelt harmony, forcing everyone to listen more closely to a song titled *Before the Deluge.*

A time warp!

Clay looked to Lynne and saw that she had tears in her eyes.

She was overcome by emotion at hearing the word deluge. A word her father had used so often. One of those meaningful coincidences that let her know she was in the right place at the right time.

Everyone sat stunned once they'd finished the song..

The musicians let the song's lyrics sink in before offering their take. The songwriter, a guy named Jackson Browne, lived during the times of their grandparents and great-grandparents. He must have been a visionary. There was no other way to explain how poignant and pertinent his message was after three-quarters of a century. It was as if the lyrics had been written for the audience that very morning.

Remember the title they implored. "*Before the Deluge.*" Check it out. It's not easy to find, but certainly available. And, please, please let music be a refuge for our souls during the storms to come. A safe harbor for our spirits.

"Wowzaaa!" exclaimed Jodie as she shot to her feet at started clapping to show her appreciation.

The audience followed her lead, delivering a loud ovation. The two musicians smiled and thanked their audience.

People forgot about their food, and left their tables to engage the two musicians. To thank them, and to fill the jar. Jodie joined them.

Lynne and Jamala surprised Clay and Hank by suggesting they part ways for the evening. They wanted some time away from the guys. Maybe even *needed* some time away from them. They hoped they'd understand. It was nothing personal. They just needed a break. A well-deserved break, though they didn't come right out and say it.

The two musicians packed the guitars into their gig bags and emptied the tip jar. They were soon on their way as Jodie returned to rejoin the others.

"Come get me for breakfast," was the last thing Lynne said to Clay.

Back in their shared bedroom, Clay checked his emails on his burner phone while Hank did the same using his Smart Glasses.

Clay finished and waited to share his thoughts until he saw Hank remove the glasses.

"This guy Perc is a real gadfly."

"What's a gadfly?" asked Hank.

"It's an annoying person," Clay replied. "Especially one who provokes others into action by criticism."

"Thanks," said Hank. "I learned a new word."

"I gotta say, I like him a lot."

"So do I," agreed the agent.

"Thought I'd check out another Podcast episode."

"No worries, said Hank reassuringly. "Thought I heard Lynne invite you over to her place in the morning."

"Yeah . . . . "

"I'm gonna sleep in."

And that ended their conversation.

Clay reached into his shirt pocket, pulled out his earbuds, and tucked them into his ears. Once he felt that they were secure, he reached for his burner phone.

It was automatic by now. Muscle memory and repetition. Hundreds, thousands, maybe millions of times.

Click. Search. Scroll.

Click!

CHAPTER 29

Podcast - *Sanctuary Earth*

Episode 6 -"Warm Water and High Seas"

Leaf: Welcome to Sanctuary Earth, where we discuss issues vital to the continuation of life on planet Earth. These programs are aired free of advertisements as a public service provided by the Plastic People's Sanctuary Movement.

I'm Leaf Aronson and we are once again talking with Perc, a radical eco-historian whose views are now shared by many scientists worldwide. What do you have in store for us today, Perc?

Perc: Today we're going to take a deep dive into "Warm Waters and High Seas."

Leaf: Where shall we start?

Perc: I'll begin with a recap.

Our oceans have lost their memory. These struggling green seas had an impressive existence once upon a time. Seafood provided the primary source of protein for three billion people.

Marine plants produced over half of the world's oxygen and ocean currents helped regulate our climate. Covering two-thirds of the earth, they absorbed one-third of the planet warming carbon dioxide human activity emitted into the atmosphere and ninety percent of the excess heat trapped by this global carbon blanket.

Mass endangerment on a level unprecedented in history made the ocean victims of acidification when global warming created more carbon than they could naturally absorb for optimal conditions. Forty percent dissolved into the seas creating carbonic acid. Once the ph. balance dropped it wasn't long before populations of shellfish saw huge reductions in numbers. More tragically, the world's coral reefs have been totally destroyed.

Massive industrialization started with the Industrial Revolution of the 1750s. By the 1860s the seas began to warm. Increased use of and dependence upon fossil fuels led to a rapid global warming. Warmer air temperatures heated the surface layer of the seas. Oceans lost their memory as fresher water at great depths depleted oxygen and starved the upper ocean of the upwelling of nutrients provided when deep waters resurface. Nutrients feed phytoplankton and move on up the food web.

For example, the lush kelp beds around the California coast that existed because of this up-welling have disappeared. Marine life worldwide has been decimated. Adding insult to injury, the species that survived were so full of micro-plastics they were inedible. Seafood eaters consumed up to 11,000 micro-plastic particles a year.

Leaf: So you're saying that in less than three hundred years we've destroyed a memory system that's lived and thrived for millions of years.

Perc: That's the sad truth, Leaf.

I mentioned at the beginning of a previous episode that warming oceans created massive glacier melt worldwide which led to rising seas and unthinkable consequences. Warmer waters eroded the base of glacier ice, erasing it like an ice cube melting in a glass of water. This erosion allowed the ice to flow faster, flowing at over a mile a minute and then faster and faster. Two-thirds of the planet is now water. We emerged from the seas and now we are being swallowed back up by the seas.

Leaf: Sorry to interrupt, Perc. For listeners who are new to this Podcast, our guest is referring to Episode 5 which is called "Catastrophic Climate Change."

Perc: No problem. Now, where was I? Oh, yeah. Hundreds of thousands of gigatons of Greenland and Antarctic ice melted into the ocean. A single gigaton equals an explosive force equal to one billion tons of TNT. This event literally blew people's minds as it occurred. Nothing had prepared humankind for this.

That, more than anything, led to the creation of the oppressive World Council. The Big Three--the United States, China, and Russia--utilized the weaponizing of food to make reluctant countries toe the line.They constructed an alternate version of history and climate related events and engaged in the suppression of truth. They became adept at ducking responsibility for what their inaction had caused to happen and for the deplorable conditions that we currently endure.

The role of the World Council cannot be overestimated. Afraid of a revolution, and of losing their grip on power and money, they clung to an outdated paradigm. Sea waters flowed into the mouths of the major rivers that hadn't yet dried up, bringing salt water that destroyed forests and farmlands along what was left of the coastlines.

Meanwhile, the major powers continued to pour hundreds of billions of dollars into defense budgets in an effort to protect themselves from so-called enemies, providing a classic example of the dictum, "we are our own worst enemy."

Finally, after the catastrophic results of giving short shrift to climate change, they created the World Council to pool their resources to fight global warming. By then it was too late. The irony is that the Council is dominated by the biggest polluters on the planet, the very ones who made the mess we find ourselves in.

The World Council's goal was not to persuade people, but to throw misinformation out to people to disorient them and have them question reality so that they could downplay the scientific evidence.

Follow the money since it's been said that money is the mother's milk of politics. The World Council allowed the interests of the fossil fuel industry and plastic manufacturers, to hold sway over the health and well-being of the people. The corporations were the real power behind the throne.

Their lack of any meaningful response to the climate emergency, one created by their own inaction, is due to the fact that it would now cost trillions of dollars for these cash strapped governments.

So we're all left to suffer, if only subliminally.

Leaf: Speaking of past episodes, you told listeners in Episode 4, which you called "Plastic Planet," that you'd talk more about the plastic islands now floating in our oceans. I assume you meant in this episode?

Perc: Yes! I've stated, rather controversially, that even if the glaciers had remained basically intact our seas were gravely endangered. These past twenty five years have been hell from an environmental standpoint. The plastic islands are no exception.

Millions of tons of plastic is either washed or dumped deliberately into our oceans, and the amount has more than doubled over the last quarter century. Most of this is in the form of single use plastic items. After this waste breaks down, and it includes toxic chemicals, it's ingested by marine animals: fish, dolphins, seals and turtles. Plastic has been discovered blocking the digestive tracks of at least 265 species.

Leaf: We've already touched on this fact, Perc. What about the islands?

Perc: I was just getting to that, Leaf. Show a little patience, man!

I was about to talk about the five major floating islands, not found on our maps, that have eradicated so much of our marine life and also contributed to climate change. These gigantic concentrations of garbage mostly consist of mirco-plastics. They float inside the oceans' eddies trapped in immense whirlpools which ocean currents group together. The five largest plastic islands coincide with the main ocean vortices: two in the Pacific, two in the Atlantic, and one in the Indian Ocean. There are other smaller and more dispersed plastic islands such as those found in the Mediterranean Sea and the Caribbean.

The Great Pacific Garbage Patch now covers an area twice the size of Texas or six times the size of France. Twice the size of France, Spain, and Germany put together. In some areas as deep as one mile. The total mass of micro-plastics is three-quarters of what's seen on the surface and in many places is estimated to be up to seven miles deep.

Also called the Pacific Garbage Vortex, it spans waters from the West Coast of America to Japan. The patch is comprised of the Western Garbage patch, located near Japan, and the Eastern Garbage patch, found between California and Hawaii. This first of the five was discovered half a century ago.

Buoyant plastics, along with nylon fish netting, is transported by converging currents and accumulates in the patches. Once they enter the vortexes they don't usually leave the islands until they degrade into micro-plastics under the effects of wave action, marine life, exposure to sunlight, and temperature changes.

The end result of ocean plastic is the devastation of fishing communities, the death of more than one million marine animals a year, damage to air quality by plastic off-gassing, and an increase in global warming.

We now have more plastic than fish in our oceans!

Leaf: Any final thoughts?

Perc: When I think about the tragedy of our oceans, I think about cruise ships.

Those floating cities, that are a billion dollar business, have always been a major polluter of the seas. All the waste from these ships ended up in our rivers and seas. Billions of gallons of raw sewage dumped into the oceans annually. Chemical and pesticide laden food waste and the dirty water from sinks, showers, toilets, and laundry facilities. Their smokestacks were cleaned by scuppers to remove toxic chemicals left by exhaust. All of the water used to scrub them down was discharged into the ocean. This acidified warm water contained heavy metals, hydro-carbons, and nitrates, all harmful to marine life. The fish eat this chemical soup and we once ate the fish and ingested these destructive toxins.

Leaf: Wow, you've covered a lot of ground, Perc.

Perc: So have our still rising seas, Leaf.

Leaf: Yes, they have indeed. And that brings us to the end of our second to last episode with Perc. Join us next week when the radical historian tackles the question that is on everyone's mind. Where do we go from here? Thank you for listening to Sanctuary Earth.

Narrator: J. J. Cooper was the producer of this episode. Our engineers are Andrew Wilson and Celeste Roberts. Our editor is Rosie Zuniga. The executive producer is Leaf Aronson.

CHAPTER 30

Clay devoted some time to reflecting upon "Warm Water and High Seas."

He'd witnessed firsthand the coastal erosion Perc had described as worldwide in its disastrous effects, but the idea that the oceans had lost their memory had never occurred to him. He'd never encountered such thoughts in his own education. He wondered what other deficiencies he might have been subjected to. Nobody can know everything his mother had once explained to him. There's too much to know.

He took comfort in this perspective, but he couldn't help but repeat to himself: the oceans have lost their memory. What a disturbing thought. The high seas of the planet had been the victims of a form of dementia or Alzheimer's disease. Were the plants and animals losing their memories? Would humanity also lose its collective memory or accept an alternative history of what had brought it to the brink?

Not if individuals like Perc had anything to do with it, Clay reasoned. Thanks, Perc, for caring enough to speak truth to power. For looking reality in the face and not flinching. For challenging us to turn things around.

Clay found himself looking forward to the final episode.

He'd taken a look at the list of episodes so he already knew that it was titled, "Where Do We Go From Here?" Leaf Aronson had mentioned it at the end of the last interview. The question begged an answer.

But morning had arrived and he'd promised Lynne that he'd come over to her place for breakfast. He looked over and found Hank fast asleep so he proceeded to dress quietly and leave their shared room without waking the wannabe agent from his slumber.

They decided to walk to the communal dining hall for lunch.
    A blue sky, filled with white marshmallow clouds, greeted them when they left Lynne's cozy nest. A dirt pathway meandered down through a sparse stand of trees, the leafy canopy blocking the full effect of the sun's rays to fill their eyes with dappled sunlight. As they walked along, Clay reflected that Lynne knew all about his sperm markers, but he knew nothing about her fertility. This wasn't quite fair in his estimation. He was born with a curious mind, so he couldn't allow the matter to remain unresolved. He felt compelled to broach the subject.
    He turned to Lynne and she met his gaze.
    "Seems like everyone and their brother knows about me and my so-called markers," he began. "I know nothing about you, Lynne. I mean, about your fertility or lack thereof. I'm curious. You must have been tested."
    Her feeble smile wasn't an answer.
    Clay waited patiently.
    "Does it make a difference?"
    He thought it over as they continued to stroll down the path. The trees gave way and the dining commons came into view in the distance. Clay wondered if he should wait to give her an answer. Probably not, he reasoned.
    "Not really."
    "I'm highly fertile by today's standards, but I've resisted conception. I keep a low profile. They're not going to turn me into some kind of Hand Maiden."
    "What the hell is a Hand Maiden?"
    "You certainly are limited, aren't you?" Lynne laughed good-naturedly. "Don't you read?"
    "Yes, of course."
    "Have you ever heard of Margaret Atwood?"

A long pause.

Clay thought back, trying to remember the name, but he came up blank.

"Sorry, can't say as I have."

"You're pathetic," she told him in a teasing tone. "*The Handmaid's Tale* is a classic."

Clay and Lynne arrived at the communal dining hall.

They entered and found a table in a far corner of the vast room. They wanted to be alone. That wasn't happening as eyes turned to study the couple as discreetly as possible.

A young waitress, dressed casually in shorts and a t-shirt, approached carrying two menus. She recognized Lynne immediately. She turned to Clay, gave him a wide smile, and then turned back to Lynne. The smile remained plastered to her face.

"Did you want to order at the counter?"

"No," said Lynne.

"Can I get you started with something?" asked the waitress as she placed two menus on the table.

"We'll have two coffees," Lynne told her. "*Chiapas Organico.*"

Lynne searched Clay's eyes while raising her brows and he nodded his approval.

"I'll be back shortly with the coffees and to take your order."

The waitress sauntered off, taking her smile with her.

"I usually order at the counter," said Lynne. "Since Jamie is new to the Sanctuary I'd like to help her out with a tip."

Clay appreciated the gesture. It seemed like everybody at the Sanctuary truly cared for one another's well-being. He found this refreshing and it kindled a sense of hope in him. Maybe the human race wasn't so bad after all. He'd have to reassess his attitude. Not allow his dark thoughts to hold sway.

"You look lost in thought, Clay," Lynne remarked just as Jamie returned to the table holding a wooden tray with two cups of steaming hot coffee, a bowl of sugar, a small pitcher of cream, and a couple of spoons. She placed the ceramic mugs on the table.

"Sugar or cream?"

"Just cream," answered Clay.

"Same for me," added Lynne.

Down came the small pitcher and two spoons.

"Did you want to order or do you need a little more time?"

"We're not sure yet."

"No worries," Jamie reassured them with a smile. "Take your time. I'll be back in a few."

Jamie executed a quick pirouette and exited with the grace of a ballet dancer, all the while holding the wooden tray high in the air above her shoulder.

Finding themselves alone again, except for the occasional glances, Clay and Lynne added cream to their coffees, stirred, and began to sip the aromatic liquid and inhale the earthy aromas of southern Mexico.

One sip and then another.

They turned their eyes to the menu, but Clay caught a disturbing movement at the edge of his peripheral vision. He looked up to find his sister heading towards the table with Jamala and Hank close behind. He reached over and patted Lynne twice on top of her hand to get her attention.

When the threesome arrived at the table they remained standing. They all had worried looks on their faces despite efforts to appear cool and collected.

"Rico discovered that one of the Copulation Cartels is heading our way," Jamala said quietly as she attempted to avoid creating a chaotic scene in the dining commons.

"Are we in danger? " asked Clay in a hushed tone.

"Yes, we are in danger!" came an emphatic reply delivered as a whisper.

Clay took one last sip of his coffee as Lynne reached into her pocket and pulled out enough currency to cover the bill plus a generous tip. She plunked the money down on the table. They rose to join the others and everyone made their way out of the communal dining hall without saying another word.

Five worried expressions.

"River is getting the switchblades ready," announced Jamala, returning to her normal voice.

"You're going to fight them with knives?" Hank said in disbelief.

"No, you moron, drones."

"Oh, yeah. I forget about those," the agent shrugged. "Isn't that old technology?"

"Surplus drones," Jamala informed them. "That's all Government will allow us to purchase."

"What are you going to do?" asked Jodie.

"We'll have to use our armed drones for the first time," replied Lynne. "We have no choice."

"You think I should turn myself over to them," Clay offered. "I'm the one who's placed you in danger."

"No way," declared Lynne. "Something like this was bound to happen sooner or later."

"She's right, Clay," Jamala agreed.

"Clay, you need to go with River," Lynne insisted without hesitation.

All eyes turned to Jodie's older brother. Would Clay put himself in harm's way or would he try to talk his way out of it. They didn't have to wait long for his response. It was almost immediate.

"Let's go!"

"Clay and I can check out the jeep from the motor pool and head up to the drone hanger," said Lynne. "The rest of you wait here until we get back."

"Be careful, Clay," warned Jodie.

CHAPTER 31

The road seemed familiar.

Clay soon realized that it was the same route Lynne had used to reach the Sanctuary, only in reverse. She had called it the "back way." Perhaps Hank was right. Maybe that was one of the Copulation Cartels following them and not Government. Probably not. Government's Mole had admitted his guilt, and why would he lie about such an action.

Before they reached the top, Lynne swerved the jeep and deftly turned a corner without slowing down to reduce speed. Clay grabbed on to his seat and fought successfully to maintain his balance. Half a mile down the road they came upon an area where the land leveled out into a wide field.

At the far side of this clearing stood a metal Quonset hut. Beyond an open door a man worked quickly, loading something into large backpacks. They couldn't make out what it was that he was stuffing into the packs, but they assumed it was the switchblade drones.

The man heard the jeep pull up and came outside to greet them.

He wore a blue tank top and long cargo pants that covered the sides of his cowboy boots. His muscles and taunt skin glowed in the noontime sun. A single tattoo, a black clef, the symbol used at the beginning of every piece of sheet music, adorned his right arm up along the thick deltoid. His hair and beard grew long and shaggy.

Lynne and Clay climbed out of the jeep.

She walked right up to the guy and gave him a big hug. An awkward moment for Clay until the guy turned to him and offered a self-assured fist bump.

"I'm River," he said, by way of introduction."

"Clay Roberts."

"I got a call," said River. "They say you're going with me."

"You okay with that?" asked Lynne.

"Of course," came the reply. "But we need to get going. Why don't you wait for us here, Lynne."

She nodded her agreement.

"Give me a hand, Clay Roberts."

No more talk. River returned to the hut and grabbed a couple of the backpacks. Clay followed him inside and did a quick glance around. He saw two more packs as well as batteries and controllers stored in the climate controlled Quonset. Clay picked up the other two backpacks. Four switchblade drones in all. They had no idea what kind of firepower they'd be facing.

River carried the backpacks over to a high clearance pick-up truck and placed them in the bed of the truck. Clay did the same. River climbed into the driver's seat. Clay was about to get into the passenger side when Lynne, who had followed them over to the truck, grabbed Clay and wrapped her arms around him. She squeezed tightly, letting him know how much she cared for him. Clay took a deep breath.

"Gotta go, lady."

"I know."

Lynne released him and watched as he climbed up into the truck next to River.

Before Clay had closed his door completely, River stepped on the accelerator and the truck's rear tires tore at the ground below. They spun out, straightened out, and then flew off down the dirt road leaving Lynne behind.

They turned back onto the main road.

River kept his eyes glued to its surface as he sped to the top of the knoll.

"So, you're the guy they call Mr. Super Sperm."

Clay winced.

"The Cartel says they're going to take you hostage," he added in a dispassionate voice.

"Sorry, man," Clay apologized. "I didn't mean to put you guys in jeopardy."

"Time we practice our defenses," asserted River. "This is going to happen more and more in the future. I can feel it coming."

They arrived at the top of the road. River pulled up on the Sanctuary side of the locked gate. He hopped out of the pick-up and Clay climbed out to join him. They went around to the side of the truck and reached in for the backpacks. They carried them to the summit of the hill and rested them on the ground.

"Anything I can do to help you," asked Clay. He wondered why they had insisted that he accompany this one-man response team. Maybe they were going to turn him over to the Cartel if it came to that.

"Go back to the truck and grab the binoculars," River instructed him. "They're in the glovebox."

Clay returned to the pick-up and followed instructions. He came back carrying a pair of wide-angled binoculars. By that time River had the drone launcher operational. Two thin metal legs spread out. Along with the body of the weapon they formed a tripod. The unzipped backpack lay off to one side.

The moment felt surreal, but Clay knew this was happening in real time. He reached down into his pocket and found his gift from little Sasha. He rubbed the talisman coin for luck. He needed it now. More than ever.

Time to focus.

Clay took a good look at the set-up. The black drone rested inside a beige launcher with a matching end cap.

"As you can tell these babies are launched out of a tube, much like a mortar. That's where the similarity ends. This little Kamikaze is equipped with a camera in its nose, a navigation system, and guided explosives."

"How fast does it go?"

"We're going to send it down the hill at full speed, one hundred miles per hour. Not nearly as sophisticated as today's drones, but it's all we can get our hands on. This model is twenty years old, but it'll do the job."

"Do you think the Cartel suspects that you have these?"

"I don't think they have a clue, but we're gonna set up a second drone just in case things get ugly."

River went about his business. He removed the other Switchblade from its pack and spread out the two metal supports. He turned to Clay, while continuing his set-up, to apprise him of the situation in more detail.

"After Rico caught wind of the Cartel's plans we sent up our MQ-1C Grey Eagle," said River as he put the binoculars up to his eyes to scan the terrain below. "It's an unmanned aerial vehicle. That's how we knew they're coming in on this road."

"See anything?"

"Three trucks with rockets."

River took off the binoculars and handed them to Clay so that he could have a look. Then he reached into one his cargo pockets and pulled out a pair of Smart Glasses. He donned them and made a call.

"You ready, Rico?"

He waited for the response.

"Aim for the back of the lead truck," advised River. "He should be slowing up real soon."

Clay lowered the binoculars and turned to hand them back to River. He felt a brief moment of surprise at the sight of the smart glasses.

"You use Smart Glasses?"

"They're more reliable out here," replied River. "I can't take a chance with that old cell phone technology. I got Rico back at the Control Center guiding this baby, and I don't trust the 25G network. It's too slow."

River took the launcher's wired detonator in his hand and slipped his index finger through a hole designed to steady his hand. He rested his thumb on a red button as he moved behind the launcher and placed one boot on a small vertical base to steady the unit from the force of the launch.

"Tell me when the lead truck hits my booby trap."

Clay raised the binoculars back to his eyes and searched the road below. The first truck came to an abrupt halt about a mile down from the gate.

"He stopped!"

"Hey, Rico, zero in on the back of that truck cause I'm gonna launch this baby right now."

River pressed the red button on the detonator and the gas propelled drone shot out from its launcher. They stared in amazement as the drone left the tube. As it began to fly the wings immediately unfolded.

They heard a loud explosion as the rear end of the rocket launching truck burst into flames.

"Bingo!" yelled River. "Good job, Rico!"

Clay experienced a rush of adrenalin as the driver of the pick-up, and his passenger, threw open the doors of the cab and ran back to one of the other trucks. They jumped on the running boards, on either side of the truck, and held tight to the rear view mirrors as the two remaining trucks spun around and sped off down the road.

Clay turned to River and found him grinning from ear to ear.

"How'd you stop that truck, River?"

"I embedded some two by fours across the road, but first I drove a bunch of sharp nails through the back sides. Not a real booby trap, but enough to puncture tires on the lead vehicle," he added with a smile on his face. "I was hoping they'd turn around after the first strike. We're not trying to hurt anybody. Just scare them off."

River began to disassemble the second drone.

"Sad that people can't just live and let live," River said to no one in particular.

"What if that didn't work?" Clay wondered. "I mean, what if they'd seen the nails and swerved around them?"

"They would have stopped to lower their tire jacks to the ground for stabilization before firing off any rockets," River informed him. "That would have given me time to launch a strike when they picked a spot."

Clay knew that River could have accomplished this mission alone or with another helper. He also realized that this experience had reinforced his earlier feelings of never living at a Sanctuary. He'd always worry he was placing decent people in danger. He decided not to dwell on these thoughts. Let them pass like clouds moving across the afternoon sky, he told himself. Move on. Think of something positive like giving River the kudos he deserves.

"You're good at this," complimented Clay. "You really know what you're doing."

"Thanks, Mr. Super Sperm," River laughed. "Now let's head back."

After securing the unused drone in the bed of his pick-up River headed back down to the Quonset Hut. Only this time at a more leisurely pace.

Lynne was waiting for them outside when they drove up.

River climbed out of the pick-up first and gave her a thumbs up. She smiled and heaved a sigh of relief. Clay got out and flashed the universal two-fingered peace sign, V for victory. Then he helped River unload the truck and take the remaining drones back into the hut. He took a moment to look around while Lynne waited for him outside. She was giving them both a little space. She could catch up on the details later.

Clay saw a complete drum kit over in one corner, and off to one side a set of weights: barbells dumbbells, and a weight bench. Not all business out here, thought Clay. The two finished putting things away and left the hut.

Outside, everyone stood around with little to say.

The situation became a bit awkward.

"I'm goin' back inside and unwind a little," announced River. "See you guys later."

Lynne turned to Clay with a smile.

"I was worried about you," she admitted. "I was so glad to see that pick-up coming back down the road."

"You heard the explosion," he asked.

"Yes, but I didn't know who was on the receiving end."

"You guys are lucky to have River on your side."

"And I'm lucky to have you," she said as she opened her arms, wrapped them tight around his waist, and gave him a big hug.

They climbed into the jeep. Lynne had left the windows up so she rolled them down to allow fresh air into the vehicle. As they drove off they could already hear River launching into a frenzied, yet somehow melodious drum solo.

CHAPTER 32

Clay and Hank stood outside the communal dining hall.

No sign of the ladies. Clay checked his burner phone. They had arrived too early. Probably a ten minute wait. The agent donned his Smart Glasses and scanned through his emails. It didn't take long. He removed the glasses and searched the horizon for signs of Jam and the others.

"I'm ready to sign that contract," Clay informed him.

That caught the agent's attention.

He turned to his soon-to-be client.

"You mean the one in your truck back at the farm," the agent laughed. "The one you kidnapped and took to the coast."

"That's the one," said Clay with a sheepish grin.

"I could be happy just being *your* friend and agent," said Hank. "I can farm out my other clients."

"Kind of like a one-trick pony, huh?"

"Exactly," agreed the agent. "We can work out the details later."

Hank extended his hand to solidify a gentleman's agreement. Clay took it and gave it a strong squeeze. This time the agent was prepared to respond accordingly and held his own as he returned the firm grip. This slid into a finger grip as they were about to let go. That morphed into a fist bump.

Both men smiled.

Clay glanced down at his phone to check the time. They must be running late. More time to pass. He turned back to Hank with a sly grin.

"Does this have anything to do with Jam?"

"Time will tell . . . " came the noncommittal answer, accompanied by a grin of his own. "I'll head back to the farm with you so I can take the rental car back. Then I'm going to help my mother and grandmother fill out their applications to join the Arm-in-Arm Sanctuary."

"You'll have some great references."

"I really feel they can live a more meaningful life out here?"

"And you?"

"I'm not sure yet, but it's a possibility."

Laughter soon filled the air and it wasn't theirs.

Clay and Hank turned their heads and discovered three familiar figures approaching.

"Hey, guys," the trio sang out in unison before breaking out into more laughter.

"Always late, but worth the wait," Jamala insisted, invoking the cliché to lighten the mood.

"If you say so," laughed Hank.

Time to leave the Sanctuary.

Though they'd spent more time at Arm-in-Arm than they had anticipated, not one of the visitors regretted it as they stood outside the Motor Pool, next to the same jeep Lynne had used to drive them to the Sanctuary days earlier.

Jamala remained with them so she could say her goodbyes. She took Jodie and Hank aside so that Clay and Lynne might have a moment alone.

"You know that I'd like to stay, right?" Clay asked with a hint of sadness in his voice.

"I know," Lynne said softly. "But I have important work to do here, and you and Jodie have a farm to run."

They both knew the real reason, but it was too painful to talk about it. The fact that Clay would never live at the Sanctuary. The attack by the Copulation Cartel had made that quite clear. Clay insisted and nobody tried to dissuade him because they all of them understood that he was doing the right thing. A self-chosen exile to protect the Plastic People's Movement from harm.

Lynne wrapped her arms around Clay's neck and pulled him closer.

They kissed.

And kissed again.

They disengaged and the threesome who'd been waiting and watching approached.

Five souls gathered together. Five individuals who, during the course of a few days, had found it easy to enjoy each other's company. Would this be the last time? Nobody knew. A bittersweet moment for everybody. Hugs and kisses. Tears and laughter.

Jamala enveloped Lynne in a warm hug: "Drive carefully, little sister."

Lynne smiled and gave a nod.

"Time to go," she said with a finality that brought the departure scene to a close.

Hank turned to Jamala: "This whole experience has been ca-ray-zee, but in a good way."

"I couldn't agree with you more," she responded with a smile.

No more lingering or sad goodbyes.

Jodie and Hank climbed into the back of the jeep.

Clay sat shotgun next to Lynne.

The battery powered engine turned over and purred quietly and they drove off from the Motor Pool. Hank turned around to look out the back window and saw Jamala blowing him a kiss. His heart suddenly beat faster. He never dreamed his visit to Arm-in-Arm Sanctuary would lead to this.

They drove out past the adobe homes with their solar panels, past a park with children running around, laughing and playing. Beyond the last row of houses and through the front gate. A different route this time. No back road. No bumpy ride. Nobody chasing them. Nothing to be afraid of.

Free as the wind.

The farmhouse felt like a long, lost friend.

It had only been days, but it seemed so long ago that they'd left for the Sanctuary and left their familiar world behind. Expanded their horizons by embracing the unknown. A world of new possibilities. An opportunity for a change of heart.

Clay made Lynne promise to wait for him at the farmhouse until he returned from driving Hank back to the university to pick up his rental car. Hank said he'd be in touch. There was a business proposition to discuss with Clay, but that could wait until later. Until he had negotiated better terms with the Sperm Bank of California. Until he had helped his mother and grandmother with their applications for Arm-in-Arm Sanctuary.

Lynne had waited, spending time with Jodie while awaiting his return.

He stood with her on the front porch.

Jodie had already said her goodbyes and disappeared inside the house.

"You good to drive back?"

"It's not that long a drive."

Clay walked Lynne out to the jeep.

He came back around to the driver's side.

"I'm going to miss you," confessed Clay.

"Call me once in a while."

"I will," he promised. "I'll be fantasizing about you."

"When we see each other again I'll make those fantasies come true," Lynne assured him.

Not much more to say. They embraced and held each other tight while making time for one last kiss, both hoping that it wouldn't be their last kiss.

Lynne pushed him playfully aside and got into the driver's seat.

Clay's heart sank as he watched her drive off.

Left standing, back on the front porch, he was also left alone with his thoughts and feelings and they came rushing in upon him. A part of him felt empty without her. Her comforting presence. All that she had given him. This woman had changed his world. Helped subdue his demons. Offered him hope for a brighter future. Now she was gone.

He didn't want to go back inside just yet. He also didn't want to spend time thinking about the days they'd be apart. He needed a distraction. Something to take his mind off Lynne. You'd better move on, he told himself.

Then he remembered something.

Before the flurry of activity leading to their departure from the Sanctuary, Clay had been eager to hear the final episode of the *Sanctuary Earth* Podcast. What was it Hank had said, "Even Perc wants the human race to survive." Even Perc, the pissed-off radical eco-historian who had so much disdain for world leaders and corporate interests, was searching for a glimmer of hope.

Clay tucked his earbuds into his ears and reached for his burner phone with eager anticipation. He almost hated for the series to end. He'd learned so much and been challenged in the process. Still, he couldn't wait. The final episode of the Podcast: "Where Do We Go From Here?"

The question burning in the heart of every living soul left on the planet.

Click. Search. Scroll.

Click!

CHAPTER 33

Podcast - *Sanctuary Earth*

Episode 7- "Where Do We Go From Here?"

Leaf: Welcome to Sanctuary Earth, where we discuss issues vital to the continuation of life on planet Earth. These programs are aired free of advertisements as a public service provided by the Plastic People's Sanctuary Movement.

I'm Leaf Aronson and this brings us to our seventh and final interview with Perc. For listeners unfamiliar with our guest please go back to episode #1 of this Podcast, titled "Perc's Personal Journey." It's been great having you join us to share your insights, Perc. Now we've reached the end of our series of episodes and the one question that I'm sure our listeners must have is where do we go from here?

Perc: I'd like to provide listeners with a summary first.

Leaf: All right.

Perc: As a species, we've reached a reproductive Spermageddon. We have less than three billion people left on the planet. Less than a billion in the Global North and two billion in the Global South where conditions today are truly catastrophic. Of all these peoples, only twenty percent are under the age of thirty-five. Only one in ten men and women in this population are possibly capable of having children. Many of them have given up hope and don't want to bring children into this world. We may not survive as a species.

It would be nice to say that we are not to blame, but we are. We could have seen it coming, but we were to inclined to ignore the warning signs. And we had many! A perilous experiment of nature called *homo sapiens* had taken dominance of planet earth and selfishly tipped the scales of planetary sustainability, thereby endangering the entirety of life in this world.

A whole new world has taken shape because the planet we call Earth has become a wasteland. Literally, as billions of tons of waste are strewn across the world, mountains of garbage made up of plastics, fiberglass, electronics, paper, food, clothing, the assorted debris of a dying species. The earth's most endangered species. The human race. *Homo sapiens*. The saps of the planet who had sapped the earth by depleting the world of its most precious elements: air and water and soil and forests and glaciers and other life forms, countless species allowed to die in the earth's waning days.

Due to our greed and ignorance of our true needs we didn't think or care about the harm we did to other species, our fellow travelers on this planet. Our friends, not our enemies. They also faced diseases, viruses, climate change, and habitat destruction. Why couldn't we have been more attuned to their suffering?

Earth. So precious. So used. So abused. This rare jewel of a planet, floating in the vastness of an infinite universe made up of galaxy upon galaxy upon galaxy, has become sick and perhaps terminally ill.

We had so many warnings on so many fronts. Such denial and short-sightedness. The lack of a sense of urgency and the failure to act led to catastrophic results: sea rise of ten feet with more to come, shortages of drinkable water, massive crop failures, devastating wildfires, torrential floods, and the total collapse of the world economy.

Now we all suffer the consequences.

Leaf: Sounds like a litany of our sins, Perc. The results of human-created climate change and other manmade calamities. Does it make any sense at all to talk about where we go from here given our dire circumstances?

Perc: Of course it does, Leaf! Imagination teaches us that there is always a way forward.

Leaf: I'd like to believe that. How long do you think our species has left?

Perc: Difficult to say. We've seen some glimmers of hope. I wish there was a magic bullet, but we both know that's not realistic. Your Plastic People's Movement towards more natural living conditions seems to have paid dividends. Some of your couples have brought children into this world naturally without resorting to alternative methods like in-vitro.

Leaf: Glimmers of hope. I like what you're saying, but what's it going to take to turn this around, Perc?

Perc: Nothing less than a Revolution!

Leaf: Whoa! Are you saying Storm the Barricades?

Perc: No, Leaf. I'm talking about a Revolution in the way we think and act. A radical reimagining of our way of life. A more mindful approach that places the needs of the earth if not first at least equal to our own. It's never too late to move towards a positive direction.

Leaf: There's been a lot of talk about leaving this planet to colonize other worlds.

Perc: Pure escapism, Leaf. What, so we can destroy other heavenly bodies like we have Earth? If we can't make a go of it on this planet we're doomed.All those expeditions into space have given us is space junk as old satellites broke apart or collided due to the rapid increase in private rockets launches. More waste for the wasteland.

Leaf: What about space bubbles? Certainly they've helped.

Perc: The "space bubbles" have helped, but not enough. For listeners not familiar with them, I'll explain. Scientists created and deployed several inflatable, thin, film-like silicon bubbles joined together like a raft. Once expanded in space to the size of Brazil, they provided an extra buffer against harmful solar radiation coming from the sun. A question of too little, too late. They weren't deployed until 2045. By then, most of the damage to the earth had been done.

Leaf: Any final thoughts? Is there a Hail Mary in the playbook, a game changer?

Perc: The ultimate game changer on the energy front is nuclear fusion! Clean and sustainable and it will be a reliable source for thousands of years. The joke has always been that it's thirty years away, but this no longer the case. My guess is two or three years. If we are lucky enough to survive as a species it may save our proverbial bacon.

Leaf: Are those tears that I see in your eyes, Perc?

Perc: You're hopeless if you don't cry when you think about what the f**k has gone down these past twenty to thirty years.

I know that my rhetoric sometimes sounds harsh, but I really would like to see the human race survive. We have so much untapped potential. If we can just start over with a newfound reverence for nature and the earth we might be able to beat the odds and create a new way of living for ourselves and future generations. That's my hope and I pray it comes to pass.

Leaf: One final question for you, Perc. I've asked it before, but I'll ask it again. Is it too late? Have our actions and inactions doomed our species to extinction along with most other forms of life on this earth?

Perc: It may very well be too late, Leaf. However, I'm a firm believer in the miraculous and regenerative powers of nature.

Leaf: We've come to the end of our series of interviews with the radical historian known as The Percolator. It's been an honor working on these Podcast episodes with you, Perc. Thank you for sharing your insights. You've certainly provided our listeners, and myself, a lot to reflect on.

Perc: It's been a pleasure, Leaf.

Leaf: Join us next week for a new series of episodes as I interview one of the world's notable energy efficiency experts, Lisa Kaminski. Our focus will be on how to integrate the four R's into our lives: Refuse, Reduce, Reuse, and Recycle.

Narrator: J. J. Cooper was the producer of this episode. Our engineers are Andrew Wilson and Celeste Roberts. Our editor is Rosie Zuniga. The executive producer is Leaf Aronson.

CHAPTER 34

A knock at the farmhouse door.

When Jodie opened it she found Lynne standing in front of her. Warm smiles of recognition. A close embrace; a drawing back. Clay's sister couldn't help but notice a slight baby bump. Lynne nodded in response to her observation. This was followed by another smile. Jodie took her back into her arms and gave her a gentle hug.

"Does Clay know?"

"That's why I'm here," she replied. "I haven't told him yet."

"He's out in the garden," Jodie said. "Come on."

She led Lynne through the farmhouse, past the kitchen, to the French doors that led outside into the garden. She opened one of them and stepped across the threshold. She motioned for Lynne to join her, but she left the door open.

"Clay!" she yelled. "You've got a visitor."

"I'll be right there, sis," he shouted back.

"I'll leave you two alone."

Jodie went back into the house, closed the door behind her, and disappeared from sight.

Clay emerged from the orchard and headed for the back door as Lynne waited with anticipation. She remembered the garden, recollected how much she had liked the farm the first time she'd visited. Then she saw him. She felt her heart beat faster.

Clay stopped in his tracks when he recognized her standing in the garden, and then his mouth opened into the widest, most heartfelt smile she'd ever seen. She hadn't called to tell him she was coming. He'd been surprised, but soon recovered from the initial shock of her presence.

He went to her.

"What are you doing here?"

"Aren't you glad to see me?" she asked, unsure of herself.

He wrapped his arms around her and gave her a warm hug.

"Of course I'm glad to see you."

"We need to talk, Clay."

He gave her a questioning look.

Lynne looked down at the slightest beginnings of a baby bump.

Clay's eyes followed hers and then it struck him. The slight curvature of her tummy. The first inklings of the new life taking shape within her. He raised his eyes to hers and gazed deeply into those dark orbs, so deep he became lost in wonderment. No words came to his lips. He stood dumbfounded.

In the midst of that silence, Lynne took his hand and pressed it gently on her belly. She left it there for a moment, waiting to gauge his response. All he could do was smile. An enchanting, compassionate smile.

"We're having a baby," she told him, giving voice to the obvious.

"How long have you known?"

"I suspected I might be pregnant about six weeks ago, but I waited until last week to verify my suspicions."

"Let's go out into the garden and sit," he suggested.

Clay led Lynne out past the raised vegetable beds and into the semi-shaded lounging area, a niche surrounded by berry vines. On the way he noticed she wore her hair in a pony-tail. First time he'd seen that. It seemed to accentuate her slender neck and, some-how though he couldn't explain why, it made her seem more vulnerable.

The L-shaped furniture still sat on large thirty inch square pavers set upon crushed gravel. The cozy-looking sectional, made with a wooden frame and wire backs, had retained its comfortable pads and pillows. The single chair, the one turning the L into a U-shape setting, stood where it had always been as did the table in the middle. The two glazed pots were no longer overflowing with Jodie's pink, white, coral, and violet geraniums. Bare soil awaited a new planting.

"Looks much the same," observed Lynne as fond memories of her first visit surfaced in her mind.

"Pretty much," agreed Clay. "I added something new over there."

He gestured over towards a bench strategically placed under the canopy of a fig tree to provide shade, relief from the afternoon sun. Not an evergreen. This tree would lose its leaves during winter. Just when one might desire a bit of warmth.

"I like it."

"I thought you might," he responded. "I thought of you. Of us . . . sitting here one day."

So they sat together on the stone bench.

Time to share more intimate thoughts and feelings.

"I wish you'd told me sooner."

"I wasn't sure how you'd react to the news."

"Are you kidding." he said with a smile. "I think it's wonderful!"

Lynne took a deep breath and let out a sigh of relief.

"It's just that," she began, and then hesitated before sharing what she was thinking. "I mean . . . you've said some things in the past."

Clay reached for her hands and took them into his own.

"I've changed since I met you, Lynne" he admitted. "You gave me a reason to believe again. To believe we might actually be able create a better future."

Clay released her hands and stood.

He got down on one knee and took a hold of one of her hands.

It seemed corny to her. Like something out of a movie.

"You're not going to propose?"

"I propose that we raise *our* child together," Clay answered calmly. "Here on this farm."

Lynne snatched her hand away and threw her arms around him, her weight knocking Clay over as they both fell to the ground laughing.

"I was hoping you'd feel that way."

Tears of joy ran down her cheeks.

"There's something I need to share with you," said Clay. He sounded tentative.

They sat up and put their backs against the bench, side by side.

He hoped the revelation he was about to make wouldn't change how she felt about him. He wasn't sure how it might alter their future together.

"I have a one year contract with the California Sperm Bank," he explained sheepishly. "Hank negotiated all the details. I supply them with a vial of sperm once a month."

"I'm sure you find it very lucrative."

"I don't do this for the money," he told her. "I do it in hopes our species might survive."

She slugged him on the shoulder. A rather hard slug. He wasn't sure how to take this. Was she mad at him or just playing around?

"I hope this doesn't change things," he said nervously. "I mean between us. Both sides can terminate the contract at any time. I don't have to continue if you want me to quit. Hank will be disappointed, but he'll get over it."

Lynne put a finger to his lips to shush him.

"I can think of a lot worse things than a lot of your little offspring running around the planet creating a new world."

"Last month was my first on the job, so to speak."

"So you're new at this?"

"The only way I could do it was by fantasizing about you," he said quietly. He looked into her eyes with longing. "What I'm trying to say is I may need your help in the future."

"That can be arranged," she teased.

"So you'll come live here at the farm."

"That's why it took me so long to share this with you," she told him. "I had to get approval to work remotely. I hoped you were going to want that for us."

"What did they say?"

"Leaf is fine with it as long as I agreed to attend monthly meetings at the Sanctuary. And, he's given me six months of Maternity Leave."

"Getting hot out here," he said. "Let's go inside."

Clay pulled Lynne to her feet and the couple headed for the house walking hand in hand.

The back of the farmhouse came into view.

Clay had a brief epiphany as they approached the French doors leading into the house.

The realization that Lynne carried in her womb a glimmer of hope and a prayer for the future. What that future might bring they had no way of knowing. Would their child even have a future? Would there be an Earth left worth inhabiting? Could humanity survive its own madness?

The only thing Clay knew for certain was they would face that future together.

ACKNOWLEDGEMENTS

This novel would not have been imagined, yet alone researched and written, if it were not for the groundbreaking research I encountered in Shanna H. Swan's essential book: *COUNTDOWN: How Our Modern World Is Threatening Sperm Counts, Altering Male and Female Reproductive Development, and Imperiling the Future of the Human Race*, written with Stacy Colino.

Swan's fascinating explanation of how modern toxic chemicals are destroying human fertility is truly eye-opening in a world still laboring under the outdated overpopulation paradigm. I took her research findings and coupled them with the ongoing and projected effects of climate change to imagine a future that's scary yet feasible.

I had written and self-published two historical novels,set in 10th century Islamic Spain (part of the Andalusian Trilogy), when I chanced upon *Countdown*. I put the series on hold to focus my energies on writing this dystopian novel because I felt the urgency of the novel's themes required an individual response.

I am grateful to my longtime editor, Visnja Murgic, who reviewed early drafts of the novel and offered helpful suggestions as well as editorial assistance. Her "eagle eye" has improved my novels on many occasions. Any deficiencies in the manuscript are the sole responsibility of this author.

Author Biography

William Mesusan lived and traveled in central Mexico where he pursued his dream of becoming a published writer. He wrote seven cover stories for *El Ojo del Lago*, Mexico's most widely read English-language magazine, along with a dozen and a half e-zine articles.

Two trips to Spain, and research into the country's past, inspired a series of novels set in 10th Century Islamic Spain. He's self-published two books in The Andalusisan Trilogy series: *The Galician Woman* and *The Bone Relic*. The final book, *The Missing Vizier*, and a prequel (*The Lost Manuscript*) are forthcoming.

Invitation to Readers

Thank you for reading this novel.

If you found the story to your liking, please consider leaving a review on your favorite book seller's website. This is the most generous act you can make to help an author find new readers.

Reviews are hard to come by and give credibility to the book. They are greatly appreciated. If you aren't interested in posting a review, please consider leaving a rating.

Thank you, again.